We, the sisterhood, hereby instate the following rules to govern the use of the Traveling Pants:

1. You must never wash the Pants.

2. You must never double-cuff the Pants. It's tacky. There will never be a time when this will not be tacky.

3. You must never say the word "phat" while wearing the Pants. You must also never think "I am fat" while wearing the Pants.

4. You must never let a boy take off the Pants (although you may take them off yourself in his presence).

5. You must not pick your nose while wearing the Pants. You may, however, scratch casually at your nostril while really kind of picking.

6. Upon our reunion, you must follow the proper procedures for documenting your time in the Pants.

7. You must write to your Sisters throughout the summer, no matter how much fun you are having without them.

8. You must pass the Pants along to your Sisters according to the specifications set down by the Sisterhood. Failure to comply will result in a severe spanking upon our reunion.

9. You must not wear the Pants with a tucked-in shirt and belt. See rule #2.

10. Remember: Pants = love. Love your pals. Love yourself.

The Second Summer of the Sisterhood

Ann Brashares

Delacorte Press

Published by
Delacorte Press
an imprint of
Random House Children's Books
a division of Random House, Inc.
New York

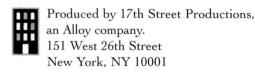

Produced by 17th Street Productions,
an Alloy company.
151 West 26th Street
New York, NY 10001

Visit us on the Web! www.randomhouse.com/teens

Educators and librarians, for a variety of teaching tools, visit us at
www.randomhouse.com/teachers

Cataloging-in-Publication Data is available from the Library of
Congress.

ISBN: 0-385-72934-0 (trade) 0-385-90852-0 (lib. bdg.)

The text of this book is set in 12-point Cochin.

Book design by Marci Senders

Printed in the United States of America

April 2003

10 9 8 7 6 5 4 3 2 1

BVG

For my mother,
Jane Easton Brashares,
with love

Acknowledgments

I would like to express my great and unending appreciation to Jodi Anderson. I also acknowledge, with admiration and warmest thanks, Wendy Loggia, Beverly Horowitz, Channing Saltonstall, Leslie Morgenstein, and Jennifer Rudolph Walsh.

I lovingly and gratefully acknowledge my husband, Jacob Collins, and the three greatest joys in my life: Sam, Nathaniel, and Susannah. I thank my father, William Brashares, my role model. I thank dear Linda and Arthur Collins, who took us in this year and even gave me a place to write this book. I thank my brothers, Beau, Justin, and Ben Brashares, for giving me the highest possible opinion of how boys are.

The Second Summer of the Sisterhood

Nothing is too wonderful

to be true.

—Michael Faraday

PROLOGUE

Once there were four girls who shared a pair of pants. The girls were all different sizes and shapes, and yet the pants fit each of them.

You may think this is a suburban myth. But I know it's true, because I am one of them—one of the sisters of the Traveling Pants.

We discovered their magic last summer, purely by accident. The four of us were splitting up for the first time in our lives. Carmen had gotten them from a second-hand place without even bothering to try them on. She was going to throw them away, but by chance, Tibby spotted them. First Tibby tried them; then me, Lena; then Bridget; then Carmen.

By the time Carmen pulled them on, we knew something extraordinary was happening. If the same pants fit—and I mean really fit—the four of us, they aren't ordinary. They don't belong completely to the world of things you can see and touch. My sister,

Effie, claims I don't believe in magic, and maybe I didn't then. But after the first summer of the Traveling Pants, I do.

The Traveling Pants are not only the most beautiful pair of jeans that ever existed, they are kind, comforting, and wise. And also they make you look really good.

We, the members of the Sisterhood, were friends before the Traveling Pants. We've known each other since before we were born. Our mothers were all in the same pregnancy aerobics class, all due in early September. I feel this explains something about us. We all have in common that we got bounced on our fetal heads too much.

We were all born within seventeen days of each other, first me, a little early, in the end of August, and last Carmen, a little late, in the middle of September. You know how people make a big deal about which twin was born three minutes before the other one? Like it matters? Well, we're like that. We draw great significance from the fact that I'm the oldest—the most mature, the most maternal—and Carmen is the baby.

Our mothers started out being close. We had a group play date running at least three days a week until we started kindergarten. They called themselves the Septembers and eventually passed that name down to us. Our mothers would gab in whoever's yard it was, drinking iced tea and eating cherry tomatoes. We would play and play and play and occasionally fight. Honestly, I remember my friends' mothers almost as well as my own from that time.

We four, the daughters, reminisce about it some-times—we look back on that period as a golden age. Gradually, as we grew, our mothers' friendship disintegrated. Then Bee's mother died. A giant hole was left, and none of them knew how to bridge it. Or maybe they just didn't have the courage.

The word *friends* doesn't seem to stretch big enough to describe how we feel about each other. We forget where one of us starts and the other one stops. When Tibby sits next to me in the movies, she bangs her heel against my shin during the funny or scary parts. Usually I don't even notice until the bruise blooms the next day. In history class Carmen absently grabs the loose, pinchy skin at my elbow. Bee rests her chin on my shoulder when I'm trying to show her something on the computer, clacking her teeth together when I turn to explain something. We step on each other's feet a lot. (And, okay, I do have large feet.)

Before the Traveling Pants we didn't know how to be together when we were apart. We didn't realize that we are bigger and stronger and longer than the time we spend together. We learned that the first summer.

And all year long, we waited and wondered what the second summer would bring. We learned to drive. We tried to care about our schoolwork and our PSATs. Effie fell in love (several times), and I tried to fall out of it. Brian became a regular fixture at Tibby's house, and she wanted to talk about Bailey less and less. Carmen and Paul evolved from stepsiblings to friends. We all kept our nervous, loving eyes on Bee.

4

While we did our thing, the Pants lived quietly in the top of Carmen's closet. They were summer Pants—that's what we had all agreed on. We had always marked our lives by summers. Besides, with the no-washing rule, we didn't want to overuse them. But not a day of fall, winter, or spring went by when I didn't think about them, curled up in Carmen's closet, safely gathering their magic for when we needed them again.

This summer began differently than the last. Except for Tibby, who'd be going to her film program at a college in Virginia, we thought we'd be staying home. We were all excited to see how the Pants worked when they weren't traveling.

But Bee never met a plan she didn't like to change. So from the start, our summer did not go the way we expected.

Oh who can tell, save he whose heart hath tried.

—Lord Byron

Bridget sat on the floor of her room with her heart pounding. On the carpet lay four envelopes, all addressed to Bridget and Perry Vreeland, all with Alabama postmarks. They were from a woman named Greta Randolph, her mother's mother.

The first letter was five years old, and asked them to attend a memorial service in honor of Marlene Randolph Vreeland at the United Methodist church in Burgess, Alabama. The second was four years old, and told Bridget and Perry that their grandfather had died. It included two uncashed checks for one hundred dollars apiece, explaining that the money was a small bequest from their grandfather's will. The third was two years old and included a detailed family tree of the Randolph and Marven families. *Your Heritage*, Greta had written across the top. The fourth letter was a year old, and it invited Bridget and Perry to please come visit whenever they could.

Bridget had never seen or read any of them until today.

She'd found them in her father's den, filed with her birth certificate and her report cards and her medical records as though they belonged to her, as though he'd given them to her.

Her hands were shaking when she went into his room. He was just home from work, sitting on the bed and taking off his work shoes and black socks as he always did. When she was very small, she'd liked to do it for him, and he'd liked to say it was his favorite thing in the day. Even at the time it had made her worry that there weren't enough happy things in his days.

"Why didn't you give these to me?" she yelled at him. She strode close enough for him to see what she held. "They are written to me and Perry!"

Her father looked at her like he could barely hear her. He looked that way no matter how loudly she talked. He shook his head. It took him some time to figure out what Bridget was flapping in his face. "I am not on speaking terms with Greta. I asked her not to contact you," he said at last, as if it were simple and obvious and not a big deal.

"But they're mine!" Bridget shouted. It *was* a big deal. It was a very big deal to her.

He was tired. He lived deep inside his body. Messages took a long time to get in and get out. "You're a minor. I'm your parent."

"But what if I had wanted them?" she shot back.

Slowly he considered her angry face.

She didn't feel like waiting around for an answer, letting him set the pace of the conversation. "I'm going there!" she shouted at him without even thinking about what she was saying. "She invited me and I'm going."

He rubbed his eyes. "You're going to Alabama?"

She nodded defiantly.

He finished with his socks and shoes. His feet seemed small. "How are you going to manage that?" he asked her.

"It's summer. I've got some money."

He thought about it. He couldn't seem to think of a reason why she couldn't. "I don't like or trust your grandmother," he told her finally. "But I'm not going to try to forbid you to go."

"Good," she snapped.

She went back to her room as her old summer dissolved and her new one dawned all around her. She was going to go. It felt good to be going someplace.

"So guess what?"

This was a phrase from Bee that always made Lena sit up and listen. "What?"

"I'm going away. Tomorrow."

"You're going away tomorrow?" Lena repeated dumbly.

"To Alabama," Bee said.

"You're kidding me." Lena was only saying that. It was Bee, so Lena knew she wasn't kidding.

"I'm going to see my grandmother. She sent me some letters," Bee explained.

"When?" Lena asked.

"Well . . . actually . . . five years ago. That's when the first one came."

Lena was stunned not to have known this.

"I just found them. My dad never gave them to me." Bee didn't sound mad. She stated it as a fact.

"Why not?"

"He blames Greta for all kinds of stuff. He told her not to contact us. He was annoyed that she tried."

Lena had so little optimism where Bee's dad was concerned that this did not shock her.

"For how long, do you think?" she asked.

"I don't know. A month. Maybe two." She paused. "I asked Perry if he wanted to come with me. He read the letters, but he said no."

Lena didn't find that surprising either. Perry had been a sweet kid, but he'd grown into a reclusive teenager.

Lena felt alarmed at this change in plans. They were supposed to get jobs together. They were supposed to hang out all summer. But at the same time she felt oddly comforted by the impulsiveness. It was something the old Bee would do.

"I'll miss you." Lena's voice wobbled a little. She felt weirdly teary. It was natural that she would miss Bee. But Lena usually registered that something was sad before she felt it. Now the order was reversed. It took her by surprise.

"Lenny, I'll miss *you*," Bee said quickly, tenderly, as startled as Lena was by the ready emotion in Lena's voice.

Bee had changed so much in the last year, but a few things had stayed the same. Most people, including Lena herself, backed away when they sensed some out-of-control emotion. Bee went right out to meet it. Right now, that was a thing Lena loved.

Tibby was leaving the next day, and she hadn't finished packing or begun shopping for their biannual break-and-enter at Gilda's. She was madly packing when Bridget appeared.

Bridget sat atop Tibby's bureau and watched her throw the entire contents of her desk on the floor. She couldn't find her printer cable.

"Try the closet," Bridget suggested.

"It's not there," Tibby answered gruffly. She couldn't open her closet because it was jammed with things she could neither keep nor throw away (like her old guinea pig's cage). Tibby feared that if she even cracked open the door, the whole mountain would tumble and crush her to death.

"I bet Nicky took it," Tibby muttered. Nicky was her three-year-old brother. He took her stuff and broke her stuff, usually the moment before she really needed it.

Bee didn't say anything. She was being awfully quiet. Tibby turned to look at her.

If a person hadn't seen Bee in a year, they might not have recognized her sitting there. She wasn't blond and she wasn't thin and she wasn't moving. She had tried to dye her hair really dark, but the dye she'd used had barely conquered the famous yellow struggling underneath. Bee was normally so thin and muscled that the fifteen or so pounds she'd gained over the winter and spring sat heavily and obviously on her arms and legs and torso. It almost looked like her body wasn't willing to incorporate the extra fat. It just let it sit there, right on the surface, hoping it would go away soon. Tibby couldn't help thinking that what Bee's mind wanted and what her body wanted were two different things.

"I may have lost her," Bee said solemnly.

"Lost who?" Tibby asked, looking up from the mess.

"Myself." Bee bounced one heel against a closed drawer.

Tibby stood. She abandoned her mess. Gingerly she backed toward her bed and sat down, keeping an eye on Bee. This was a rare mood. Month after month Carmen had subtly tried to pry introspection out of Bee, but it hadn't come. Lena had been maternal and sympathetic, but Bee hadn't wanted to talk. Tibby knew this was important.

Although Tibby was the least physical of the group, she wished Bee were sitting next to her. And yet she knew intuitively that Bee was sitting on her bureau for a reason. She didn't want to be sitting on a low, soft place within easy range of comfort. She also knew that Bee had chosen Tibby for this conversation because as much as Tibby loved her, she would listen without overwhelming her.

"How do you mean?"

"I think about the person I used to be, and she seems so far away. She walked fast, I walk slow. She stayed up late and got up early, I sleep. I feel like if she gets any farther away, I won't be connected to her at all anymore."

Tibby's desire to go closer to Bee was so strong she had to clamp her elbows against her legs to make them stay put. Bee's arms were wrapped around her body, containing her.

"Do you want . . . to stay connected to her?" Tibby's words were slow and quiet, seeming to make their way to Bridget one at a time.

Bee had made every effort to change herself this year. Tibby quietly suspected she knew the reason. Bee couldn't outrun her troubles, so she'd entered her own version of the witness protection program. Tibby knew how it was to lose someone you loved. And she also knew how tempting it was to cast off that sad, ruined part of yourself like a sweater you'd outgrown.

"Do I want to?" Bee thought about the words carefully. Some people (like Tibby, for instance) tended to listen in a muffled, sheltered way. Bee was the opposite.

"I think I do." Tears flooded Bee's eyes, gluing her yellow eyelashes into triangles. Tibby felt tears fill her own eyes.

"You need to find her then," Tibby said, and her throat ached.

Bee stretched out one arm and left it out there, her palm turned up to the ceiling. Tibby got up without thinking and took the hand. Bee laid her head on Tibby's shoulder. Tibby felt the softness of Bee's hair and the moisture from her eyes against her collarbone.

"That's why I'm going," Bee said.

Later, when Tibby pulled away from Bee, she wondered about herself. She wasn't as destructive as Bee. She had never been as dramatic. Rather, she'd slipped carefully, stealthily away from her ghosts.

Late that afternoon, Carmen lay in her bed feeling happy. She'd just returned from Tibby's, where Bee and

Lena had turned up too. They would gather again tonight for the second annual Pants initiation at Gilda's. Carmen had thought she'd be feeling miserable right around now, feeling sorry that she wasn't going anywhere. But she often found good-byes easier than expected. She took care of most of the dreading beforehand. And besides, seeing Bee had made her happy. Bee had a plan, and Carmen was glad. Carmen would miss her like crazy, but something inside Bee had shifted for the good.

The summer didn't look so bad from where she lay. They had drawn straws to determine the route of the Pants, and Carmen would get them first. She had the Pants *and* a date tomorrow night with one of the best-looking guys in her class. That was fate, wasn't it? That had to mean something.

All winter she'd tried to imagine what the Pants would bring her this summer, and now, with the convergence of her date and the Pants, she saw the big clue she'd been hoping for. This summer, they'd be the Love Pants.

Carmen sat up when she heard a familiar trill from her computer. It was an instant message from Bee.

Beezy3: Packing. Do you have my purple sock with the heart on the ankle?
Carmabelle: No. Like I'd wear your socks.

Carmen looked from her computer screen down to her feet. To her dismay, her socks were two faintly different shades of purple. She rotated her foot to get a view of her anklebone.

Carmabelle: Ahem. Might possibly have sock.

The door of Gilda's Aerobics Studio in upper Bethesda had a lock that was laughably easy to pick. But when they got to the top of the stairs, the smell of old sweat was so pervasive Carmen wondered why anyone besides them would choose to be there, never mind take the trouble to break in.

They got right to work, with a feeling of grandness in the air. It was already late. Bee was boarding a bus to Alabama at five thirty in the morning, and Tibby was leaving for Williamston College in the afternoon.

As a matter of tradition, Lena set up the candles and Tibby laid out the Gummi Worms, the deformed cheese puffs, the bottles of juice. Bridget set up the music, but she didn't turn it on.

All eyes were on the bag in Carmen's arms. They had each inscribed the Pants and ceremoniously put them away in September after Carmen's birthday, the last of the four. None of them had seen them since.

There was a hush as Carmen opened the bag. She drew out the moment, proud that she was the one who had found the Pants—though, granted, she was also the one who had almost thrown them away. She let the bag fall to the ground as the Pants seemed to flutter open in slow motion, swirling the air with their memories.

In silent awe, Carmen laid the Pants on the floor, and the girls arranged themselves in a circle around them. Lena unfolded the Manifesto and laid it on top of them.

They all knew the rules. They didn't need to look at them now. They had already diagrammed the route of the Pants, and the logistics were a lot easier this summer.

They held hands.

"This is it," Carmen breathed. The moment was all around them. She remembered the vow from last summer. They all remembered it. They said it together:

"To honor the Pants and the Sisterhood
And this moment and this summer and the rest of our lives
Together and apart."

It was midnight, the end of together . . . and in another way, the beginning of it.

There is nothing like

returning to a place that

remains unchanged to

find the ways in which

you yourself have altered.

—Nelson Mandela

Though the town of Burgess, Alabama, population 12,042, lived large in Bridget's mind, it didn't warrant a lot of fanfare as a stop on the Triangle bus line. In fact, Bridget almost slept straight through it. Luckily, when the driver threw the parking brake, it jolted her awake, and she groggily hopped around, grabbing her bags. She raced off the bus so fast she forgot her rain jacket bunched up under the seat.

She walked along the sidewalk to the town's center, noticing the fine, straight lines between the paving stones. Most sidewalk cracks you saw were fake joints pressed into wet cement, but these were real. Bee stepped on each crack forcefully, defiantly, feeling the sun beating down on her back and a burst of energy in her chest. Finally, she was doing something. She didn't know what, exactly, but action always suited her better than waiting around.

In a quick survey of downtown, she noticed two churches, a hardware store, a pharmacy, a Laundromat, an ice cream place with tables outside, and what looked like a courthouse. Farther down Market Street she saw a quaint-looking bed-and-breakfast, which she knew would be too expensive, and around the corner from that, on Royal Street, a less quaint Victorian with a weather-beaten red sign that said ROYAL STREET ARMS, and under that, ROOMS FOR RENT.

She walked up the steps and rang the bell. A slight woman in her fifties or so answered the door.

Bridget pointed up to the sign. "I noticed your sign. I'm looking for a room to rent for a couple of weeks." Or a couple of months.

The woman nodded, studying Bridget carefully. It was her house, Bridget could see. It was big and had probably even been grand once, but it, and she, had obviously fallen on hard times.

They introduced themselves, and the woman, Mrs. Bennett, showed Bridget a bedroom on the second floor at the front of the house. It was simply furnished but big and sunny. It had a ceiling fan and a hot plate and a minifridge.

"This one shares a bathroom and costs seventy-five dollars a week," she explained.

"I'll take it," Bridget said. She would have to finesse the issue of ID by putting down a giant deposit, but she had brought $450 in cash, and hopefully she'd find a job soon.

Mrs. Bennett ticked off the house rules, and Bridget paid up.

She wondered at the speed and simplicity of the whole transaction as she moved her bags into the bedroom.

She'd been in Burgess less than an hour, and she was set up. Itinerant life was easier than it was cracked up to be.

There wasn't a phone in the room, though there was a pay phone in the hallway. Bridget used it to call home. She left a message for her dad and Perry that she'd arrived safely.

She pulled the cord to start up the ceiling fan and lay down on the bed. She found herself banging her heel against the bottom of the white metal frame, thinking about the moment when she would introduce herself to Greta. She had tried to picture that moment so many times, and she couldn't. She just couldn't. She didn't like it. The thing she wanted from Greta, whatever unnamable thing it was, would be crushed in the first dutiful embrace. They were strangers, yet they had so much heaviness between them. Brave though Bee was, she was scared of this woman and all the things she knew. Bee wanted to know them and she didn't want to know them. She wanted to find them out in her own way.

Bee felt an old familiar buzz of energy in her limbs.

She got out of bed. She looked in the mirror. You could sometimes see a new thing in a new mirror.

At first look she saw the usual devastation. It had started when she'd quit soccer. No, really it had started before that, at the end of last summer. She'd fallen for an older guy. She'd fallen harder for him and gone further with him than she'd meant to. The trick Bee always had was to keep moving, moving at a pace so fast it was thrilling and even reckless. But after last summer she'd paused for a bit, and the painful things—old, supposed-to-be-forgotten things—had caught up with her. By November she'd quit soccer, just as the college scouts were swarming around her. At Christmastime the world had celebrated birth and Bee had remembered a death. She'd hidden her hair under a coat of Dark Ash Brown #3. By February she'd been sleeping late and watching TV, resolutely turning bags of donuts and boxes of cereal into personal gravity. The only thing that had kept her in the world was the constant attention of Carmen, Lena, and Tibby. They would not let her be, and she loved them for it.

But as she looked longer in this mirror, Bridget saw something different. She saw protection. She had a blanket of fat on her body. She had a coat of pigment on her hair. She had the cover of a lie if she wanted it.

She didn't look like Bee Vreeland. Who said she had to be her?

"This is like a preview, isn't it?" Tibby's mom said excitedly as her dad pulled the silver minivan into a parking space behind Lowbridge Hall.

It probably wouldn't have bothered Tibby so much if it had been the first time her mother had said it.

Just how excited was she to be shipping Tibby off to college? Did she have to be so obvious about it? Now Alice could enjoy her photogenic young family without the perplexing teenager skulking in the background.

It was supposed to be that the kid was happy about leaving home and the parents were sad. Instead, Tibby was feeling sad. Her mother's happiness was forcing a role reversal. *We could both be happy*, Tibby thought briefly, but the contrarian in her shot it down.

Carefully Tibby zipped her new iBook back into its case. It was an early birthday present from her parents, another example of being bought off. At first Tibby had felt vaguely guilty about all the stuff: the TV, the separate phone line, the iMac, the digital movie camera. Then she'd figured she could just be ignored, or she could be ignored and have a lot of fancy electronics.

The Williamston campus was a classic scene of college life. There were the brick paths, the lush grass, the ivy-covered dormitory. The only things that weren't convincing were the wide-eyed students milling around the lobby. They were like extras turned loose on a very realistic movie set. They were still in high school, and they looked as fraudulent as Tibby felt. It reminded her of the times Nicky marched around the house wearing Tibby's backpack.

A paper posted by the elevator listed the room assignments. Tibby scanned it anxiously. *A single. Please let it be a single.* There she was. Room 6B4. There appeared to be nobody else in room 6B4. She poked the elevator button. Things were looking up.

"A little over a year from now, we're going to be doing this all over again. Can you believe it?" her mother asked.

"Amazing," said her father.

"Yeah," said Tibby, rolling her eyes to the ceiling. Why were they so sure she'd be going to college? What would they say if she stayed home and worked at Wallman's?

Duncan Howe had once told her she could make assistant manager in a few years if she dropped the attitude and let the hole in her nose close up.

The door of room 6B4 was open, and a key was dangling from a tack on the bulletin board. There was a bunch of papers on the desk welcoming her and so on. Besides that there were a single bed, a nightstand, and a very beat-up wooden bureau. The floor was brown linoleum with vomity white flecks.

"This is . . . wonderful," her mother declared. "Look at the view."

In her five years as an agent, Tibby's mother had mastered the art of real estate spin: When there is absolutely nothing with any charm in a room, point out the window.

Her father put her bags down on the bed.

"Hello?"

All three of them turned.

"Are you Tabitha?"

"Tibby," Tibby corrected. The girl had on a Williamston sweatshirt. Her brown hair frizzed out of her ponytail all around her hairline. She had pale skin and a lot of moles. Tibby counted the moles.

"I'm Vanessa," the girl said, giving a big, arcing wave to all of them. "I'm the RA. That stands for resident assistant. I'm here to help out in any way. Your key is there." She pointed. "Your baseball cap is there." Tibby winced at the Williamston cap balanced jauntily on the corner of the nightstand. "Orientation materials are on the desk, and instructions for the phone system are on the nightstand. Just let me know if there's anything I can do."

She said all this in the rushed, half-memorized manner of a waiter with a lot of specials.

"Thank you, Vanessa," her father said. After he'd passed his fortieth birthday, he'd taken to repeating everyone's name a lot.

"Terrific," her mother said. At exactly that moment, her mother's cell phone went off. Instead of ringing, it played Mozart's Minuet in G. Tibby felt embarrassed every time she heard it. It didn't help that it was the last piece of music Tibby had struggled to play before her piano teacher had given up on her completely when she was ten.

"Oh, no," her mother said, after listening for a moment. She groaned and glanced at her watch. "In the pool . . . ? Oh, my . . . Okay." She looked at Tibby's dad. "Nicky got sick in swimming class."

"Poor kid," her dad said.

Vanessa looked trapped and uncomfortable. Nicky getting sick in swimming probably wasn't covered in her handbook.

"Thanks," Tibby said to Vanessa, turning away from her parents' discussion. "I'll find you if I, you know, need to ask anything."

Vanessa nodded. "Okay. Room six-C-one." She jabbed a thumb over her shoulder. "Right down the hall."

"Great," Tibby said, watching her flee. When she turned back to her parents, they were both facing her. They had that look.

"Honey, Loretta has to take Katherine to music class at

one. I've got to dash back to . . ." Tibby's mother drifted for a moment. "I'm trying to think. . . . What did he eat for breakfast . . . ?" Then she remembered she was right in the middle of disappointing Tibby. "Anyway, we're going to have to postpone our lunch plan. I'm sorry."

"That's fine." Tibby hadn't even wanted to have lunch with them until they'd canceled it.

Her dad turned to her and hugged her. Tibby hugged him back. It was still her instinct. He kissed the top of her head. "Have a great time, sweetie. We'll miss you."

"Okay," she said, not believing him.

Alice stopped in the doorway and turned around. "Tibby," she said, opening her arms as if she hadn't been so distracted she'd almost forgotten to say good-bye.

Tibby went over and hugged her, too. For an instant she allowed herself to sag into her mother's body. "See ya," Tibby said, straightening up.

"I'll call tonight to make sure you're settled in," Alice promised.

"You don't need to. I'll be fine," Tibby said heavily. She said it for her own protection. If her mom forgot to call, which could happen, both of them would have that as an excuse.

"I love you," her mother said on the way out.

Yeah, yeah, Tibby felt like saying. Parents could feel good by telling their kid that a few times a week. It was nearly effortless and gave them so many parent points.

She clutched the instruction booklet for the campus telephone system. She bent over it, studying it carefully so she wouldn't feel sad.

By page eleven, paragraph three, Tibby had discovered that not only did she have her own voice mailbox and her own password, but she also had five messages in her box. She played them, and smiled as she heard the voices. One was from Brian. One was from Lena. Two were from Carmen. Tibby let out a little laugh. Even Bee had left a scratchy message from a pay phone on the road.

Fine, blood was thicker than water. But friendship, it struck Tibby, was thicker than both.

"Honey, I just want to stop in here for a minute."

Lena's mom had recruited her to sit in the car while she picked up a prescription so she didn't have to park. But inevitably, this led to further errands. This was how her mom secured quality mother-daughter time—through stealth and trickery. Lena would have out-and-out refused, but she didn't have a job yet, which undercut her sense of self-worth.

Lena gathered her heavy hair away from her sweaty neck. It was too hot for sunroofs. It was too hot for parking lots. It was too hot for mothers.

"Fine." "Here" was Basia's, a boutique filled with women like her mother. "Do you want me to wait so you don't have to park?" Lena asked even as her mother swooped into a wide-open spot smack in front of the store.

"Of course not," her mom replied airily, always deaf to the irony in Lena's voice.

Lena had spent so much time missing Kostos earlier in the year that she'd gotten into the habit of imagining he was present. It was a little game she had. And somehow, his imagined presence gave her perspective on her value as a person. Now she imagined him sitting in the backseat of the car, listening to Lena act like an ungrateful wiseass.

She is horrible, she imagined Kostos thinking as he sweated on the dark leather seat.

No, I'm only horrible to my mother, Lena imagined defending herself.

"It'll just be a minute," her mother promised.

Lena nodded gamely for Kostos's benefit.

"I want to get something for Martha's graduation brunch." Martha was her cousin's goddaughter. Or her goddaughter's cousin. One of those.

"Okay." Lena followed her mother out of the car.

The store was cold as February. That was a plus. Her mother went right to the racks of beige-colored clothing. On the first pass she picked out a pair of beige linen pants and a beige shirt. "Cute, no?" she said, holding them up for Lena.

Lena shrugged. They were so boring they made her eyes glaze over. Whenever her mom went shopping, she always bought things exactly like all the things she already had. Lena overheard the conversation with the salesperson. Her mother's clothing vocabulary made her wince. "Slacks . . . blouse . . . cream . . . ecru . . . taupe." Her Greek accent made it that much more embarrassing. Lena fled to the front of the store. If Effie were here, she would be cheerfully trying on flowered things in the dressing room next to her mother.

Lena looked through the sunglasses and hair doodads on the counter. She glanced out the front windows. DETNAW PLEH, said the sign on the door.

Her mom finally narrowed the heap of beige to an "adorable eggshell blouse" and a "darling oatmeal skirt." She topped them off with a large pin Lena wouldn't have worn even for a joke.

As they were finally leaving, her mother stopped and seized Lena's upper arm. "Honey, look."

Lena nodded at the sign. "Oh, yeah."

"Let's go ask."

She U-turned them right back inside. "I noticed the sign on your door. My name is Ari, and this is my daughter Lena." Mrs. Kaligaris's real name was Ariadne, but nobody called her that except her own mother.

"Mom," Lena whispered through clenched teeth.

With a couple hundred fresh dollars in the register, the saleslady introduced herself as Alison Duffers, store manager, and listened eagerly to Mrs. Kaligaris's pitch.

"This job might be perfect, don't you think?" Ari finished eagerly.

"Well—," Lena began.

"And Lena," her mother interrupted, turning to her, "think of the discounts!"

"Uh . . . Mom?"

Mrs. Kaligaris chatted amicably, gathering lots of useful information, like the hours (Monday through Saturday, ten till six), the money (starting at six seventy-five an hour plus a seven percent commission), and the fact that they would need her to fill out some paperwork and supply her social security number.

"Wonderful, then." Mrs. Duffers beamed at them. "You're hired."

"Hey, Mom?" Lena said as they walked to the car. She couldn't help smiling in spite of herself.

"Yes?"

"I think she just hired you."

Carmen was pulling on the Traveling Pants for their great inaugural journey of the second summer when the phone rang.

"So guess what?" It was Lena's voice. Carmen turned her music down.

"What?"

"You know that place Basia's?"

"Basia's?"

"You know, off Arlington Boulevard?"

"Oh, I think my mom goes there sometimes."

"Exactly. Well, I got a job there."

"Seriously?" Carmen asked.

"Well, actually, my mom got a job there. But I'll be reporting for duty."

Carmen laughed. "I never pictured you having a career in fashion." She studied herself in the mirror.

"Thanks a lot."

"Hey, do you really think I should wear the Pants tonight?" Carmen asked, fishing.

"Of course. They look gorgeous on you. Why not?"

Carmen turned to get the back view. "What if Porter thinks the writing is weird?"

"If he can't appreciate the Pants, then you know he's wrong for you," Lena said.

"What if he asks me about them?" Carmen asked.

"Then you're in luck. You won't run out of things to talk about for the entire night."

Carmen could practically hear Lena smiling into the phone. Once, in eighth grade, Carmen had been so worried about running out of things to say on the phone to Guy Marshall, she'd written out a list of topics on a pink index card. She wished she'd never told anybody about that.

"I'm going to get my camera," Carmen's mother announced when Carmen walked into the kitchen a few minutes later. She was unloading clean dishes from the dishwasher.

Carmen glanced up from the raw place next to her thumbnail. "Do that only if you want me to commit suicide. Or homicide. Or matricide, I think they call it." She resumed picking her thumb skin without mercy.

Christina laughed, jangling the silverware basket. "So why can't I take a picture?"

"Do you want the guy to run screaming from our apartment?" Carmen drew her sore, newly spare eyebrows down in consternation. "It's just a stupid date. It's not the prom or anything."

Carmen's casualness was betrayed by the fact that she'd spent almost the entire day with Lena doing manicures, pedicures, facials, waxing, and conditioning treatments. Actually, Lena had lost interest after the pedicure and spent the rest of the time reading *Jane Eyre* on Carmen's bed.

Carmen's mother looked at her patiently and offered up her martyred mother-of-a-teenager smile. "I know, *nena*, but it happens to be your first date, stupid or not."

Carmen turned wide, horrified eyes on her mother. "If you say that when Porter is here —"

"Fine. Okay!" Christina held up her hand. More laughing.

Anyway, it wasn't her first date, Carmen comforted herself sullenly. She just hadn't yet had one of these nineteen-fifties–style jobs where the guy picks you up at your house and causes you extreme mortification at the hands of your mother.

According to the stark-faced clock on the kitchen wall it was 8:16. This was a tricky business. Their date was at eight. If Porter came earlier than 8:15, for example, that would seem overeager. It would impart strong loser over-tones. If, on the other hand, he came after 8:25, that would mean he didn't like her all that much.

Eight sixteen ushered in the official grace period. Nine minutes and counting.

She bustled into her room to get her watch. She refused to fall victim to the evil kitchen clock any longer. With its large black numbers, unmistakable minute marks, and fat, relentless second hand, it was the least forgiving clock in the house. According to it, she was constantly late for school and virtually never made her twelve o'clock curfew. She made a mental note to give her mother a replacement clock for her birthday. One of those stylish museum clocks with no numbers or markings of any kind. A clock like that would cut you a break now and then.

The phone rang as soon as she went back into the kitchen. Her mind raced. It was Porter. He was bailing. It was Tibby. Telling her not to wear the plastic mules that made her feet sweat. She studied the caller ID panel, waiting for her destiny to appear. . . . It was . . . the law firm where Christina worked. Bleh.

"It's the Stalker," Carmen said irritably without picking up.

Christina sighed and strode past her. "Don't call Mr. Brattle the Stalker, Carmen."

Christina put on her slightly pinched office face and picked up the phone. "Hello?"

Carmen was already bored with her mother's conversation, and they hadn't even started talking. Mr. Brattle was Christina's boss. He wore a class ring and used the word *proactive* a lot. He always called with big emergencies like not being able to find the letterhead.

"Oh . . . yes. Of course. Hi." Her mother's face unpinched. Her cheeks went pink. "Sorry. I thought you were . . . No." Christina giggled.

It couldn't have been Mr. Brattle. Mr. Brattle had never once in his life said anything to cause anyone to giggle, even accidentally. Huh. Carmen was considering this mystery when the buzzer sounded from downstairs. Inadvertently, her eyes flashed to the evil wall clock. For once, the news wasn't bad: 8:21. Very good, in fact. She pushed the button to open the lobby door. She wouldn't subject Porter to intercom trauma.

"Hi," she said to him, after waiting the appropriate number of seconds before answering the door. She tried to seem as though she'd just been belt-sanding a dresser rather than plain old waiting for him.

The state of his hair (smooth, medium long), the set of his face (alert, interested) didn't change now that he was standing inside her apartment instead of outside her locker in the hallway at school. She didn't see a more intimate version of him.

He was wearing a gray button-down shirt and nice jeans. Which meant he liked her more than if he'd just worn a T-shirt.

"Hey," he said, following her inside. "You look great."

"Thanks," Carmen said. She shook her hair a little. Whether or not it was true, it was the right thing to say.

"You, uh, all set?" he asked brightly.

"Yeah. I'll just grab my bag."

She went into her room and grabbed the fuzzy turquoise bag from her bed, where it perched like a prop. When she came out, she expected her mom to pounce. Oddly, Christina was still talking on the phone in the kitchen.

"Okay, well. All set," Carmen said. She put her bag over her shoulder and hesitated by the door. Was her mom seriously going to miss this milestone chance to embarrass her?

"Bye, Mom," she shouted.

Carmen meant to breeze out of there, but she couldn't help turning around to check. Her mother had appeared in the kitchen doorway, phone at her ear, waving eagerly. "Have fun," she mouthed.

Very strange.

They walked side by side down the narrow hallway. "I'm parked right outside," Porter informed her. He was looking at the Pants. His eyebrows were slightly raised. He was admiring them.

No, he was confused by them.

Was it possible that she couldn't tell his confusion from his admiration? Maybe that wasn't a good sign.

I've had a perfectly

wonderful evening, but

this wasn't it.

—Groucho Marx

Bee would have ordered a huge bowl of spaghetti. She wouldn't care if she had noodles hanging out of her mouth like tentacles. Bee didn't subscribe to the list of acceptable date foods.

Lena did. She would have ordered something neat. A salad, maybe. A neat salad.

Tibby would have ordered something challenging, like octopus. She would challenge her date with octopus, but she wouldn't order something that would end up between her teeth and cause true discomfort.

"Sautéed breast of chicken," Carmen said to the darkly freckled waiter, failing to acknowledge that he was a sophomore in Tibby's pottery class. Chicken was safe and boring. She had come within a breath of ordering a quesadilla, but had realized that could bring up annoying ethnicity issues. Momentarily she was struck with fear that Porter would order something Tex-Mex to make her feel at home.

"I'll have a burger. Medium rare." He handed in his menu. "Thanks."

Very no-nonsense and masculine. It probably would have bothered her if he'd ordered something girlish and trendy, like a wrap.

She bunched up her napkin in her hands and smiled at him. He was very nice-looking. He was tall. In fact, he seemed especially tall sitting across from her. Hmm. Did that mean he had short legs? Carmen had an irrational fear of short legs, since she suspected she herself had them. Her mind leaped about. What if she fell in love with him and they got married someday and they had children with very, very short legs?

"Do you want another Diet Coke?" he asked politely.

She shook her head. "No thanks."

If she had another Diet Coke, she would have to go to the bathroom right away and give him an opportunity to notice her short legs.

"So . . . have you thought about where you're going to school?"

The question hung out there, and Carmen wished she could suck it right back in. This was the kind of question her mother would have asked him if she hadn't been on the phone when he'd arrived. You didn't ask that of a fellow sufferer. The trouble was, they'd covered all the "How many siblings do you have"–type bases before they'd even ordered.

Gabriella, Carmen's worldly cousin, had told her that you could judge the success of a date by how quickly it went. Maybe running out of things to say before you ordered your food was a bad sign.

Carmen glanced down at her watch. Her eyes froze. Uh-oh. Was that rude? Quickly she glanced back up.

Porter didn't look offended. "I'll probably go to Maryland," he answered.

Carmen nodded with great interest.

"What about you?"

This was good. This would buy at least three sentences of conversation. "Williams is my first choice. It's pretty hard to get in, though."

"Great school," Porter said.

"Yep," she agreed. Her grandmother hated it when she said "Yep" or "Yeah" or "Uh-huh" instead of straight-up "Yes."

Porter nodded.

"My dad went there," she said, unable to keep a note of pride out of her voice. She recognized that she worked that tidbit of information into conversations a little too often. When you didn't have an actual father around, you tended to rely more on the facts.

Just then Kate Barnett walked into the restaurant with Judd Orenstein, wearing the shortest skirt Carmen had ever seen. It was denim with a lime green hem. In this case, the hem kind of *was* the skirt.

Carmen wanted to laugh about this. Badly. But glancing at Porter, she somehow doubted that he would want to laugh with her. Carmen squeezed her eyes shut so she wouldn't start laughing and took a mental snapshot to share with Tibby later.

A date was good. A date was fine. But if she said "Kate Barnett borrowed a skirt from her four-year-old sister," her date would think she was catty and possibly even mean.

One problem with her date, she realized, was that he was a boy. She didn't know much about those. The regular cast in her life consisted of her mother, Bee, Tibby, and Lena. Just beyond that circle were her aunt, her female cousin, and her grandmother. In the old days she'd hung out with Bee's brother, Perry, but that was before they'd hit puberty, so it didn't totally count. There was Paul. But Paul was different. Paul was as sturdy and responsible as any forty-year-old man. He was on a higher plane.

The truth was, Carmen loved the idea of boys. She liked how they looked, how they smelled, how they laughed. She'd read enough magazines to know the rules and intricacies of dating. But when you got right down to it, having dinner with one was kind of like having dinner with a penguin. What were you supposed to talk about?

Dear Kostos,

How are you? How is your bapi? How is the football team?

So guess what? I got a job. At a clothing store about a mile from our house. It pays $6.75 an hour plus commissions. Not bad, huh?

Effie is a busgirl at the Olive Vine, did I tell you that? She charmed them by using all seven of the Greek words she knows (most of them having to do with making out). Last night I heard her in the shower practicing the Olive Vine birthday serenade.

Say hello to the old people from me.

Since February, when she'd broken it off with Kostos, Lena had written these brief, chatty, pal-to-pal letters once a month or so. She didn't know why she wrote him at all anymore, really. Maybe it was that girl thing of wanting to stay friends with old boyfriends so they wouldn't go around spreading bad rumors about you. (Not that she really believed Kostos would do that.) Or maybe it was so they couldn't get over you completely.

Her old letters had been different—frequent and agonizing. She wrote in pencil before pen. She held the paper up to her neck so that it might absorb a little of her. She put it in the envelope but didn't seal it for a few hours. She sealed it but didn't stamp it for a day. She always hesitated at the mailbox, hovering before opening the door, hovering before closing it, as if her future were in the balance.

Lena had thought that since she'd broken it off, she would stop thinking about him and missing him so much. She'd thought she'd be free. But it hadn't quite worked out that way.

Well, it might have worked out that way for Kostos, ironically enough. He'd apparently stopped thinking about and missing her. (Which was fine.) He hadn't written her a letter in months.

Lena studied the bottom of her paper, wondering how to sign off.

If she hadn't actually feared that she loved Kostos, she would have written *Love, Lena*, no problem. She wrote *Love* at the end of notes and letters to people she didn't love at all. She signed thank-you notes to Aunt Estelle (her uncle's needling ex-wife) *Love, Lena.* When you stopped to think about it, there was terrible love inflation in letters generally. It was easy to write *Love* when the word was meaningless.

Did she still love Kostos?

As Tibby liked to say, give Lena a choice of A or B and she'll always choose C.

Did she love him?

A: No.

B: Yes.

C: Well, you might suspect that, considering she did think about him a lot. But maybe it had just been attraction last summer. How did you separate attraction from love? And how could you possibly think you loved someone you barely knew and hadn't seen in almost nine months and quite possibly would never see again?

In those last hours in Santorini, Lena had certainly believed she loved him. But what lunatic would base her whole life on a few hours? And anyway, she knew better than to trust her desire-drenched memory. The Kostos she remembered probably had less and less in common with the actual Kostos as the months passed.

She pictured the two Kostoses as being like the film-strip of mitosis she'd watched in ninth-grade biology. The film had started with the one cell that spread and expanded, stretching and pulling apart until—*foop*—two cells. And the more time those two cells spent apart (one going off and helping make a brain, maybe, and the other going off and helping make, say, a heart) the more different they became. . . .

Yes, her answer was a resounding C.

Lena signed the letter *Yours*, folded it carefully, and slid it into its envelope.

On her way down the hall with Porter, Carmen reviewed the major points of the evening so she could answer what were sure to be a million questions from her mother.

"Hello?" she said quietly as she opened the door.

There she was, Carmen Lucille, sixteen, almost seventeen, in her darkened apartment with a date. She waited for her mother to pad around the corner, all worried about catching them kissing.

Carmen waited. What was going on? Had her mother fallen asleep in front of *Friends* reruns again?

"Mom?" Carmen checked her watch. It was after eleven.

"Sit down," she invited Porter, pointing to the sofa. "I'll be right back."

She checked her mother's room. To her astonishment, she wasn't there. Carmen was starting to feel slightly afraid when she flicked on the light in the kitchen. Her mother was not there, but a note was sitting in the middle of the table.

Carmen,

I went out to dinner with a friend from work. Hope you had a fabulous time.

Mama

A friend from work? *Fabulous?* Had her mother mistakenly switched bodies with a different person? Christina didn't say *fabulous*. She didn't have any friends from work.

Stunned, Carmen walked back to the living room. "Nobody here," she said, not recognizing the possible implications of her words until she looked at Porter.

He didn't look lecherous exactly, but he was probably wondering what she meant. She had invited him to come up, after all.

Her mother had left the apartment to Carmen on the night of her first actual, official date? What was she thinking?

Carmen could march Porter right into her bedroom and go the whole damn way if she felt like it. Yes, she sure could.

She looked at Porter. His hair was sticking up a little at the back. The soles of his tennis shoes were oddly wide and flat. She looked through the open door of her bedroom. It made her vaguely uncomfortable to think that Porter could see her bed from where he sat on the sofa. Hmm. If a guy seeing your bed made you feel embarrassed, it was probably a sign that you were not ready to get in it with him.

"Listen," she said. "I have to get up early to go to church tomorrow morning." She yawned for effect. It started out fake but turned real in the middle.

Porter stood quickly. The combination of God and the yawn had done the trick. "Okay. Yeah. I better get going."

He looked slightly disappointed. No, maybe he looked relieved. Was it possible she couldn't tell the difference between disappointed and relieved? Maybe he didn't like her. Maybe he was glad to be getting out of there. Maybe he thought the storied Pants on her short legs looked like the weirdest thing he'd ever seen.

He had a very, very nice nose, she realized as it came toward her. He was standing close and hunching over a bit as they stood together in the doorway. "Thanks a lot, Carmen. I had a great time." He kissed her on the lips. It was quick, but it wasn't disappointed or relieved. It was nice.

Did he have a great time? she wondered, musing at the closed door, or was he just saying that? Was his idea of a great time different from her idea of a great time? Sometimes Carmen marveled at the sheer volume of thoughts cramming her head. Did other people think this much?

The success of any date was all about expectations, really, and Carmen possessed a singular genius for stacking hers straight up to the sky.

She turned to face the empty apartment. Where the hell was Christina? What in the world was her mother thinking? How was Carmen supposed to transform raw experience into a good story without her mother here to tell it to? What was the deal?

She went into the kitchen and sat restlessly at the small Formica table. When her parents had still been together, they'd lived in a small house with a yard. Since then, she and her mother had lived in this apartment. Her mother seriously believed that you couldn't have a lawn without a man to mow it. The kitchen window looked at three other kitchen windows. The area between them

was what real estate agents called a courtyard but what
ordinary people called an airshaft. Carmen had long ago
gotten into the habit of not picking her nose or anything
when she sat in the kitchen.

This wasn't right. She couldn't just go to bed. This
night was crying out for narration. She couldn't call Bee
in Alabama. She tried Tibby's dorm room, feeling as
though she were calling a different universe, a future universe. It rang and rang. In this future universe, it
appeared, you weren't there to pick up your phone at
eleven thirty. She was hesitant to call Lena at this hour in
case she woke up Lena's dad, and his temper along with
him, but she went ahead and did it anyway.

She braced herself for two long rings.

"Hello?" It was Lena's whisper.

"Hi."

"Hi." Lena sounded sleepy. "Hi. *Hi.* How was your
date?"

"It was . . . good," Carmen pronounced.

"Good," Lena said. "So . . . so do you like him?"

"Like him?" Carmen repeated this as though the question were not entirely relevant. She had thought about
many things over the course of the evening, but she
hadn't really thought about that.

"Do you think he has short legs?" Carmen asked.

"What? No. What are you talking about?"

"Do you think *I* have short legs?" This was clearly the
more tender question.

"Carma, *no.*"

Carmen was thoughtful for a minute. "Len, did you ever run out of things to say to Kostos?"

Lena laughed. "No. I had more the problem of not being able to shut up. But we only got together at the very end of last summer, after a lot of crazy stuff had happened."

Usually Carmen spoke to Lena as freely as she spoke to herself, but for some reason she felt shy about admitting that her famously big mouth had shriveled in the presence of an actual boy. Instead, she launched into a long consideration of the whereabouts and motivations of her mother.

Lena was silent so long Carmen suspected she'd fallen asleep. "Len? Len? So what do you think?"

Lena yawned. "I think it's nice that your mom is out having fun. You should go to bed."

"Fine," Carmen said sulkily. "It's obvious who needs to go to bed."

After that Carmen still couldn't fall asleep, so she wrote an e-mail to Paul. Paul was so sparing with words that writing to him was somewhat like writing to nobody, but she did it often even so.

Then she decided to e-mail Tibby. She began by describing how Porter had looked. She was going to say something about the color of his eyes, but when she stopped and tried to picture Porter's eyes, she realized that she hadn't really looked at them.

On the other hand, you

have different fingers.

—Jack Handey

"Tomko-Rollins, Tabitha."

Tibby winced. Silence. She wished she could change her birth certificate. And her school transcript and her social security card.

"That's, uh, just Rollins. Tibby Rollins," she said to the screenwriting instructor, Ms. Bagley.

"What's Tomko?"

"My . . . middle name."

Ms. Bagley checked her list again. "So what's Anastasia, then?"

Tibby sank down in her seat. "A typo?" She heard laughter around her.

"Okay. Tibby, you said? Fine. Tibby Rollins." Bagley wrote a note on the list.

It was one of the many ironies in her life that Tibby was the only member of her five-person family who still hauled the stupid name Tomko around. It was her mother's maiden name. When her parents had been hippies and communists and feminists and everything, her mother had derided women who changed their names when they got married. She'd been Alice Tomko then, and she'd stuck Tibby not only with the name but with the hyphen. Thirteen years later, when Nicky came along, her mother had actually dropped the name Tomko herself. "It just makes everything so complicated," she had muttered, becoming Alice Rollins. She vaguely pretended the Tomko didn't exist for Tibby anymore either. But the birth certificate didn't lie.

It took a while for Tibby to recover enough dignity to drag her eyes up off her desk and look around the room. One girl two seats over she recognized from the sixth floor. A few kids she'd met at the orientation dinner and party last night. Many of them had hungry looks on their faces. They needed to make friends fast; it didn't much matter with whom.

Two kids didn't have the hungry look. One was a noticeably good-looking guy. His hair was long in the front, messed up and half in his eyes, like he'd just gotten out of bed. He was slouched far down in his chair, so his legs stuck out into the room. The other was a girl next to him. Her hair was pixie short, both black and maroon, and she wore pink-tinted rimless glasses. Her T-shirt looked like a size 6X. Clearly they knew each other from before.

Sophie, the girl in 6B3, had already invited Tibby to have lunch today. The roommates Jess and somebody else whose name also started with a *J* from somewhere in

6D were eager for Tibby to hang out tonight. But Tibby felt herself eschewing all the kids who were desperate and friendless like she was.

She watched Bed Head and Pink Glasses. Pink Glasses whispered something to Bed Head, and he laughed. He looked sort of hungover. He slouched lower in his chair. Tibby's ears tickled with the desire to know what the girl had said.

Tibby wanted these two, who didn't need to make any friends.

"Okay, folks." At last Bagley was done with her list. "Let's play a little game to get to know each other and help remember each other's names."

Pink Glasses raised an eyebrow at her friend and slouched down to join him. Tibby felt herself slouching a little too.

"Ready? Here's how it goes. Tell us your name and two of your favorite things that begin with the same letter that starts your name. I'll go first." Bagley considered the ceiling for a moment. She was in her thirties, Tibby guessed. Her dark eyebrows crept in toward her nose, Frida Kahlo style. For some reason, Tibby suspected this meant that she didn't have a husband. "Caroline. Uh, crawfish and . . . Caravaggio."

Tibby watched Pink Glasses whispering to her friend some more while a girl named Shawna told everyone she liked shish kebab and Shaquille O'Neal. Pink Glasses looked up, surprised, when she realized it was her turn. She obviously hadn't been listening to anything anyone had said. "Oh, uh . . . my name is Maura and . . . I'm supposed to say two favorite things?" she asked.

Bagley nodded.

"Okay, uh, Milk Duds and, um . . . *film*."

A couple of people snickered. Tibby shook her head. If Maura had just said "movies" like a normal person, she would have gotten the assignment right.

Bed Head's name was Alex, and he liked aardvarks and acorns. He drew out the *a* sounds. Tibby had the suspicion he was trying to make both the teacher and Maura feel like idiots. But he had a nice, kind of growly voice, and he flashed Maura a dazzling half smile.

I want one of those, Tibby found herself thinking.

He wasn't wearing socks with his Pumas. Tibby wondered if his feet smelled.

It was Tibby's turn. "My name is Tibby," she said. "I like Tater Tots and . . . tweezers." Tibby didn't know what had possessed her to say that. She slowly turned forty-five degrees and saw Alex looking at her from under his hair. He smiled at her.

On the other hand, she did know what had possessed her. Or, anyway, who.

Bridget took a lot of extra steps up the front walk of the two-story brick house. There were little anthills along one side. Grass pushed up triumphantly through the concrete in many places. A doormat said HOME IS WHERE THE HEART IS in large letters decorated with pink and yellow flowers. Bridget remembered that doormat, and she also remembered the brass door knocker in the shape of a dove. Or a pigeon. Maybe it was a pigeon.

She banged on the door a little harder than she'd meant to. She needed to keep it moving. "Come on, come on," she mumbled to herself. She heard footsteps. She shook out her hands to keep the blood flowing.

Here we go, Bridget thought as the doorknob turned and the door swung open.

And there she was.

The old woman was the right age to be Greta, though Bridget did not actually recognize her.

"Hello?" the woman said, squinting into the bright sunlight.

"Hi," Bridget said. She stuck out her hand. "My name is Gilda, and I just moved to town a couple of days ago. Are you Greta Randolph, by any chance?"

The old woman nodded. Well, that was that.

"Would you like to come in?" the woman invited her. She looked a little suspicious.

"Yes, thank you. I would."

Bridget followed her over white wall-to-wall carpet, amazed by the smell of the house. It was distinctive in some unidentifiable way . . . or maybe it was familiar. It stopped her breath for a moment.

The woman invited her to sit on the plaid couch in the living room. "Can I offer you a glass of iced tea?"

"No, not just now. Thank you."

The woman nodded and sat in the wing chair across from her.

Bridget wasn't sure what she had been looking for, but this wasn't it. Greta Randolph was overweight, and the fat was distributed clumsily around her upper body. Her hair was gray and short and permed-looking. Her teeth were yellow. Her clothes looked straight from Wal-Mart.

"What can I do for you?" she asked, looking at Bridget carefully, probably to make sure she didn't swipe any of the crystal doodads on the bookcase.

"I heard from your neighbors you might need a little help around the house—you know, odd jobs. I'm looking for work," Bridget explained. The lie came effortlessly.

Greta looked confused. "Which neighbors?"

Bridget arbitrarily pointed to the right. Lying was easier than most people thought, she decided. Which was key, because liars preyed on the general truthfulness of everybody else. If everybody lied, then it wouldn't be easy anymore.

"The Armstrongs?"

Bridget nodded.

The woman shook her head, puzzled at the thought of that. "Well, we all need a little help, I guess, don't we?"

"Definitely," Bridget said.

Greta thought a moment. "I do have a project I've been meaning to do."

"What's that?"

"I'd like to clean out the attic, then maybe turn it into an efficiency and rent it out in the fall. I could use the extra money."

Bridget nodded. "I could help you with that."

"I warn you, there's a lotta junk up there. Boxes and boxes of old things. My kids left all their stuff in this house."

Bridget shrank back. She hadn't imagined that would come up quite so fast, even indirectly. In fact, as she sat there, she'd sort of forgotten the connection she had to this woman.

"You tell me what to do and I'll do it."

Greta nodded. She squinted at Bridget's face for a long moment. "You're not from around here?"

Bridget tapped her toes inside her sneakers. "No. I'm just here for, uh, summer vacation."

"Are you in high school?"

"Yes."

"And your family?"

"They are . . ." These were answers Bridget should have prepared ahead of time. "Traveling. I wanted to work to earn some extra money. For college next year."

She stood up and stretched her legs a little, hoping to ward off follow-up questions. She looked through the hallway to the back porch, her memory stirring at the big pink dogwood in the backyard with good low branches for climbing.

She turned to look at the mantel. A framed photograph of six-year-old versions of her and her twin brother, Perry, looked back at her. Her breath caught. Maybe this wasn't such a great idea. She sat back down.

Greta pulled her eyes off Bridget and consulted her knotty knuckles for a while. "Fine. I'll pay you five dollars an hour. How would that be?"

Bridget tried not to grimace. Maybe that was the pay scale in Burgess, Alabama, but in Washington you wouldn't flip a burger for that. "Uh, okay."

"When can you start?"

"Day after tomorrow?"

"Good."

She got up, and Bridget followed her to the front door. "Thanks a lot, Mrs. Randolph."

"Call me Greta."

"Okay, Greta."

"I'll see you day after tomorrow at . . . how's eight?"

"That's . . . fine. See you then." Bridget groaned inwardly. She had gotten very bad at waking up in the morning.

"What did you say your last name was?"

"Oh. It's . . . Tomko." There was a stray name that could use a new owner, even temporarily. Besides, she liked thinking of Tibby.

"How old are you, if you don't mind my asking?"

"Just about to turn seventeen," Bridget said.

Greta nodded. "I have a granddaughter your age. She'll be seventeen in September."

Bridget flinched. "Really?" Her voice warbled.

"She lives up in Washington, D.C. You ever been there?"

Bridget shook her head. It was easy to lie to strangers. It was harder when they knew your birthday.

"Where are you from, anyway?"

"Norfolk." Bridget had no idea why she said that.

"You've come a long way."

Bridget nodded.

"Well, nice to meet you, Gilda," the woman who was her grandmother called after her.

"The restaurant was really fabulous. I thought we'd just go to a neighborhood place, but he'd made a reservation at Josephine. Can you believe that? I was worried I was underdressed, but he said I looked perfect. Those were his exact words. 'You look perfect.' Can you believe that? I spent the longest time trying to figure out what to order so I wouldn't end up with béarnaise sauce down the front of my blouse or salad in my teeth."

Christina laughed so heartily it was as though no one had ever soldiered through that predicament before her.

Carmen looked down at her whole-wheat toaster waffle. The four middle squares contained full pools of syrup and the rest of it lay dry. The things her mother was saying were things Carmen should have been saying. She couldn't help noting the irony with a certain amount of sourness. Carmen wasn't saying them because her mother was saying them and saying them and saying them and not shutting up.

Christina widened her eyes dramatically. "Carmen, I wish you could have tasted the dessert. It was to *die* for. It was called *tarte tatin*."

The overeager French accent with the uptilting snap of Puerto Rican just under the surface made Carmen unable to be as mad at her mother as she wanted to be.

"Yum," Carmen said dully.

"He was *so* sweet. Such a gentleman. He opened the

car door for me. When was the last time that happened?" Christina looked at her like she really wanted an answer.

Carmen shrugged. "Never?"

"He graduated from *Stanford* University. Did I say that already?"

Carmen nodded. Christina looked so pathetically proud, Carmen couldn't help thinking shamefully about her own pride the night before when she'd said her dad went to Williams.

Carefully Carmen tipped the syrup bottle, attempting to fill each individual square of her waffle with its own small puddle. "What's his name again?"

"David." Christina seemed to enjoy the taste of it even more than *tarte tatin*.

"How old did you say he was?"

Christina depuffed a little. "He's thirty-four. That's only four years' difference, though."

"More like five," Carmen said. It was a mean thing to say masquerading as a true thing to say. Her mother was turning thirty-nine in less than a month. "But he does sound really nice," Carmen added to make up for it.

That was all her mother needed. "He is. He really is." And she proceeded to rattle on about just how nice he was straight through two additional waffles. About how he had brought her coffee a few times at the office and helped her when her computer froze.

"He's a third-year associate," Christina blabbed informatively, as if Carmen would care at all. "He didn't go to law school right after college. He worked for a newspaper in

Memphis. I think that's what makes him so *interesting*."
Christina said the word like it had only ever deserved to be
used this one time.

Carmen poured herself a glass of milk. She hadn't had a
glass of milk since she was about thirteen. She wondered,
with a scientific sort of curiosity, how long her mother
would keep talking if she herself didn't say *anything at all*?

"He's always been so friendly and helpful, but I never
imagined he would want to take me out on a date.
Never!" Christina took the opportunity to circle the small
room a few times. Her church shoes *clack clacked* on the
peach linoleum.

"I know it's probably not a good idea to date somebody from the office, but on the other hand, we don't
work in the same department or even on the same floor."
She waved her arm, grandly allowing the concept of an
office romance before she'd even finished disallowing it.

"I mean, last night, watching you go, I felt so old and
lonely thinking about how it would be with you gone
next year. And then this! The timing is straight from
God, I think."

Carmen made herself not mention that God had a lot
of better things to think about.

"I shouldn't leap ahead. What if it goes nowhere?
What if he isn't looking for a real relationship? What if
he's in a different place than me?"

First off, Carmen hated when her mother used the
word *place* like some great metaphysician. And second,
since when was her mother looking for a relationship?

She hadn't gone out with a guy since Carmen was in fourth grade.

Not answering didn't do the job. Even going to the bathroom didn't stem her mother's flow of words. Carmen wondered whether actually leaving the apartment would make her mother stop talking.

At last Carmen consulted the clock. It was never on her side. For the first time in Carmen-Christina history it said they were not late for church. "We oughta get going," Carmen suggested anyway.

Her mother nodded and followed her companionably from the kitchen, talking all the while. She didn't take a break until they pulled into the church parking lot.

"Tell me, *nena*," Christina asked as she dropped her keys into her purse and steered Carmen into church. "How was *your* evening?"

Lenny,

I know you're just a few blocks away and I'll be shoving the Pants into your arms in about five (okay, ten) minutes when I pick you up (okay, late) for work. But it made me a little sad not to be writing a letter from a faraway place, and then I thought, well, hey, just because we can e-mail and call and see each other all we want this summer doesn't meant I can't write a letter from a near place, does it? That's not exactly a felony, is it?

So, Lenny, I know it's not like last summer. You

59

don't miss me, because you saw me several times yesterday and then I blabbed you into a near coma last night. But even though you are about to see me and possibly yell at me for being late (again), I can still take this opportunity to tell you that you are the best, greatest, awesomest Lenny ever and I love you a lot. So go crazy in these Pants, chickadee.

Carmen Electrifying

Men occasionally stumble

over the truth, but most

of them pick themselves

up and hurry off as if

nothing had happened.

—Winston Churchill

Lena didn't go crazy in the Pants. The first day she left them at home in her room on top of the pile of letters from Kostos. The second day she wore them to work, got reprimanded by Mrs. Duffers, and had to take them off before lunchtime. She left them on the chair in the back of the store, where a customer saw them and tried to buy them.

Her heart was still pounding from the horror of that experience when Effie strode in. It was closing time, and Lena hadn't finished cleaning out the fitting rooms.

"So guess who called today?" Effie demanded.

"Who?" Lena hated Effie's guessing games, especially when she was tired.

"Guess." Effie followed her back to the fitting rooms.

"*No!*"

Effie looked sour. "Fine. *Fine.*" She cast her eyes upward for patience. "Grandma. I talked to her."

"You did?" Lena stopped picking up clothes. "How is she? How's Bapi?"

"They're great. They had a big anniversary party in the old restaurant last month. The whole town was there."

"Ohhh." Lena could picture it. Her mind drifted slowly to Fira, to the view of the Caldera from the terrace of the restaurant her grandparents owned. "That's so nice," she said distantly. Picturing the harbor of course made her picture Kostos. Picturing Kostos gave her that zoomy feeling in the bottom of her abdomen.

Lena cleared her throat and resumed gathering clothing. "How are the Dounases?" she asked evenly.

"Good."

"Yeah?" Lena didn't want to ask about Kostos outright.

"Sure. Grandma said Kostos brought a girl from Ammoudi to the party."

Lena tried very hard not to move her face one single millimeter.

Effie's eyebrows went down. "Lenny, why do you look like that?"

"What do you mean?"

"Like . . . that." Effie pointed at Lena's tight, miserable face. "You're the one who broke up with *him*."

"I know." Lena bumped her foot spasmodically against the mirror. "Your point being . . . ?" Lena needed to play stupid. Otherwise she might cry.

"I don't get you. If you feel this way, why did you break up with him?" Effie asked, not seeming to care that they weren't having the same conversation.

"Feel what way? How do you know I feel any which way?" Lena asked. She began sorting pants by size.

Effie shook her head, as though Lena were a hopeless and pitiable moron. "If it makes you feel better, Grandma doesn't like the girl he brought."

Lena pretended very hard not to care about that.

"And she also said, and I quote, 'Dis girl is not nearly as boootiful as Lena.'"

Lena kept up with the pretending.

"Does that make it any better?" Effie wheedled.

Lena shrugged, impassive.

"So I said, 'Grandma, that girl probably didn't break up with him for no reason.'"

Lena threw the clothes down. "Forget it," she stated. "You are not getting a ride to work."

"Lenny! You promised!" Effie said. "Besides, what do you care? I thought you said you didn't care."

Effie always won. Always.

"I *don't* care," Lena mumbled babyishly.

"So drive me to work like you promised." Effie was a genius at turning a favor into an obligation.

The sky had turned so dark Lena couldn't believe it wasn't nighttime. Cradling the Pants in one arm, she locked the front door and pulled down the gate. Outside, heavy, warm splashes of rain landed in her hair and dripped down her forehead. Effie ran to the car and Lena walked, protecting the Pants under her shirt. She liked rain.

The Olive Vine was less than two miles from the shop. Effie bounded into the restaurant in a couple of giant strides.

Lena drove on. The rain drummed and the windshield wipers squeaked. She liked being alone at the wheel when nobody was expecting her anyplace. Sometime in the last few months she had passed into the stage of driving where she didn't have to think consciously about how to do it anymore. She didn't have to think *Okay, blinker. Brakes. Turn.* She just drove. It left her mind free to wander.

She found herself driving past the mailbox where she used to mail the old letters, before she had stopped caring so much. Or before she had started pretending she had stopped caring so much.

She still held the Pants close to her body. She'd worn them when she and Kostos had kissed so exquisitely at the very end of the summer. She took a deep breath. Maybe a few of his cells still clung to them. Maybe.

Having the Pants with her now on this rainy night, far away from Kostos, gave her a deep, melancholic feeling of loss.

So that was how it was. Kostos had a new girlfriend. Lena had a mean sister and a job selling beige clothing.

Who, exactly, had come out on top?

At first Bridget thought she remembered nothing from Burgess. Then, as she ambled around town, a few little things jogged her memory. One was the peanut machine outside the hardware store. Even as a six-year-old, she'd thought it was weird and old-fashioned that the gumball machine dispensed peanuts. And yet, here it still was. She strongly suspected the peanuts were as old as she was.

Another thing was the rusted black cannon from the Civil War, in the grassy patch in front of the courthouse.

A pyramid of stuck-together cannonballs stood by its base. She remembered clowning around—sticking her head in it as though she were a cartoon character and making Perry laugh.

She also remembered climbing on the high wall next to the bank, and her grandmother shrieking at her to get down. She'd been such a monkey as a little kid. She'd been the best tree climber in her neighborhood, even among boys and older kids. She'd felt so light and rubbery then compared to now.

Bridget let her feet guide her, because they seemed to have a better memory than her head. She walked farther along Market Street until the village stretched out a little. There were hydrangeas in bloom in front of every house—big purple balls.

Past the Methodist church, a wide field stretched out, green and lush. It went along for three blocks, bordered by giant, ancient oak trees and pretty iron benches. At the far end she noticed soccer goals marking a beautiful green regulation field. She felt breathless as she looked at it. There was a rumbling, creaking feeling in her brain as it searched its many dusty, unconsidered files.

She sat on a bench and closed her eyes. She remembered running and she remembered a soccer ball, and then she started remembering many, many things all in a rush. She remembered her grandfather teaching her and Perry how to kick the ball when they were only three or four. Perry had hated it and tripped over his feet, but Bridget had loved it. She remembered holding her hands behind her back to remind herself that soccer was only kicking.

She remembered dribbling past her grandpa and him shouting proudly after her, "Folks, I think we have a natural!" even though there was nobody else on the field.

The summer she was five, her grandpa had stuck her in the Limestone County Boys' League, amid loud protests from the other parents. Bridget remembered forcing her grandmother to cut her hair short, like a boy's, and she also remembered her mother crying when she saw Bridget at the end of the summer. Bridget led the Burgess Honey Bees to a trophy for two summers straight, and the parents stopped complaining.

God, she had forgotten about that team until this very minute. And it had been so meaningful to her then—the coincidence of her nickname and the team name. "She's the Bee-all! She's the Bee's Knees!" her grandpa used to shout from the sidelines, thinking he was so funny. Her father had never cared for sports, but her grandpa had adored them.

Had her father known when her grandfather died?

She let her mind drift. She'd never stopped to think about how soccer had started for her, but this was it. This was the beginning.

There was a strange thing about her memory, and she had noticed it before this. When she was eleven and the terrible stuff had happened, her brain had sort of erased itself. Everything from that time or before she'd either forgotten completely or remembered as though it had happened to somebody else. They'd made her see a psychiatrist for a few months after her mom died, and he had said her brain had formed scar tissue. She had never liked that image much.

She sat there, resting her scarred head on the back of the bench for a long time, until, as though in a dream, she heard footsteps and shouts and the beloved *thunk* of a foot against a soccer ball. She opened her eyes and watched, startled, as a group of boys took over the field. There were fifteen or twenty of them, and they appeared to be around her age, maybe a little older.

When one of the boys passed close by, she couldn't help flagging him down. "Are you part of a team?" she asked.

He nodded. "The Burgess Mavericks," he said.

"Is there still a summer league?" she asked.

"Sure." He was holding a soccer ball. Though Bridget hadn't touched one in more than nine months, she looked at his with longing.

"You have practice now?" she asked.

"Tuesday and Thursday evenings," he answered in his twangy Alabama way. People seemed to talk with more syllables down here.

She remembered loving that accent, listening to it magically insert itself into her own vowels and consonants by the middle of August. And then she'd go back up north, her friends would giggle at the way she talked, and by October it would be gone again.

The guy kept turning his head to look at the drills starting up on the field. He was polite, but he didn't want to talk to her anymore.

"And you play games on Saturday?" she asked.

"Yep. All summer long. I gotta go."

"Okay. Thanks," she said after him as he joined his friends on the field.

It was still strange to her how she related to the world now. A year ago, this same boy would've taken a look at her hair and been happy to tell her anything she wanted to know. He would have been show-offy and loud so his friends would see that he was talking to her.

Between the ages of thirteen and sixteen Bridget had attracted more wolf whistles and phone numbers and corny pickup lines than she could count. It wasn't because she was—had been—beautiful. Lena was beautiful, truly and uniquely, and boys mostly looked scared when she passed by. It was that Bridget had been thin and striking and outgoing, and, of course, she'd had the hair.

She watched them kick around and run a few drills. When they started a scrimmage, she walked a bit closer to the sidelines. Already some girls—probably girl-friends—had appeared. As she studied the faces of the players, a few of them transformed from strangers into long-ago teammates before her eyes. Amazing. There was a ball hog she definitely recognized, what was his name? Corey Something-or-other. And the midfielder with red hair. He looked and played almost exactly the same as when he was seven. She was sure she recognized one of the goalies, and then there was . . . *Oh my.* Bridget clasped her hands to her chest. The name jumped right into her head: Billy Kline. *Oh, my God!* He had been the second-best player on the team and her best pal off the field. She remembered him distinctly now. She probably even had a letter or two from him stuffed away somewhere back home.

Unbelievable.

He had grown up very nicely, she couldn't help noting. He was both wiry and muscular, her favorite type. His hair was darker and wavier, but his face was the same. She'd loved his face when she was a little kid.

She watched him with a pounding heart and a scrambling mind. His house was down close to the river. They'd spent hours and hours collecting rocks together, certain that every one was an ancient arrowhead and that they could sell it for big bucks to the Indian Mound Museum in downtown Florence.

Billy threw the ball in from the sidelines. She moved quickly out of his way. He looked at her and through her.

She wasn't worried about him recognizing her. Back then she'd been skinny, yellow-haired, and full of joy. Now she was heavy, muddy-haired, and full of care. She might as well be a different person.

It was a relief, in a way. Sometimes it felt like a relief to be invisible.

Tibby sat on the outside of a group of kids in the film program. There was a lot of dark clothing and heavy footwear, and quite a few piercings glinting in the sunlight. They had invited her to sit with them while they all finished up their lunches before film seminar. Tibby knew that they had invited her largely because she had a ring in her nose. This bugged her almost as much as when people excluded her because she had a ring in her nose.

A girl named Katie complained about her roommate while Tibby chewed listlessly on pasta salad. It had as much taste as her sleeve. She chewed and nodded, nodded and chewed. It was a good thing she'd been born with her friends, Tibby realized, because she was terrible at making them.

A few minutes later she followed the group up the stairs of the arts building and into the classroom. She sat on the edge so there would be empty seats next to her. Partly she wanted to lessen her commitment to this particular group. Mostly she was waiting for Alex.

Her heart sped up when he arrived with Maura and sat down next to Tibby. Maura sat on his other side. Granted, they were the only two empty seats together left in the room.

The instructor, Mr. Russell, organized his papers. "All right, class." He held up his hands. "As you know, this is your project seminar. This class is not about listening but about doing."

Alex was taking notes in his binder. Tibby couldn't resist glancing at them.

Class about doing.

Was he joking? He glanced at Tibby. Yes, he was joking.

"You're each going to make a film this summer, and you'll have nearly the entire term to do it. You'll spend a lot of time out in the world and a little time in this class."

Alex was now drawing a picture. It was Mr. Russell, only his head was very tiny and his hands were very large. It was a pretty good picture. Did Alex know Tibby was peeking at it? Did he mind?

"The assignment," Mr. Russell went on, "is to make a biographical piece. Focus the film on somebody who's played an important role in your life. You are welcome to use scripts and actors or to make a documentary. It's up to you."

Tibby had an idea of what she wanted to do. It just arrived in her head. It arrived in the image of Bailey. Her friend Bailey, last summer, sitting against the slatted blinds in Tibby's bedroom window with the sunlight sliding through in the last month of her twelve-year-long life. It made Tibby's eyes ache. She looked to her left.

Up to you, Alex wrote in flowery calligraphy under the picture of Mr. Russell.

Tibby rubbed her eyes. No, she didn't want to do that idea. She couldn't do that idea. She didn't permit herself to even give that idea a worded tag in her brain. She let it float back out the way it had come.

For the rest of the class she felt haunted by the feeling of the idea, even though the idea itself was gone. She forgot about Alex and his notes. Her eyes seemed to focus only a few inches in front of her face.

She forgot about him until he was talking right next to her ear. It took her a few moments to realize he was talking to her ear. Or rather, to her.

"Do you want to get coffee?" he seemed to be asking.

Maura was looking at her expectantly too.

"Oh . . ." When Alex's words arranged themselves into the proper order, Tibby discovered she was pleased. "Now?"

"Sure." Maura appeared to have taken over the planning. "Do you have another class?"

Tibby shrugged. Did she? Did it matter? She stood up and lifted her bag over her shoulder.

They sat in the back of the café at the student union building. It turned out both Alex and Maura were from New York City, which Tibby might have guessed. It also turned out Maura's room was on the seventh floor of Tibby's dorm. Maura was particularly interested in Vanessa, the RA.

"Did you see her room?"

Tibby's attention was drifting over to Alex. Maura wasn't willing to let it go.

"Seriously, did you see it?"

"No," Tibby said.

"It's full of toys and stuffed animals. I swear to God. The girl is a *freeeeak.*"

Tibby nodded. She didn't doubt that, but she was more interested in listening to Alex talk about his project. "It's pure nihilism. Think Kafka, but with a lot of explosions," he was explaining.

Tibby laughed appreciatively even though she didn't know what *nihilism* meant and she couldn't name a single thing Kafka had written. He was a writer, wasn't he?

Alex had a wry smile. "Kafka meets early Schwarzenegger, and the whole thing takes place in a Pizza Hut."

He is smart, Tibby thought. "And how is this biographical?" she asked.

Alex shrugged and cast her a low-level smile. "Dunno," he said, like he couldn't be bothered.

"So what's your project going to be? Do you know yet?" Maura asked her.

Tibby didn't even allow herself the idea of her first idea, though it cast its shadow from high above her head. "I don't know. . . . I'm thinking probably I'll . . ."

Tibby had no idea how she was going to end this sentence. She looked down at Alex's Pumas. She wanted her movie to be funny. She wanted Alex to smile at her the way he had in Bagley's class.

She thought of the stuff she'd already filmed this summer. She'd caught this hilarious bit of her mom bustling around the kitchen, unaware that she had Nicky's lollipop stuck to the back of her head. It was a dumb gag, but it was funny.

"I'm thinking I'll probably do kind of a comic one . . . about my mom."

Carmen wished the ride to the Morgans' were longer so she could complain longer. She could tell Lena felt the ride was long enough.

"I understand, I really do," Lena said sweetly but with diminishing patience as she pulled up in front of the large white clapboard house. "I'm just saying, your mom hasn't gone on a date in a long time. It's exciting for her."

Lena glanced at Carmen's sour face. "But then again, she's not my mom. If she were, maybe I'd feel exactly the same way."

Carmen studied her suspiciously. "No. You wouldn't."

Lena shrugged. "Well, I don't think my mom ever kissed a guy other than my dad, so it's pretty hard to picture," she reasoned diplomatically. "But if she did—"

"You would be kind about it," Carmen finished.

"No one is kind to their mom," Lena said.

"You are," Carmen accused.

"Oh, no, I'm not," Lena said with feeling.

"You get annoyed and maybe huffy sometimes, Len, but you're not openly bratty."

"Annoyed and huffy can be even worse than bratty," Lena argued.

The shiny red front door opened, and Jesse Morgan stood waving at them from the top step.

"I have to go," Carmen said. "Can you pick me up? I'll drive tomorrow."

"You can't drive tomorrow. If you do, I'll be late again," Lena said.

"You won't be. Seriously. I'll get up early. I promise."

Carmen often promised this but never actually did it.

"Oh, all right." Lena always gave her another chance. It was a little dance they did.

"Hi, Jesse," Carmen said, hurrying up the walk. She grabbed him in a brief headlock as she passed through the door. Jesse was four and liked to keep track of who came and went on Quincy Street. Also, he liked to yell puzzling things to people on the sidewalk from his second-story bedroom window.

Carmen walked straight back to the kitchen, where Mrs. Morgan was cleaning Rice Krispies off the floor with one hand and holding Joe, the nine-month-old, with the other.

Carmen had already learned not to give the kids Rice Krispies, because they were harder to clean up than, say, Kix. That was something an outsider could figure out in a day and a mother would never think of. Wet, walked-on Rice Krispies were part of Mrs. Morgan's unquestioned burden.

"Hi, everybody," Carmen said. She held out her hands to Joe, but he clung to his mother. Joe did like Carmen, but only when his mother was out of the house.

"Hi, Carmen. How are you?" Mrs. Morgan threw some Saran-wrapped objects from the refrigerator to the garbage can. "I'm going out to run some errands. I'll be back at noon. I'm on the cell if you need me."

Prolonging the inevitable, Joe surveyed Carmen from where his head lay on his mother's shoulder. Carmen remembered what Lena had said about not being kind to your mother. Joe was kind to his mother. He adored her. Had Carmen been kind to her mother when she was a baby? Maybe you were kind only when you were very young or very old.

She accepted a wriggling, protesting Joe from Mrs. Morgan.

As soon as she had him settled on the floor with stackable buckets, he took off his sock and started chewing on it. The sock had a little rubber tic-tac-toe pattern on the bottom. For traction, Carmen figured.

"No, Joe. Don't eat your socks."

Jesse was watching the cars go by through a small pane of glass just the height of his face at the side of the front door. "Hey, Jess. What do you see?"

Jesse didn't answer. Carmen liked the fact that though grown-up people felt the need to check in with a lot of useless questions and statements, children rarely felt the need to answer them.

"I have to make a pee," he said after a while. Carmen picked up Joe and followed Jesse upstairs. For some reason Jesse only liked to use the bathroom upstairs. She decided to change Joe's diaper while she was up there. She laid him down on the diaper pad and let him gum the tube of ointment. Could zinc oxide hurt you if ingested?

She opened the top drawer of his bureau, admiring the neat assortment of socks, all carefully matched, all primary colors, all with the little tic-tac-toes on the bottoms. Mrs. Morgan seemed like an intelligent woman to be spending so much energy on socks. Hadn't she gone to law school? Could you be overqualified for this job?

Carmen thought of her mother sitting at the kitchen table of the old house, dragging a fork along the bottoms of Carmen's new birthday-party shoes so Carmen wouldn't slip on the shiny floors at Lena's house.

Downstairs, Carmen called her mom at work. "Hi," she said when her mom answered. That was really all she wanted to say.

"*Nena*, I'm glad you called." Christina was breathless. "I'm going out for dinner with David tonight. If that's okay. There's, uh, lasagna in the freezer." Her mother sounded distracted. Not distracted as in looking for the stapler, but deeply distracted.

"Really? Again?" Carmen paused awhile, wishing her mother would pick up on her mood.

"I won't be late," her mother assured her. "It's crazy this week."

"Well. Okay." Carmen's voice was soft. "Bye."

There had definitely been a time, maybe as recently as the day before, when Carmen would have loved the idea of a night with the apartment all to herself. But right now she didn't.

An hour or so later she checked her messages. There was one from Paul, returning a call of hers. There was one from Porter. The notorious after-date phone call. If a guy called within three days, he liked you. If he waited a week, that meant he didn't have any better options and was probably just trying to get lucky. If he didn't call at all, well, that was obvious.

Porter's call fell just inside the three-day mark. And an hour before, this also would have mattered to her.

Tibby,

Well, here are the Pants. I admit I didn't exactly set the world on fire. I got scolded by my boss and watched a trendy fifty-year-old try to buy them. I hope you'll do better.

78

Anyway, I don't know what Carmen told you, but I'm totally okay about Kostos and his new girlfriend. I was the one who broke up with him, remember?

Have fun with the Pants. I miss you. Call me later tonight if you are not out being cool and sophisticated with your cool and sophisticated new filmmaker friends.

Love,
Lena

. . . You can see only as far as your headlights, but you can make the whole trip that way.

—E. L. Doctorow

Lena loved Carmen's kitchen. It felt safe and contained, unlike the sprawling renovation at her house, with all its gleaming white and silver steel and too-bright halogen bulbs. Also, Lena loved the food Carmen's kitchen had in it. It was all avocados and low-fat chips and herbal teas — girl stuff. None of the giant twelve-packs of beer and endless pork chops that jammed up the fridge at her house. There were so many fewer compromises in an apartment for two than in a house for four.

"Honey, would you like a glass of iced tea?"

Lena looked at Carmen's mom. She appeared to be rearranging the pots in the lower cabinets. Her hair was back in a ponytail, and she looked like she was about twenty. Christina was always pretty, but Lena had never seen her look as animated and happy as she looked today.

"I'd love one," Lena said.

Carmen was scanning the movie section of the newspaper. "I'll have one too," she said without looking up.

"How's your mom?" Christina asked over the noise of the sink. She always asked this of Lena in a slightly guilty way, as if she were trying to pick up her dry cleaning without the ticket.

"She's all right."

"And how is your boyfriend? What's his name?"

"Kostos," Lena said reluctantly, never eager to discuss her love life. "But he's not my boyfriend anymore. We broke up."

"Ohhh. I'm sorry. Was the long-distance thing too hard?"

Lena liked that explanation. It was succinct and it didn't necessarily make her sound like a lunatic. "Yes. Exactly."

Christina took a full pitcher from the refrigerator. "Reminds me of your mother. She must know what you're going through."

Lena was bewildered. "We haven't really talked about it."

Christina didn't seem to realize that not all mothers talked to their daughters about everything all the time.

"Anyway, I don't think she knows anything about long-distance relationships," Lena said.

Christina lined up three glasses. "Of course she does. She was with Eugene for at least four or five years."

Lena looked doubtfully at Christina.

Christina and Lena's mom hadn't been close for a long time. Christina's memory seemed to be getting jumbled, maybe on account of her own love affair.

"Who's Eugene?"

Carmen had now torn herself from the movie section. She was looking back and forth from Lena to Christina.

"Who's Eugene?" Christina repeated. The look on her face

slowly transformed from surprise to uncertainty to anxiety.

"Uh . . ." She turned her back to the girls and poured the tea.

"Mama? Hello? Helloooooooo?"

Christina took a long time stirring in the sugar. When she turned back around, her face didn't look open anymore. "Never mind. I might be mixed up. It was all a long time ago."

Christina was a lovable, big-hearted, totally sweet person, but she was a bad actress and a horrible liar. Lena *had* believed she was mixed up before. Now she felt certain she wasn't.

Carmen's eyes were narrowed like laser beams on her mother's face. "Never mind? *Never mind?* Are you joking?"

Christina cast a longing look at the door. "I've got to call Mimmy, honey. It's already afternoon."

"You're not going to tell us?" Carmen looked as if she were ready to explode.

Christina's eyes darted around nervously. "There's nothing to tell. I was mistaken. I was thinking about someone else. It's not important." She snapped her mouth shut and left the kitchen in a hurry. She knew as well as anyone that Carmen didn't let a person off the hook easily.

"It's not important?" Lena echoed faintly.

Carmen looked at Lena knowingly. "That obviously means it is."

"Who's Eugene?"

Lena let it drop quietly between dinner and dessert as her mother loaded the plates into the dishwasher. Lena was clearing the table. It was just the two of them in the kitchen. Effie was at a friend's, and their dad was reading the newspaper in the dining room.

"What?" Ari turned around.

"Who's Eugene?"

Right away Lena knew she was causing a disturbance.

"Why are you asking me that?" Her mother was holding a plate in each hand.

"I just . . . want to know."

"Who told you about him?"

"Nobody," Lena said. If her mother wasn't giving any information, then she didn't feel like giving any either. Besides, she didn't want to get Carmen's mom in trouble.

Ari's face took on a frustrated, unpolished look. She seemed to be calculating in a hurry. "Well, I have no idea what you are talking about."

"Then why are you whispering?"

Lena hadn't meant to torture her mother, but that was how it was working out.

"I'm not," she said, also in a whisper.

Lena stopped. This was feeling a little out of control. She wanted information, badly. The harder it was to get it, the more critical it seemed. On the other hand, the look on her mother's face scared her a little.

Lena's dad ambled into the kitchen. "How about some cheesecake?" he asked agreeably.

Lena's mother cast her a look that said, in no uncertain terms, *Do not open your mouth or I will ground you until you are an old woman.*

84

"I'm going upstairs," Lena informed the granite countertop.

"Nothing sweet?" her dad asked. They had a common love of dessert.

"Not tonight," she said.

"Do you think Mom had a boyfriend before Dad?" she asked Effie when she appeared in Lena's room awhile later.

"No. Nobody important."

"What makes you so sure?" Lena asked.

"Because she would've told us about it," Effie reasoned.

"Maybe not. She doesn't tell us everything."

Effie rolled her eyes. "Mom has a very boring life. Maybe there isn't anything to tell."

Lena thought for a while. "I think Mom had a boyfriend named Eugene. I think she lived here and he lived in Greece, and I think she might have really loved him."

Effie raised her eyebrows. "You do, do you?"

Lena nodded.

"Well, I think you should stick with your own tragic love story."

"David wants to take us both out to dinner," Christina announced that evening, as though Ed McMahon had just arrived with the giant novelty check.

"Why?"

"Car*men*!" Christina was too happy to be mad. "Because he wants to meet you!"

Christina had the Weight Watchers cookbook open on the counter and onions sizzling in a pan.

"When?"

"Tomorrow night?" Christina suggested.

"I'm going to the movies with Lena."

"Thursday?"

"Baby-sitting."

"Friday?"

Carmen studied her mother in annoyance. Usually a person got the hint by the third try. "I'm . . . going out with Porter," she said, satisfied with her answer even though it was a lie. Her mother wasn't the only one in the world with a boyfriend.

Christina's eyes turned from disappointed to pleased. "Bring him! We'll go out, all four of us!"

"David wants to take us out to dinner," Carmen announced into the phone an hour later. Her tone was somewhat different than her mother's had been.

Tibby exhaled. "It sounds like it's getting serious. You know, time to meet the parents. Except the other way around."

"I told her I was going out with Porter, and she wants him to come too."

"A double date with your mother?" Tibby said, at least partly enjoying the absurdity of it.

"I know," Carmen moaned. "It might be better this way, though. I'll have something else to pay attention to. And maybe the guys can talk about tire irons or something."

"Maybe." Tibby sounded doubtful.

"The only thing is, I don't actually have a plan to go out with Porter. I made that up."

"Oh, Carmen."

"Yeah, so now I have to ask him."

Tibby laughed, but Carmen could tell it was appreciative. "Do you like him?" she asked.

"Who?"

"Porter!"

"Oh. Uh, I guess so."

"You *guess* so?"

"He's really good-looking. Don't you think?"

"He looks fine," Tibby said a little impatiently. "But Carmen, you shouldn't ask him out if you don't like him. It kind of sends the wrong message."

"Who said I didn't like him? Maybe I do like him," Carmen snapped.

"Gosh. You make it sound so romantic."

Carmen laughed. She bit at a loose piece of skin next to her thumbnail. "Did I tell you my mom put us on a diet?"

"No."

"Yes."

"Poor you."

"Except I walked to Giant and bought three flavors of Ben & Jerry's."

Tibby laughed again. "Atta girl."

Hey Bee Bee,

I am a big fat loser, but what else is new? The big event on my social calendar is a double date with my mother. I am totally serious.

87

How did this happen? A week ago my mom's big plans were a dentist appointment. Now she's doing something with David like every other night.

Don't say you're happy for her. You said that last time. You're not the one eating the frozen pizza.

Last night she went out wearing this cropped shirt. I swear you could see her belly button. Not pretty, Bee.

This morning I called her at the office to see if I could go to a ten o'clock movie and she said, "Use your judgment." !!!! How come my judgment was never good enough to use before David came along?

Am I just being a selfish brat? Be honest.

But not too honest.

Write soon and tell me everything about Gilda Tomko. I miss you so much.

Love,

Carmen "the Brat" Lowell

"Meet us for breakfast if you want," Maura called later that night as the elevator door closed. "We're walking down the highway to IHOP."

"All right," Tibby said through the door. Being New Yorkers, Maura and Alex liked to joke about how other places didn't have sidewalks, only highways. Tibby nodded along like she was a New Yorker too, not a product of pure suburbia.

The pulsing sleep light of her iBook greeted her. "Hi," she said to her computer.

"Hi," it said back.

Tibby started. She felt her blood zooming around her body.

The computer laughed. It had the voice of Brian. Tibby switched on the overhead light.

"Oh, my God! Brian! You scared the crap out of me."

He came over to her and pulled on her arm. "Hey, Tibby." His smile was giant.

Her smile was giant too, and automatic. She had missed him. "What are you doing here?"

"I missed you."

"I missed you too," she said without thinking.

"And also, I thought I'd bring you home."

"You mean for the weekend?"

"Yeah," he said.

"That's not for three days."

"That's true." He shrugged. "I missed you."

"How did you get in here?"

"Somebody let me in downstairs." He pointed to her door. "And you could pick that lock with anything."

"Really? That's comforting." She missed Bee when she thought of lock-picking.

"Is it okay if I . . . ?" He pointed to a dark green sleeping bag in a roll on the floor.

"Sleep here?" she asked.

He nodded.

"Yeah. Of course. I mean, where else are you going to go?"

He looked a little uncertain. "Are you sure it's okay?"

When she stopped to think about it, Tibby realized it was pretty profound having a boy stay all night in your room. It was really like college in that way.

But then again, Brian wasn't a boy. Well, he was, technically speaking. But Tibby didn't act or feel around him the way she did around any other boys she had ever known. Much as she loved him, Brian was about as sexy as tube socks.

She studied him for a moment. It was funny how much he had changed since the day she met him. He was much taller. (It helped that he'd been eating dinner at her house two or three nights a week.) He washed his hair sometimes. (Tibby was always taking showers; she suspected he had learned by example.) He wore a belt. (Okay, so maybe she had bought him one.) But still he was Brian.

"I could get in trouble, though," Tibby said. "If the RA or anybody sees you."

Brian nodded solemnly. "I thought of that too. I'll make sure nobody sees me."

"Okay." She knew her parents wouldn't get mad about it. That wasn't the issue.

He sat down on her night table.

"I saw Nicky and Katherine yesterday," he told her.

"Yeah?"

"Katherine fell down the steps. She wanted you to fix it."

"She wanted me?"

"Uh-huh."

Tibby felt her cheeks warm. Mostly she kept those two small creatures at bay. She knew how much her parents wanted her to interact with them. Every time Tibby let Katherine climb on her lap, she felt her mother's opportunism, her constant desire for free baby-sitting. When Bugs Bunny looked at Daffy Duck on the desert island, he saw a big, juicy roasted duck. When Alice looked at Tibby, she saw an able-bodied teenage baby-sitter.

"I played Dragon Spots with Nicky."

"He must have loved that." Brian was fostering in Nicky an early love of video games.

She felt a little bit uneasy that Brian was still going to her house when she wasn't there. Was it really Tibby he liked or was it the Rollinses' tinies?

"How's it going here?" Brian asked. He looked at the sketches and notes scattered over her desk.

"Pretty good."

"How's your movie? Did you decide what it's going to be about yet?"

Tibby had spoken to Brian many times since she had decided and started working on the movie. But for some reason she hadn't told him about it. She gathered the sketches into a pile. "I think so."

"What?"

"Maybe about my mom." She didn't feel like elaborating.

His face lit up. "Really? That's a great idea."

Brian had an annoying tendency to like Alice.

"Yeah."

"How are your friends?" Brian asked. "I mean, those

new ones you met." His eyebrows peaked over his nose in that earnest way he had.

"They're . . ." She was going to say *nice*, but the word didn't fit. *Great* seemed to carry the wrong connotation too. ". . . all right."

"I'll meet them tomorrow, hopefully." Brian began unrolling his sleeping bag.

"Sure," she said. She wasn't quite sure about that.

He kept his toothbrush and toothpaste in a crumpled plastic Wallman's bag. Her bathroom kit was made of thick, see-through blue plastic with a zipper. "You can go first," she offered. She peered out the door. The bathroom was only a few yards down the hall. "Go ahead," she said.

While she waited for him, she decided to fish her extra blanket down from the closet shelf to give him a little extra padding on the hard floor. A big Jiffy envelope with Lena's handwriting on it came down with the blanket.

The envelope seemed to stare at her critically. She knew the Pants were in there, and yet she hadn't even opened it. Why not?

She knew why, really. When she opened the Pants, she would remember about last summer and Bailey and Mimi and everything else. She would have to see the crooked red heart she'd embroidered onto the side of the left knee. She would have to remember those strange, long days after Bailey's funeral when she'd sat alone on the back screened porch making endless ragged stitches. Maybe she wasn't ready to think about it right now.

A few minutes later the room was dark and Tibby and

Brian were both lying on their backs looking up at the ceiling. Her first-ever sleepover with a boy.

"Did you quit Travel Zone?" Tibby asked.

"Yeah."

Brian moved from one job to the next. He was a skilled Webmaster and all-around techno-dork. He could get hired at twenty bucks an hour no matter what he did.

They were quiet. She listened to his breathing. She could tell he wasn't asleep yet. Her throat felt tight and achy.

In the first few months of their friendship, there had been quiet, full moments between them, and Brian had brought up the subject of Bailey. It was hard for Tibby every time he did. After a while she asked him not to. She said when they were quiet together, they would both know who they were thinking about.

Tonight in this small dorm room in this strange place, they both knew who they were thinking about.

lovers alone wear

sunlight

—E. E. Cummings

David didn't have any obvious physical deformities. His teeth were all there. He had hair even. Carmen surveyed David's clothing in a quick glance. Acceptable. He wasn't wearing a *Star Trek* shirt or anything. She studied his feet for evidence of an orthopedic shoe.

"This is Porter," Carmen said. "Porter, this is my mom, Christina." She turned back to David. "And this is David."

She watched Porter and David shaking hands, trying to pretend they hadn't just stepped into the weirdest date of their lives.

"Porter is going to be a senior next year," Christina said to David, as if they were dear old friends. "He and Carmen are friends from school." Carmen winced inwardly. Christina seemed to feel she needed to lay the world out for David.

The hostess showed them to their table. It was a booth. Carmen found herself wishing it weren't a booth. Christina and David sat on one side, and Carmen and Porter sat on the other. David pushed close to Christina and draped his arm loosely around her waist. Carmen felt her back stiffen.

Carmen stared at her mother, wondering what this nondeformed man could possibly see in her. Did David realize that her mother was old? That she wore briefs instead of bikinis? That she sang along to Carpenters songs, and not in tune? Was he some kind of weirdo with a fetish for Hispanic legal secretaries?

But the truth was, Carmen realized, gazing at her mother's vivid face, Christina was kind of pretty. Her hair was thick and curled nicely at her shoulders. She didn't even need to dye it. She wasn't a supermodel, but she wasn't exactly obese, either. She had a nice, free, tinkly laugh, and she used it a lot. Especially whenever David opened his mouth.

"Carmen?"

Porter was gazing at her with the expectant look of someone who has just asked a question, possibly more than once.

Carmen opened her mouth. "Uhhhh."

"Or not?" he prodded politely.

"Uhhhh?"

Now all three of them were looking at her like that.

Carmen cleared her throat. "Sorry. What?"

"Do you want to share the sesame noodles appetizer?" Porter asked, probably regretting the idea now that he had had to ask several times.

"Um. Sure," she said awkwardly. It seemed like a caricature of a double date to be eating off the same plate.

But wouldn't it be mean to say no after she'd already ignored him?

"Could we have an extra plate?" Carmen asked the waitress while they were ordering, feeling as uptight as Tibby's eighty-one-year-old grandma Lois.

She felt about as romantic as Grandma Lois as she divvied up the noodles and cut hers with her fork.

Her mother didn't look anything like Grandma Lois. She was leaning into David, laughing at something he'd said. Her cheeks were flushed. She ate a dumpling off David's plate without a trace of awkwardness.

"See, good, huh?" he asked her. David's voice and eyes were asking Christina and Christina alone. He might as well have been asking her if she loved him. And she might has well have been answering yes. Their eyes stuck on each other in a way that would have been embarrassing if they had been at all embarrassed.

They were the caricature. *Your happiness is generic,* Carmen thought stingily.

"Carmen?"

Porter had that look again. "I'm sorry," Carmen said. "What was that?"

He wasn't yet comfortable enough with her to call her back from her mental travels, or better yet, tease her about it. Instead, he just looked bewildered. Sort of like Grandma Lois's husband. Late husband.

"Nothing. Don't worry about it."

Carmen cut up more noodles, feeling the odd sensation of watching the dinner progress without actually attending it.

At some point she realized that the humming conversation had come to a stop. David was looking at her.

"Your mom says you're baby-sitting for the Morgans this summer."

David was giving her one of his straight-in-the-eyes looks. An unwavering, direct, "I come in peace" sort of look. Carmen's eyes flitted and danced around the restaurant. "Uh-huh. Yep. Do you know them?"

"Jack Morgan is a partner at the firm. Cute kids, huh? That little boy, what's his name?"

Carmen shrugged. "Jesse?"

"Yeah, Jesse. He's a piece of work." David laughed. "At the firm picnic he counted all the ice cubes."

Christina and Porter laughed. Carmen forgot to.

"He called me a wildebeest from his bedroom window when I went by to pick up Carmen yesterday." Christina laughed very admirably, Carmen thought, at being called a wildebeest. Carmen wasn't sure she herself would have admitted that in front of a date.

Carmen watched, semientranced, as David kissed her mother's hair. Then Porter said something, but Carmen didn't listen to what it was.

When at last the bill came, David paid it in a way that was decisive but not show-offy. "Next time," he said to Porter respectfully as Porter fumbled with his wallet.

Gallantly David got up and fetched Christina's jacket from its hook. Carmen snuck a look to see if he had short legs. He didn't.

❖   ❖   ❖

Lena got up from her bed and put on the Lucinda Williams CD Kostos had sent her back in January. Tibby was gone, Bee was gone, Carmen was out on her demented double date. The music made Lena yearn for a feeling she'd had in Santorini and lost. She'd barely had it. Maybe she'd only glimpsed it. She couldn't name it. It was rough and ragged and dangerous, but soaring and wonderful too.

Lena knew she had spent too much of her life in a state of passive dread, just waiting for something bad to happen. In a life like that, relief was as close as you got to happiness.

Lena wondered about her dread. Where had it come from? What did she fear? Nothing terrible had happened to her. Was it a case of past lives? Otherwise, she hadn't lived long enough to explain it. Unless she lived in dog years. Did she live in dog years? Did she live at all?

She went to her closet and drew out her worn shoe bag. She spilled the letters on her bed. She tried not to do this too often, especially since she had learned about the girlfriend, but tonight she couldn't help herself.

She used to read Kostos's letters so often she had pulled out every possible nuance, every meaning, every drop of emotion. She had sucked them so dry she was surprised they didn't burst into powder. She remembered the joy when a new letter would arrive—full of potential, unread. She remembered thinking that the multitude of fresh, unfelt feelings made the new envelope sit heavy in her hands.

She perched cross-legged, hypnotically opening them one by one. In the beginning she had often been struck by the formality of Kostos's writing, constantly reminding her that he wasn't an American or a teenager. Then it had all fallen away and he was just him.

The first one was from early last September, soon after she'd left him and Santorini for home.

The memories are so close I feel your presence everywhere. And I see forward so clearly and sadly to a time when the memories will be distant. I won't be able to picture your painting things scattered on the flat rock in Ammoudi or your bare feet soaking up the sunshine on Valia's garden wall. Now I see them. Soon I will remember them. Long after that I will remember remembering. I don't want any more hours to pass to separate me from you. Tonight I was packing for London, hating to leave this place where we were together.

The next one, sent later that month, had a postmark from England, where Kostos had moved to study at the London School of Economics.

There are five of us in a three-bedroom flat. Karl from Norway, Yusef from Jordan, and a couple of Brits from up north who've barely moved in. London is loud and shiny and thrilling. I've waited for it for a long time, and still, it's startling to be here. Classes begin Tuesday. Last night I had a couple of pints (cupla is the term—no matter how many) with Yusef at a pub on our street. I couldn't help telling him about you. He understood. He has a girl back home.

The next letter was from October. She remembered her surprise at the Greek postmark. It had been written just after Kostos's grandfather had his heart attack. Kostos had dutifully gone back home to Santorini. Instead of studying macroeconomics with world-famous professors, he was making boat fittings in the archaic family forge. That was the kind of person Kostos was.

Lena, please don't worry about me. It was my choice to come back. Really. The LSE isn't going anywhere. I've already received a deferment. It was no trouble finding a guy to take over the flat. I'm not sorry about it. My bapi is recovering quickly now. He sat in the forge with me while I worked today. He claims he'll be back to full schedule by Christmas and I'll be back in school for the new year, but I don't need to rush. I'll take care of Bapi's business first.

I went swimming in our olive grove the night I got back. I was delirious thinking of you.

He'd originally written *making love to you*, then crossed it out about a thousand times. But when Lena read the letter from the back in the perfect light, she could read the censored words. And as many times as she read them, their impact never faded. Each word burst like a firework in her brain. Longing. Agony. Bliss. Pain.

Had he made love to this new girlfriend? The thought seared her brain like a hot coal, and she tossed it out as fast as she could.

The next letter she pulled from the pile was from December. The letters from this period still evoked a throb of shame in Lena's chest. She was only glad she didn't have possession of her own letters.

Your last letter sounded so distant, Lena. I tried to call you on Monday. Did you get the message? Are you feeling all right? How are your friends? Bee?

I tell myself your spirits were down the day you wrote. You're fine and we're fine. I hope it's true.

Then came fateful January. Whatever courage had bloomed inside her last August had withered in the cold winter. She'd become huddled and impermeable again. She'd written a cowardly letter and he'd responded.

Maybe it's just too far. The Atlantic Ocean seemed small in September. Now, even the Caldera looms for me like the edge of an uncrossable distance. I have dreams where I swim and swim and I always end up on a different shore of this island. Maybe we've been apart too long.

And then she'd broken it off completely, promising herself she would be whole again. But she wasn't whole again. She was still missing him.

Of course I understand, Lena. I knew this could happen. If I were away in London, working hard in university, it would all feel different to me. Just being here on this island, longing to be somewhere else . . . I will miss you.

For long nights over many months she imagined that he did miss her. Slowly, stopping and rewinding and stopping again, she played rumbling, narcotic, sometimes X-rated scenarios of what might happen when two people who missed each other that much saw each other at last. No matter that Lena was self-conscious, uninformed, and a virgin many times over. A girl could dream.

But now Kostos had a girlfriend. He'd forgotten her. They'd never see each other again.

The dreams weren't as pleasing when they had no chance of coming true.

Brian was dressed and sitting patiently at her desk when Tibby woke up the next morning.

She was conscious of how her hair stood up when she first got out of bed. She flattened it with both hands.

"Are you hungry?" he asked her companionably.

She remembered about breakfast. She remembered the IHOP and walking down the highway. She meant to tell Brian about the plan and have him come along. She meant to, but she didn't.

"I have an early class," she said.

"Oh." Brian didn't bother to hide his disappointment. He didn't play any of those games where you try to act like you care less than you care.

"Could you meet me for lunch?" she asked. "I'll get sandwiches from the cafeteria and we can eat 'em by the pond."

He liked that idea. He did his thing in the bathroom while she dressed. They walked down together. She plotted her getaway. Not that it was so tricky. Brian would never suspect her of being the nasty kid she was.

She pointed across the way to the student union building. "They have Dragon Master in the basement."

"They do?" Brian looked more interested in college than he ever had before.

"Yeah. I'll meet you there at noon." She knew Brian could play for hours on a dollar.

She scuttled toward Masters Hall. Alex's room was on the first floor. That was where they usually met. He was sitting at his computer with his headphones on. Maura was reading one of his hip-hop magazines on the bed. Neither of them looked up or said anything.

Tibby loitered by the door, knowing they would come when they were ready. She was pleased with the way she had learned their code.

Alex was mixing his soundtrack, she guessed. There were piles of CDs on his desk. Mostly homemade things and obscure labels she only pretended she'd ever heard of. He unplugged the earphones so she and Maura could hear the end of it. There was high-pitched, disturbing reverb and a sort of low, grinding sound underneath. She wasn't sure if it was supposed to be music or not. Alex looked satisfied. Tibby nodded, wanting it to make sense to her.

"Yo, Tomko. Must have caffeine," he said, getting up and leading them out the door. Tibby wondered if he had stayed up all night.

They were supposed to sign out when they left campus, but Tibby never brought that up anymore.

They walked for a little less than a mile on the shoulder of the road as cars and trucks whizzed by.

She felt a little sad when the waitress, the gray-haired

one with the visor, brought her a huge stack of pancakes. Brian loved pancakes as much as anyone.

Alex was talking about the pimply, chess-playing kid in the room next to his, one of his favorite targets for ridicule.

Tibby thought about Brian, with his Dragon Master T-shirt and his thick, smudgy glasses with their heavy gold frames.

She laughed at something Alex said. Her laugh sounded fake to her own ears.

She wondered. Had she not brought Brian because she was worried about how he would seem to Alex and Maura? Or was it because she worried about how she, Tibby, would seem to Brian?

Bee,

I'm not doing so well with the Pants right now, so I figured I'd just go ahead and send them to you.

Anyway, I'm thinking about you all the time. I was so happy you called last night. Finding Greta right away, it just makes me know you are onto something good.

Go easy on the great state of Alabama, Bee, and remember how much we love you.

Tibby

Life isn't fair. It's just

fairer than death,

that's all.

—William Goldman

The first few days in Greta's attic were pure manual labor, pulling boxes down from giant stacks and carrying pieces of furniture and loads of books down to the basement.

The morning of the fifth day, the Traveling Pants appeared in the box Bridget had set up at the post office. She was pleased at first, because the rougher work in the attic was about to start, and she needed them. But the anxiety set in when she got back to her room.

She shuffled around the carpet as she opened the package. With her breath held and every loose part of her sucked in, she began to pull them up. She met resistance at the thighs. She had to stop. She couldn't keep going with them. What if she ripped them? How horrible would that be?

She pulled them off fast and pulled on her shorts, breathing hard.

She didn't want to read too much into this. It didn't have to mean anything. So she needed to drop a few pounds. She sat down on the bed and rested her head against the wall and tried very hard not to cry.

She held the Pants. She couldn't just leave them here and ignore them. Maybe the Pants didn't actually have to be on your person to work their magic. Right? Maybe?

Numbly, Bridget strode from the room, clutching them. She carried them all the way to Greta's, where she let herself in the side door, as instructed. Greta was in the kitchen, pricking her finger for blood. Quickly Bridget looked away. She'd suspected already that Greta was diabetic. She'd seen the familiar-looking equipment around. Bridget knew about diabetes, because her mother had developed it in the last few years of her life.

"Good morning, Greta," she said, keeping her eyes down.

"Morning," Greta replied. "Would you like some breakfast?"

"No, thanks," Bridget said.

"Orange juice?"

"No. I'll take some water up with me, if that's okay." She went to the refrigerator to get it herself.

Greta was squinting at the Pants. "Are those yours?" she asked.

Bridget nodded.

"Would you like me to wash 'em for you? A little bleach would clean that whole mess right off them."

Bridget looked aghast. "No! No, thank you." She cradled them protectively. "I like them how they are."

Greta clucked and shook her head. "To each her own," she muttered.

You have no magic in you, Bridget thought.

It was hot in the house, and at least fifteen degrees hotter in the attic. Bridget was already soaked with sweat by the time she got up the stairs.

She had left a pile of boxes in the corner that said MARLY on them in black marker. This was where it got tricky. It was both the part she wanted and the part she dreaded. She perched the pants on a bookshelf and got down to work. Putting her hands on the first box, Bridget didn't let herself think too much, she just opened it.

Carefully she pulled out some composition books. They were from grade school. Bridget felt a slight ache in her chest at the sight of her mother's careful cursive. *Social Studies, English, Algebra.* There was an envelope full of photographs below those. There were birthdays, ice cream outings, a school fair. Her mother seemed to grab Bridget's eyes in every picture. Her hair glowed and her face never stood still. Bridget had always known she had her mother's hair.

The box contained many pieces of artwork, mostly on paper plates and crumbling construction paper. Bridget saved what she could and threw the rest in a Hefty bag.

The next box seemed to date from high school. Bridget waded through textbooks and notebooks before she came to the photographs. Marly dancing, Marly cheerleading, Marly posing for cheesecakey shots in her bathing suit, Marly flirting, Marly going to party after party after party with one smug-looking date after another. There were four yearbooks, each filled with photographs of the same sort. Marly was dramatically overrepresented in each one.

Fourteen yellowed editions of *The Huntsville Times* contained Marly's photograph. There were dozens more pictures of her clipped from the local weekly papers. In every one, Marly was magnificent. She was like a movie star, smiling, laughing, shouting, preening. Bridget couldn't help feeling proud. It wasn't just her beauty—although that was striking, Bridget mused—but her intensity in every single shot.

Bridget was deeply struck by this girl, but she didn't feel she knew her personally. This Marly didn't relate in any obvious way to the woman she had known as her mother. For less than a second Bridget flashed back to her own more recent image of her mother, in the darkened room where she had lain day after day.

"Gilda!"

It was twelve. Greta was calling her down for lunch.

Numbly Bridget went down the stairs. She watched Greta laying out bologna sandwiches and potato chips, her lumpy, arthritic fingers spending an inordinate amount of time folding a paper napkin.

How did she *ever come out of* you? Bridget found herself wondering.

Carmen spent her afternoon at Lena's making brownies and M&M cookies and putting them into care packages for Bee and Tibby. Now that it was dinnertime, she was especially glad to be at Lena's. She didn't actually love Lena's dad's cooking or the overbright halogen lights over the table or the smell of Effie's quick-dry nail polish that camped out in her nose. But she was glad not to be in her own empty house for the third night in a row.

Tonight her mom and David had gone to a baseball game. Her mother had put her hair back in a ponytail and worn an Orioles cap, which Carmen had found frankly embarrassing.

"This is delicious, Mr. Kaligaris," Carmen said, sweeping her fork through something that involved spinach.

"Thanks," he said, nodding.

"So, Carmen," Effie said, picking up her fork gingerly so she wouldn't mess up her nails. "I heard that your mom is madly in love."

Carmen swallowed hard. "Yeah, sort of." She glared at Lena, searching for signs of disloyalty.

"I didn't hear it from Lena," Effie said, picking up on the vibe. "I heard from Melanie Foster. You know her? She's a hostess at the Ruby Grill. She saw your mom and her boyfriend kissing at the table."

"Do we need to hear this?" Lena asked.

Carmen felt the spinach thing coming back up.

"Don't you like the guy?" Effie asked.

"He's fine," Carmen said shortly.

Mrs. Kaligaris appeared to be interested, embarrassed, and slightly appalled at the same time. "Nice for your mom that she's met somebody she really cares for."

"I guess it's nice," Carmen said after a silence. She closed her face off.

Effie, not being an idiot, backed away from the topic.

Carmen glanced at her watch. "Speaking of . . . she's

111

supposed to be picking me up in a couple minutes." She looked around to make sure that everyone was more or less finished with dinner. "I should probably go get my stuff." She cleared her plate. "Sorry to . . . you know . . . eat and run."

"That's fine, honey," Mrs. Kaligaris said. "I'm sorry to be eating so late tonight."

The Kaligarises always ate late. Carmen figured it was the Greek way.

For the next fifty-five minutes, Lena sat with Carmen in the living room, waiting for Christina.

"She could at least call," Carmen said. She had said that a few times already. It suddenly occurred to her that it was the kind of thing her mother used to say about her.

Lena yawned. "It takes forever to get out of the stadium. I'm sure she's stuck in the parking lot or something."

"She's too old to go to a baseball game," Carmen muttered.

Mrs. Kaligaris came down in her bathrobe to get something from the kitchen. Almost all the lights in the house were off. "Carmen, you know you'd be welcome to sleep over if you'd like."

Carmen nodded. She felt like crying.

At 10:44 a car pulled up outside. David's car.

Lena, the early riser, was practically asleep on the sofa. She roused herself and touched Carmen on the elbow as Carmen stomped to the door. "It's okay," Lena said gently.

"*Nena*, it was a *mad*house," Christina erupted as soon as Carmen opened the car door. "I am so sorry."

Christina's face was too happy and excited to look

as if she were so sorry or really cared very much at all.

"Carmen, I feel bad. I apologize," David said earnestly.

Then why are you smiling like that? Carmen felt like asking. She slammed the car door and sat in silence.

Christina and David whispered things to each other as they pulled up in front of the apartment building. Carmen made no effort to hear what they were saying. She leaped out of the car so she didn't have to watch the good-night kiss.

Carmen didn't try to hold the elevator doors, so her mother had to run to make it. In the close confines of the elevator car, Carmen perceived with disgust that her mom's breath smelled of beer.

"Sweetheart, really," Christina said. "I know we were late, but if you had seen the traffic . . . The game was sold out, and . . . well, you've never minded having extra time at Lena's house. . . ."

Her eyes had a bright and tipsy look. She badly wanted Carmen to let this one go and leave her in her happy world.

Carmen walked ahead of her mother down the hall and used her keys to open the door. She wasn't going to let it go.

"I hate you," she told her mother, filled with shame and desperation as she stomped off to bed.

That night, Tibby stayed in with Brian. She could have sneaked him into the cafeteria, but she rejected the idea. Instead, they ordered a pizza and had it delivered to the room.

Afterward they both lay on the floor with paper and pens and pencils. Brian had the radio tuned to a classical station.

"What's that?" he asked, looking at the path of squares she was making over two large sheets of paper.

"It's kind of a . . . a storyboard, I guess."

He nodded, interested.

He too was hard at work. He was drawing a comic, Tibby guessed. His people had large heads and eyes. They weren't very good. They reminded her of those cheesy shiny-eyed sad-children paintings. He bit the inside of his cheek when he concentrated. He moved his lips around when he shaded with his pencil.

Tibby was considering her frames when she noticed the music. It was some sort of symphony, maybe. She realized that Brian was whistling. The crazy thing was, he was whistling along with the music. Hundreds of notes, and he seemed to hit all of them.

She stopped and looked at him. He didn't notice her. He was shading and whistling.

The music was beautiful, whatever it was. How did Brian know it so well? How did he know it note for note? Tibby lifted her hands from her papers. She rested her chin in her hand. Had he always been such an in-tune whistler?

She didn't want to say anything. She was worried that if she did, he might stop, and she didn't want him to.

She laid her head on the floor. She closed her eyes. A chill fluttered up her scalp. She felt like crying, and she had no idea why. Her papers wrinkled under her cheek.

Shading and whistling. The violins screeched and soared. The cellos sucked at the bottom of her stomach. The piano pounded away, unaccompanied by anything but whistling for a while.

Then it was over. Tibby was unaccountably sad. It felt like she had lived in the world of the music, warm and jubilant, and now she'd been cast out of it. It was cold out here.

She gazed at Brian. He was quietly drawing. He still hadn't looked up. "What was that?" she asked finally.

"What?"

"That music?"

"Uh . . . Beethoven, I think."

"Do you know what the thing is called?"

"It's a piano concerto. The fifth one, maybe."

"How many are there?"

Brian looked up at her, a little surprised by her intensity. "Piano concertos? That Beethoven wrote? Uh, I'm not sure. Maybe just five."

"How do you know it?"

He shrugged. "I've just heard it a bunch of times. It comes on the radio now and then."

Tibby's eyes bored into his with such force, Brian sensed she wanted more.

"Also, my dad used to play it."

Tibby swallowed abruptly. She dropped her eyes, but Brian didn't.

"My father was a musician—a pianist. Did you know that? He died."

Tibby gaped. No, she hadn't known that. She didn't

know anything about Brian's life, and this was a hard place to start. She swallowed again, poking her finger into the point of her pencil. "He did? I mean, he was?"

"Yeah." Brian took off his glasses, and she was struck by how deeply set his eyes were. He took a lot of pains in rubbing his glasses into the hem of his T-shirt.

"He played that?"

"Yes."

"Oh."

Tibby bit savagely on the inside of her cheek. What kind of friend was she, that she didn't even know this single most important thing? She knew Brian had had a lonely, sad life so far. She knew it, and yet she'd never bothered to find out why. She'd avoided it like she avoided so many things.

And Tibby knew, in that way you just know things sometimes, that Bailey had known. Bailey had known that Brian's father had been a musician and that he was dead. Bailey had probably known how he died. She'd probably learned it inside the first hour she met Brian.

Tibby, on the other hand, had spent hundreds and hundreds of hours with Brian striving for the comfort of not knowing.

Some things have to be

believed to be seen.

—Ralph Hodgson

"Rusty is getting open."

Billy Kline turned around and walked two steps toward Bridget. "Sorry?"

"Rusty there. Your teammate? He's faster than you think he is." Bridget had never been great at keeping her mouth shut on the soccer field.

He shook his head as though to confirm the reality of the strange girl sitting on the sidelines giving him pointers.

She shrugged. She was sitting in the sunshine chewing a piece of grass like she used to do when she was a little kid on this same field. She'd forgotten how much she loved watching the game, even when it was a bunch of amateurs. "Just a thought," she said.

He was fairly cute when he scowled. "Do I know you?"

She smiled at his accent, his grown-up voice. She couldn't help it. She shrugged again. "I don't know. Do you?"

Her manner seemed to throw him off. "I've seen you on this field a few times, I guess."

"That's because I'm a fan," she said.

He nodded at her as though she were most likely a stalker, and moved back onto the field.

If she had still been her old self, he would have known she was flirting with him and he would very possibly have asked her out by now. As it was, he didn't.

During the final minutes of the scrimmage, Rusty got open, and Billy, after waiting a beat, passed it to him. Virtually undefended, Rusty scored.

Bridget cheered from the sideline. Billy looked over at her, and he couldn't help smiling.

Carmabelle: Hey, Len. Talked to Tibby finally. Told her we'd be there when she gets home around seven. Brian's visiting her and driving home with her.

Lennyk162: I talked to her too. She's funny. Still has no idea that Brian's in love with her.

Carmabelle: You think Brian loves her in that way?

Lennyk162: I think he loves her in every way.

"Tibby, turn it off. *Please?*"

"Fine. I'll go film somebody else," Tibby said.

As happy as Lena was to see Tibby, she was not happy to see her video camera. She always felt horribly awkward in front of it.

"Do you want to do a dozen more or call it a day?" Tibby's mom asked, holding up a brown paper bag full of corn. "Up to you."

Lena checked her watch. She had half an hour before she needed to be at work. "I'll do it," she offered. She actually enjoyed husking corn. She was sitting at the round table in the Rollinses' kitchen. Tibby's mom was making some sort of salad for the Fourth of July party the following day, and Loretta, the housekeeper, was watching Nicky and Katherine splash each other in the inflatable pool on the grass outside.

Lena took a piece of corn from the bag and gingerly pulled back the husk. You never knew when you were going to find a fat beige worm or a nasty black hole full of scurrying creatures. This one looked perfect, though. She liked the silk because it reminded her of Bridget's hair. The way it used to be, anyway.

"So, Lena, how is your boyfriend?" Tibby's mom asked. She wiggled her eyebrows as if to indicate that this was dishy, and wasn't she just one of the girls for knowing about it.

Lena tried not to wince openly. She wasn't comfortable with the term *boyfriend* even when she did have one, and she hated everybody knowing her private business.

"We broke up," she said lightly. "You know, the whole long-distance thing."

"That's too bad," Alice said.

"Yes," Lena agreed. She couldn't help feeling that the mothers were a little eager on the boyfriend issue, as if life would really start once the boyfriends were under way. Lena resented that. She waited in silence for a while for that subject to die off before she introduced a new one.

"Um . . . Alice?" As soon as the girls had learned to talk, Tibby's mom had insisted they call her by her name.

"Yes?"

Lena had first had this idea a few days before. Originally she'd dismissed it as being too diabolical. The truth was, it was pretty unlike her. But now that she was presented with the perfect opportunity, she didn't really see how she could do harm with it.

She took a deep breath. She wanted to make sure her voice came out casual and innocent. "Did my mom ever talk to you about Eugene?" she asked.

Alice paused over her potatoes. In the sunlit room, Lena could see Alice's freckles—all-over freckles like Tibby's but very faint. "Eugene?" Her eyes got a slightly glazed, nostalgic look. "Sure. That was the Greek boy your mom was so crazy about, right?"

Lena sucked in her breath. She had scored information more quickly than she'd expected. "Right," she said, feeling dishonest about pretending to be the one with the information.

Alice still had a distant look on her face. "He broke her heart, didn't he?"

Lena faced the corn. Blood rushed to her head, turning her cheeks pink. She hadn't been expecting to hear that. "Yeah, I guess he did."

Alice put her knife down and gazed up at the ceiling. She seemed to be enjoying her stroll down memory lane. "God, I remember when he came to visit when you were just a baby." She looked at Lena. "I'm sure she told you about that."

Lena bit the inside of her cheek. "Um . . . she might have." She was starting to feel uncomfortable. She had found more treasure than she was prepared to carry home.

Treasure in such large amounts stopped feeling precious.

Lena couldn't help staring at Alice. She had the sense that Alice wasn't being careful enough, that she didn't care enough about other people's secrets.

"Well, I'm sure she'll tell you about it sometime," Alice said quietly. She seemed to consider that she had said more than was wise. She turned back to her potatoes. "Anyway, why do you ask about him?"

That was a good question. Lena tried to think of a good answer very quickly.

Luckily Katherine stumbled through the sliding doors, crying and slipping and trying to explain something about Nicky and her bucket. She trailed water and dirt and bits of grass all over the clean kitchen floor. Lena felt grateful to both Nicky and Katherine, because Tibby's mom instantly shooed the baby out of the kitchen and began cleaning the floor, sending all thoughts of Eugene the heartbreaker back to distant memory.

Bridget woke up in a sweat. It was hot, that was the reason, but it was also her dreams. By day, she studied and touched her mother's things, and by night, she dreamed about them. The dreams gave her as fragmented a vision of Marly as the boxes in the attic did. There were a thousand dramatic episodes, but very little sense of the person linking them together.

Bridget had gotten to like taking slow showers in the past year, but here, on the third floor of the Royal Street Arms, in this bathroom that she shared with two grizzled day laborers, she made them very quick. She consoled herself with the thought that the brownish water going down the drain was from her hair dye, but still, she had the unpleasant feeling she was getting dirtier in the shower rather than cleaner.

Greta had breakfast waiting for her. Juice and whole-wheat toast with butter and jam, just the way she liked it. She had mentioned that in passing a few days before, and Greta had had it all set up the next day.

Bridget ate and drank fast. She didn't feel like chatting with Greta. She wanted to get back to her mother.

Upstairs, Bridget came across an admittance form for Shepherd's Hill in one of the boxes. It was dated the year after Marly graduated from high school. At first Bridget assumed it was a summer school or a cheerleading camp or something, but it wasn't. Bridget realized, with her heart clunking around noisily, that it was a mental institution. From the paperwork, Bridget could see Marly had been there for a little under three months. She'd been prescribed a drug called lithium. One doctor reported that Marly had talked about suicide. Bridget watched the clean black type bend and bow as her eyes filled.

She laid the papers down and sat in the window, watching the mail truck make its way down the street. She didn't think she could keep going today.

She'd been so excited and dazzled by the images of young Marly, belle of the town, she'd almost let herself forget how the story really ended.

She was relieved when Greta called her down for

lunch. Bridget had mentioned the day before about how she hadn't been eating vegetables lately, and she felt touched when she saw the carefully peeled carrots on her plate.

"Thank you, Greta," Bridget said.

"Aw, don't mention it, honey."

Since the first week, Greta had stopped calling her Gilda and started calling her honey.

They ate their sandwiches quietly, but after they finished, Greta didn't get up from the table. She seemed more in the mood for Bridget's company today than for her sweat.

"I had two kids, did you know that? You probably figured it out from all the stuff upstairs."

Bridget nodded. This was another thing that she both wanted and dreaded.

"My daughter died six and a half years ago."

Bridget nodded, looking down at her hands. "I'm so sorry to hear that."

Greta nodded too, slowly and with her whole body. "She was a beautiful girl. Her name was Marlene, but everybody called her Marly."

Bridget couldn't make herself look up yet.

"She was famous in Limestone County when she was your age. People said if she'd run for Miss Alabama she would have won."

"Really?" The absurdity of this comment somehow gave Bridget an opportunity to pull herself together.

"Sure." Greta smiled. "But she was too busy going out

with boys. She wouldn't learn the baton twirling or whatever it was those pageant girls had to do."

Bridget smiled too.

"She was homecoming queen as a junior *and* a senior. I can tell you that never happened before or since."

Bridget nodded, trying to look impressed enough to suit Greta's pride.

"You want some more iced tea?" Greta asked.

"No, I'm fine. Thank you." Bridget stood up. "I should get back to work."

Greta waved her hand. "It's hot as blazes up there. Why don't you sit here for a while longer?"

"Okay," Bridget said.

Greta poured them both more iced tea. Even though Bridget had said she didn't want it, it turned out she really did.

"Honey?"

"Yeah?"

"Your folks know where you are?"

Bridget's face felt warm. "Yes." It was true. Her one folk, anyway.

"You know you can use my phone if you ever need to."

"Okay. Thanks."

"They're traveling, you say?"

Bridget nodded, staring into her iced tea. She didn't want Greta her to ask more questions. Sure, lying was easy, but Bridget wasn't enjoying it anymore. She wished her lies would just evaporate when she was done with them.

Bridget cleared her throat. "Did Marly go to college around here?" she asked.

Greta seemed to like talking about her daughter. "She went to Tuscaloosa. That's where her father went too."

"Did she enjoy it there?"

"Well . . ." Greta thought about this. Bridget knew she'd be honest about it, even before she opened her mouth. "She had some troubles there."

Bridget sipped her iced tea.

"Marly was real moody. High as a kite one week, and couldn't get out of bed the next."

Bridget nodded again and put her feet flat on the kitchen floor. It was hard for her to hear this. It sounded too familiar.

"She fell down hard in her first year of college—I'm not exactly sure of all the details. A doctor diagnosed her with a mental disease and put her in a hospital for a few months. I think it helped her, though she hated it at the time."

Bridget knew this was the Shepherd's Hill part.

"The next year at school, she fell in love with her history professor—a young man from Europe. It was crazy behavior for a girl of nineteen, but I'll be darned if she didn't marry him."

Bee was surprised. She had known her father had taught in Alabama, and that her parents' paths had first crossed then, but she had had no idea it was like that.

"It was sad, really, because Franz—that was her husband—he lost his job because of it."

Bridget nodded. That explained why her father had

gone from a university job to teaching at a private high school.

"He got a job in Washington, D.C., so that's where they went."

"Oh."

Greta studied her thoughtfully. "You look tired, honey. Why don't you have a nice shower in the guest bathroom and lie down and take a little nap?"

Bridget stood up, feeling so grateful she wanted to kiss Greta on the head. Because a nap and a shower were exactly, exactly what she most needed.

Bee,

I wish I could call you. I hate not being able to e-mail or call you fifty times a day. I'm not patient enough for letters. But I'll keep writing anyway, because I have to be with you somehow.

I loved hearing about your grandma and about Billy. You mighta mentioned, though, that your grandma still doesn't know who you are. (Heard it from Tibby, btw.) When are you going to tell her? How is it going to help if she doesn't know?

Can't bear to bore you now with tales of my bad behavior toward my mom, or my fizzling love life. Maybe later.

Call me this week. Otherwise, no more brownies, ya hear?

Love,

Carma

Time is what keeps

things from happening

all at once.

—Graffiti

Now Lena was the one trying to get time with her mother instead of the other way around. For days she had eagerly awaited a call to sit in the car while her mother returned videos or whatever. By now she'd realized that her mother was avoiding her.

What could it be? she wondered. What did Eugene mean to her? Why did she need to be so secretive about him?

She continued her streak of diabolical behavior when she finished her shift at work that evening and called her mom for a ride. The truth was, she really didn't have a car, and it really was raining. And there really was a fairly attractive blouse—beige, of course—that she thought her mom might want to see.

Once they were in the car together on the way home, Lena pounced.

"Hey, Mom?"

"Yes?"

"I know you're uncomfortable about it for some reason,

but could you please tell me who Eugene is? It's just me. I won't, like, put it on *Sixty Minutes* or anything. I won't say anything to anybody—not even Dad—if you don't want me to."

Her mother's lips pressed together. This was not a good beginning.

"Lena." She sounded like she was trying to be patient but it wasn't easy.

"Yes," Lena said timidly.

"I don't want to talk about it. I think I've made that pretty clear."

"But *whyyyyy?*" Lena knew she could only sound that whiny with her mother. She very purposely did not summon Kostos or his new girlfriend into the car with her at that moment.

"Because I don't want to. It's my business, and I don't feel like sharing it. Understand?"

"Yes," Lena said, quietly defeated. What else could she say?

"I don't want you to bring it up with me again."

"Okay."

Rain began to splash against the windshield. Lightning cracked the sky. This had the makings of a great summer lightning storm. Lena loved those.

"What about the next time I don't want to share something in my life with you?" Lena asked. She couldn't help adding that. She couldn't come away totally empty-handed.

Ari sighed. "It depends what it is. But just so we keep things straight, I'm the mother, you're the daughter."

"I know that," Lena mumbled.

"It's not always fair."

It's never fair, Lena felt like saying, but for once she managed to keep her mouth closed.

Her mother pulled into their driveway. She turned off the engine, but she didn't make a move to get out.

"Lena, can I ask you something?"

"Yes," Lena said, wishing and hoping her mother had suddenly decided to alter her course.

"Who told you about Eugene?"

This was not what she had been hoping for. She kneaded her hands and cleared her throat. "I don't think I feel like sharing that with you."

Joe, the baby, was playing with cars on the floor, and Jesse was watching a TV show involving cats that spoke English with a Chinese accent. Carmen felt a little guilty, not doing more to earn her money, but Jesse liked the show a lot and it was on channel thirteen, so that meant it was good for him, right?

Besides, she had a lot of things to worry about, and she could do that better when the kids were quiet. She wanted to call Bee because she hadn't heard her voice in eight days, but she couldn't, so she called Lena at work.

"My job is much harder than your job," Lena said accusingly when she picked up.

"You are so wrong. Have you ever spent time with a four-year-old boy?" Carmen demanded. This was part of a running argument.

"So how come you're always calling me, if it's so hard?"

"Because I care about you so much."

Lena laughed. "Seriously, the Duffer is withering my soul with her eyes right now. I can't talk."

"Have you heard from Bee?" Carmen asked.

"No."

Suddenly a howl filled the room. Then two louder ones. Jesse was taking Joe's cars. "See?" Carmen said smugly to Lena before she hung up.

"Jesse!" Carmen intervened. "Let Joe play with the cars!"

"*Nooooooo! They're miiiiiiine.*"

"Come on, Jesse. Just give him the cars. Don't you want him to be quiet so you can hear the TV?" Carmen felt nefarious, as if she were offering him a cigarette.

"No!" Jesse shouted. He wrenched the car out of Joe's fat hand. Joe's cry was so passionate it made no sound. His face turned purple, except for the creases around his nose and forehead, which turned greenish.

"Jesse, can't you share?" Carmen begged.

When Joe's cry finally picked up noise, it nearly blew the roof off.

Carmen scooped Joe off the floor and ran him around the room. "Want to play with my cell phone?" she asked in desperation.

It was Joe's favorite off-limits pastime. He had once called Carmen's father at work.

She thrust the phone at the baby, wincing as he accessed her speed-dial menu. Joe's face returned to a normal color instantly. "Careful, honey, I'm over my minutes," she pleaded as he pressed all the buttons.

Jesse stomped over and stuck his hand out. "I want the phone," he said.

Carmen sighed. She was out of her depth here. What did she know about sharing? She was an only child. She never shared anything. She'd missed that lesson.

Carmen was ready to give up all hope when Joe magnanimously handed Jesse the cell phone. Jesse didn't actually want the cell phone if Joe didn't, so he dumped it on the floor. Then Jesse kindly handed the yellow car to Joe and kept the blue one for himself.

Five minutes later, both boys were crawling happily around the floor, one car apiece. Carmen sat on the couch and watched the boys play, wondering if maybe that lesson she'd missed had actually contained something valuable.

"His left isn't for shit," Bridget said to Billy.

Billy, though still frightened of her, had gotten a little used to her.

Burgess was playing their third game of the season, and they were still without a win. It was the first one Bridget had attended, and she watched it as avidly as if it were the World Cup.

Billy came a little closer to her. The dark green game jersey matched his eyes.

Bridget dropped her voice and leaned in to him. "Mooresville goalie. No left."

She knew Billy wanted to ignore her, but he couldn't completely.

Two possessions later, Billy smacked it hard and wide

to the goalie's left side. It went into the net without a fight.

Everybody screamed on the sidelines. Billy turned and gave Bridget a thumbs-up. It was a stupid gesture, but she smiled at him anyway.

Burgess won 1–0. The guys on the team and their friends and all their pretty groupies went out to celebrate, and Bridget went home to her boardinghouse alone. But she was too ramped up to stay in her room, so she dug her running shoes out of the bottom of her suitcase. She hadn't used them in months. She put them on and stepped outside.

She ran straight down Market Street all the way to the river. She remembered the pretty, overgrown path that ran alongside it. The place with the arrowheads. On the far side of the river she saw the ancient, broken-down oak trees giving shelter to hardy weeds and climbers at the expense of their own failing branches.

She'd run so many miles in her life, her body seemed to welcome the exercise. On the other hand, it started to complain after only a mile or so in the July heat. She felt all the extra weight on her hips and shoulders and arms. It wrecked her stride and it wrecked her breathing.

Her mind flashed to the Traveling Pants. Just this morning she'd sent them on their way. She hadn't even worn them. She felt angry at herself, and it made her run faster and farther. And the longer she ran, the more she felt like she was carrying a burden and she wanted it off.

Lena distinctly remembered the last time the Rollinses had had their Fourth of July barbecue, because she had thrown up all over the red-and-white checkered tablecloth. She had always blamed the watermelon, but one could never be certain. They had been ten years old that summer.

The barbecue had been an annual tradition from when they were babies, but the year they were eleven it went on long-term hiatus. Though nobody ever said so, Lena knew it was because of Bee's mom. The relationships between the grown-ups were never easy after that.

She wasn't exactly sure why it had been resurrected now, six years later. For a brief moment she had feared it was because Bee was away this summer, but she realized that Tibby's mom had issued the invitations before Bee had impulsively up and gone.

Lena had another troubling thought: Had this party made Bee want to leave town?

But Lena didn't really believe that. Bee had willingly — willfully — endured gatherings that had been harder than this one. In May she had inexplicably decided to attend the annual mother-daughter sports dinner, in spite of all their efforts to make other plans for her that night.

As they pulled up to the Rollinses' groomed and gardened house, all the Kaligarises together for a rare family appearance, Lena promised herself to go easy on the watermelon.

"Now, who husked that beautiful corn?" Tibby's mom asked by way of greeting as Lena and her family made their way to the backyard. Lena could see that the corn, speckled light and dark yellow, was piled pyramid-style on a blue platter.

"That would be me," she said modestly.

She watched the mothers hug and kiss, one shoulder pat, one cheek each. Lena noticed that her mom seemed particularly stiff. The fathers shook hands with each other and talked in deeper voices than they used at home.

Lena spotted Carmen standing several yards from her mom. Carmen wore a short denim cutoff skirt, a white tank top, and a red scarf tied at the back of her long hair. Lena was always impressed. Today Carmen managed to look sexy and patriotic at the same time.

Tibby was skulking around the periphery of the yard with her movie camera. She was wearing a bleach-spotted army green shirt and mangy khaki shorts. She didn't look sexy or patriotic.

The three girls found each other quickly, like parted bits of mercury, and clumped together on the side of the deck. They watched as Christina and Ari repeated the stiff hug-and-kiss gestures.

"What's up with your mom?" Carmen asked.

"She doesn't look happy, does she?" Lena noted.

"Is she still mad at you about the Eugene thing?" Carmen asked.

"I think so," Lena said. "She's been weird."

Carmen looked at the sky. "I miss Bee."

"I miss her too," Tibby said.

Lena felt sad. She grabbed one of Tibby's hands and one of Carmen's. They squeezed and dropped them before it got sappy. They sometimes did this when one of them was missing.

"She has the Pants still," Carmen mused.

"I hope she's all right," Lena said.

Silently, they considered the various ways in which Bee was crashing around Alabama, armed with the Pants.

"I gotta go," Tibby held up the camera. "I'm working this weekend."

"Are we still going to the thing at the Mall tonight?"

"Sure," Lena said unenthusiastically. Every year on the Fourth, a big group of kids from their high school gathered by the reflecting pool to hear bands and watch the fireworks. Lena felt it was incumbent upon her as a teenager to go, but she didn't like crowds and she didn't like parties.

Effie appeared with two hamburgers, a mountain of potato salad, and two ears of corn.

"Hungry?" Lena asked.

Effie ignored her. "I want that skirt," she told Carmen.

"You can borrow it," Carmen offered magnanimously. As an only child, Carmen appreciated the novelty of Effie.

Lena surveyed the party. In the old days it had been full of counterculture types. Tibby's parents used to be the young, cool ones. Somebody had always pulled out a guitar and played folk songs and the odd Led Zeppelin tune, which her parents never knew that well on account of being Greek. Lena suspected in hindsight that a lot of the grown-ups had been enjoying bong hits in the finished basement while the kids chased each other around on the lawn. Six years later, the Rollinses' friends were a lot less scruffy. Most of them had toddlers and babies.

Suddenly Lena realized why this party had been reborn. The Septembers and their parents were vestiges of the Rollinses' first phase of parenting. Tibby's mom had invited them again for old times' sake, but this party was really about their second-phase friends, the parents of all of Nicky's and Katherine's friends. In fact, Lena strongly suspected she was going to get hit up for baby-sitting before the night was over.

It made her feel a little bit sad. She understood better how it was for Tibby. She considered how she would have described this feeling to Kostos if she were still writing real letters to him. Maybe it was just the sadness of time passing. Maybe it was a regular-life kind of heartache.

Lena, Effie, and Carmen ate on the grass and watched the babies run around. Then Lena watched with some foreboding, when the dessert platters came out, as the little kids scarfed pounds of drooly pink watermelon.

The sun had hardly begun its descent when Lena's mother appeared at her side looking out of sorts. "Lena, we're going to go. You're welcome to stay if you can get another ride home."

Lena looked up at her in surprise. "You're going already? It's pretty early."

Ari cast her the "I don't want to talk about it" look. Lena had been getting a lot of those lately.

"I'll come too," Lena said. When at parties, Lena often yearned to be home in her room. Even Effie decided to leave with them. Lena guessed that was because the only available guys were under four years of age.

Out of the corner of her eye, Lena saw Carmen's mom beckoning Carmen over. Christina wore the Christina version of the look Ari was wearing. What was going on?

Ari went straight for the car without making any apparent good-byes. Lena zipped to Carmen's side. "What's going on?" she murmured.

"I don't know." Carmen looked equally bewildered.

They both bore down on Tibby in the empty kitchen. "What's going on?" they asked her.

"God, I don't know." Tibby looked a little shell-shocked. "They were closed up in the dining room, the three of them. Your mother thinks my mom and Carmen's mom told you some big secret about Eugene. They were whispering, but you could tell they were pissed."

Lena groaned. She heard the engine revving outside. "I'll call you guys later. My mom is about to drive away." The three of them hugged quickly, parting as friends while their mothers left in anger.

Lena sat in the backseat on the drive home feeling a whole new kind of sad. She'd had some unarticulated hopes for this thing. On some level she'd had a fantasy that their mothers would remember how much they loved their daughters and each other and effortlessly strike up their old friendship again.

Now Lena felt like she understood how it was for Carmen, with her divorced parents. It was a basic human desire to long for the people you loved to love each other.

Lena watched her mother's tense face through the rearview mirror. Effie cast Lena questioning looks. Her father, seemingly oblivious, finished the piece of watermelon he'd brought with him. At least Lena hadn't thrown up.

Carma,

Stop worrying, okay? You didn't say so on the phone yesterday, but I could tell. So stop it. I'm fine. I need to be here, and pretty soon, I may even figure out why. Did I mention Billy? Oh, I guess I did. About fifteen times.

So here are the Pants, back to you again. Did they seem to go around fast this time, or is it just me? I can't tell you how I did with the Pants. I can't talk about it. You have to wait till the end of the summer and then I'll have some big things to say. I just know I will.

Hey. Have fun at the big old Rollinspalooza. Give Nicky and Katherine a little tickle torture from me. And tell Lenny to go easy on the watermelon.

Love, love, love. All ways all the time, Carmabelle.

Bee

Sometimes you need to

make a mess.

—Loretta, the Rollinses'

housekeeper

Tibby felt the heat of Alex's body as he leaned close to her. His chin was probably less than six inches from her shoulder.

"I love this," he said.

No, I love this, she thought.

It was a series of fast clips of her mother not having enough time. It had been a setup, really. Tibby had told her mom she wanted to do an interview, and Alice had spent most of the weekend putting her off. First with the towel on her head and her toenail polish drying. "Honey, can we do it later?" Then poking her head out of the bathroom. "Sweetie, I just don't have time this minute." Then frustrated and shiny up to her elbows in pink ground beef, making hamburgers for the cookout. "Can you just wait till I'm finished making these?"

Tibby ran the clips shorter and faster as they mounted. Gradually she increased the speed of the video so her mother's voice got higher and her movements increasingly jerky as the documentary progressed.

"Why don't you throw this in?" he asked. It was a close-up of red Popsicle juice running down Nicky's forearm.

"Why?" she asked.

"'Cause it's a cool shot. Also, you don't want it to get predictable."

Tibby turned her face slightly, so she could see more of him. She was both awed and chastened. He was so good at this. Whereas her ideas were predictable.

Subtly he was pushing her past the pure slapstick humor she had begun with, toward a darker, more chaotic portrait. Tibby knew it was more cutting, but it was also more challenging.

For good measure, she threw in a random shot of a yellow patch of grass in her otherwise green backyard.

"Brilliant," he said, nodding.

He was a good teacher. She was a good student. And Tibby felt some tiny, evil pleasure in the fact that Alex had taken such an interest in her movie, and that Maura had barely begun filming.

Tibby glided all the way back to her dorm on the word *brilliant*.

When she got to her room, Brian was there.

"Hey," she said, surprised.

"I came back. Is that okay?"

She nodded. Part of her wasn't so sure.

"I wanted to see how your movie was coming."

"Thanks," she said. She knew the last time he'd come, he'd made himself indispensable to a local copy shop whose computer network had been on the fritz. At least he'd be working.

She looked at Brian's thoughtless clothing. What was his home like that he seemed to want to be in it so little? She wondered, and yet she didn't ask him about it, did she? For years his life had been a video game in front of a 7-Eleven. Now, it appeared, it was Tibby.

"I have to work a lot," she said. "I'm supposed to show the first cut on Sunday. We're giving a little film festival for Parents' Day," she explained.

"That's okay. I have stuff to do too." Brian settled himself on the floor with his notebooks and pencils to demonstrate.

Tibby set her computer up at her desk. She needed to lay in the soundtrack tonight. She had thought she knew what songs she wanted, but now that she'd seen what Alex was working on, she was worried hers were too . . . predictable. She thought of all his hand-printed CD cases. He probably knew all the musicians personally. She felt like a stupid teenybopper, buying her CDs at Sam Goody.

She set about finding some lesser-known songs from lesser-known bands. She could create a hodgepodge and vary the speed so the actual songs would be almost unrecognizable.

She played the sequence she and Alex had worked on. She played it over. She cued up the song she wanted and sped it up to herky-jerky speed. She was deep in concentration when she realized Brian was looking over her shoulder. She turned around, trying to block his view of the screen with her head.

"What?"

"Is that it?"

"A part of it," she said a little defensively.

His eyes were troubled. "Do you think your mom might be upset if you show her in the bathroom with a towel on her head?" He asked it as a real question, not an accusation.

She looked at him as if he were some kind of doofus. "It's a *film*. Her feelings aren't the point. It's supposed to be . . . you know, like, art."

Brian wasn't backing off, art or not. "But if she sees it, it might make her sad," he said simply.

"For starters, she isn't going to see it. Do you seriously think my mother would show up for Parents' Day? She doesn't have time to read my report card."

"But won't you feel bad, making a movie about her that you wouldn't let her see?"

"I'm not saying I wouldn't let her see it!" Tibby snapped. "It's totally fine if she sees it. I don't care. I'm just saying, there's no way she's showing up for the festival, so it's kind of irrelevant."

Brian didn't say anything more, and he didn't watch any more of her movie. Quietly he drew as she played a loud section of a song again and again and again at varying speeds. That night there wasn't any whistling.

"I guess she's still angry. I'm not sure. She isn't talking to me," Lena said, squeezing the phone to her ear with her shoulder as she used both hands to hang up blouses.

There was always so much clothing to put back. For

every twenty pieces of clothing a shopper tried on, she usually bought about one. And when Lena had anything to do with it, she bought none. Lena had no knack for sales.

"What a surreal party. At least I got a lot of it on film," Tibby said.

Lena noticed the disjointed music in the background. Tibby was too progressive to like anything that just sounded good.

"Did you film the argument?" Lena asked heavily. She wasn't sure why the mothers' discord bothered her so much. Well, unless you considered that it was all her fault. There was that detail.

"Some of it. By mistake I erased the end of it, though, when I was filming my mom racing around the house with a diaper wipe stuck to her heel."

Lena laughed anemically. "Oh."

"My mom is a freak. When I left, she was still rambling and muttering about how your mother should be more open with you. Like my mom would spend ten seconds telling me anything."

Lena clamped a bunch of hangers under her arm. "Yeah," she said absently.

There was silence on the other end.

Lena suddenly realized she had broken a basic rule. You could rail against your mother. You could listen patiently while your friend railed against her mother. But you must never rail against your friend's mother or agree with aforementioned railing.

Lena hadn't meant to do it, but it was too late now.

"It's not like she's the only freak," Tibby said, a little quietly.

"Yes. No. I mean, no." Lena was trying to get a slippery blouse onto a hanger. She'd never been good at doing two things at once.

"And maybe you shouldn't have tricked her into telling you about that guy."

"Tibby, I didn't trick her." Lena stopped herself. Yes, she had. "I mean, I'm sorry if I tricked her, but still, she didn't have to—" By mistake, Lena pushed a number with her cheek. *Beeeep.*

"She didn't have to what?" Tibby snapped combatively. "Tell you all that stuff you were trying to get her to tell you?"

"No, I mean . . ."

"Excuse me. Uh, hello?" A woman was waving at Lena from a fitting room. Lena could hear her voice and see the arm.

In her anxiety, Lena let the blouses swish to her feet. She stepped on the arm of one. "Tibby, I—I can't—"

"The sad thing is, my mom was trying to be big pals with you."

Lena's frustration bubbled over.

"Tibby! I'm not criticizing your mom! You're the one making a film of her trailing a diaper wipe around the house!"

Tibby was quiet. Lena felt horrible. "Tib, I'm sorry," she said gently.

"I've gotta go. Bye," Tibby said, and she hung up.

The four of them had a policy that they never hung up

on each other, no matter how mad they were. Tibby had come about as close as you could get.

"Excuse me?" the shopper called again.

Lena felt like crying. She dragged herself over to the fitting room. "Yes. Can I help you?"

"Do you have these in the next bigger size?" The woman waved a pair of pants over the curtain.

Lena grabbed them and headed for the racks. Women always seemed to bring the size they wished they were to the fitting room, rather than the size that would actually fit. Lena fetched the pants in a twelve.

"Here you go," she said.

A minute later the woman appeared in the twelves. She had faded red hair and a pale complexion. "What do you think?" she asked Lena, looking hopeful.

Lena was preoccupied. She was still staring at the phone as though it had pinched her. "Well, I'd say they look a bit tight." Lena tended to favor truth over charity.

"Oh. Maybe you're right." The lady disengaged quickly from the mirror.

"I think we might have them in a fourteen," Lena offered.

The woman didn't seem to want to consider that. She left a few minutes later without buying anything. Better not to buy anything than to face life as a size fourteen when you believed you were a size ten.

Lena still held the phone as she watched her sole customer trudge out of the store. Maybe it wasn't such a mystery why Lena didn't earn any commissions.

❊   ❊   ❊

Carmen punched her mother's cell phone number into her own cell phone. She stuck a finger in her free ear to lessen the noise of the coffee shop.

It wasn't in service. Christina had turned it off. Unbelievable! What if Carmen were in an accident? What if she were lying by the side of the road, bleeding? She wished she *were* lying by the side of the road, bleeding.

"Is everything okay?" Porter asked.

Carmen realized she had inadvertently been making a by-the-side-of-the-road-bleeding face.

"Yeah." She tried to rearrange her face. "I just can't get hold of my mom."

"Is it urgent? Because we could . . ."

No, it's not urgent, Carmen felt like snapping at him. *I have nothing to say to her at all. I just want to bother her and ruin her date.*

Porter's lips were moving and he seemed to be suggesting some possible course of action, but Carmen wasn't listening.

She waved her hand. "It's fine. It's nothing." She stared grimly at her pink milk shake.

"Okay, well . . ." Porter pushed his own milk shake glass aside. To his credit, he didn't make a loud burbling, sucking effort to get at the last bit. He got his wallet. "The movie is starting in fifteen minutes. We should probably get going."

Carmen nodded blankly. Her mind was already fixed on another subject. Her mother had been whizzing around the house all day like Martha Stewart on amphetamines.

She had repapered the shelves in the kitchen and arranged tulips over the mantel in the living room. Carmen had figured Christina was just shedding happiness and beauty all over the world, but now she had a darker suspicion. What if Christina had said okay to Carmen's 10:20 movie because she secretly intended to bring David back to the apartment? What if they were going to . . .

Okay, no. Carmen didn't need to think about that.

But seriously, did her mother think it was okay to just bring a guy back to her apartment—to *Carmen's* apartment and—and—

Carmen was mad now. This was not okay.

She put her palm to her head. "You know what, Porter?"

He looked at her doubtfully, check in hand. "What?"

"I think I have a sinus infection." She could have just said headache, but this sounded more authentic. "I'm thinking I should probably skip the movie tonight."

"Oh. That's too bad." He looked disappointed. And for the first time he looked like it might have dawned on him that he was getting jerked around.

"I'm sorry," she said. She *was* sorry. She didn't want to be the jerk jerking him around.

"I'll give you a lift home, then," he mumbled, standing up.

"I could just walk," she mumbled back.

"I'm not going to let you walk home if you're sick," he said. There was a glint in his eye that challenged her. It conveyed some kind of understanding.

A few minutes later she let herself into the apartment with a self-conscious amount of noise. She considered being quiet, but God knew what she'd see if she didn't give a little warning. She banged the door shut behind her. She jangled her keys again. She took several strides into the living room and jangled them yet again.

Silence.

They weren't in the kitchen or the living room. That basically left Christina's bedroom, the worst of the alternatives. Carmen sucked in her breath and ventured that way, not quite sure what she would do when she got there.

Her heart pounding, she entered the short hallway that led to the bedroom. One step. Two.

She stopped. The door was open, she could see that now. Christina's bed was just as she'd left it—piled high with rejected date outfits.

"Hello?" Carmen called out in general. Her voice cracked. She sounded pathetic.

There was nobody there. Even though that should have made Carmen happy, it made her sad.

She sat stiffly in the kitchen. She realized after a while that she was still gripping her bag and her keys.

Fear is that little dark-

room where negatives

are developed.

—Michael Pritchard

The kitchen clock had literally stopped. It was broken. That must be it. It hadn't budged since 12:42. Or . . . oh, 12:43.

It was way too late to call anybody. Carmen didn't want to e-mail Paul. She didn't want to read the bile that would slip from her fingers. If she put it in words and actually typed them out, Paul could take all the time he liked to judge her in that silent way of his. He would probably save it to his hard drive. Maybe he would forward it to his whole address book by mistake.

She had an idea. She would pack up the Pants for Tibby. That was a perfectly wholesome thing to do. She'd been meaning to all day. She would put in the letter and address the package and everything.

She walked, as if in a trance, to her bedroom. She moved piles around aimlessly. She forgot what she was looking for until she remembered. She looked harder. With a certain effort she pulled her mind into the task.

The Traveling Pants. The Pants. Sacred. Not okay to lose.

Robotically she dug through her drawers. They were not in her drawers. Nor were they in the very large pile of clothes at the foot of her bed.

Suddenly she pictured them in the kitchen. Yes, she'd carried them into the kitchen earlier that evening. She lumbered back into the kitchen and scanned the small room.

They were not on the counter.

Worry about her mother began to vie with worry about the Pants. She checked the laundry, in case some terrible accident had brought the Pants into forbidden contact with the washing machine. Her bones and muscles seemed to rev up. She checked the bathroom hamper. Pants-worry was officially beginning to edge out mother-worry.

Carmen was dashing hopelessly toward the linen closet when the front door swung open and both worries appeared in its frame.

At the sight of her mother, Carmen stopped with a skid like a cartoon character's. Her mouth wagged open.

"Hi, sweetheart. What are you doing still up?" Her mother looked shy, not quite up to meeting Carmen just now.

Carmen gasped and sucked air, fishlike. Her lungs were very shallow. She pointed.

"What?" Christina wore her perma-flush. It served both giddiness and shame. At this moment it was shifting from the former to the latter.

Carmen poked her finger in the air, unable to summon words that could possibly convey her indignation. "Y-you . . . ! Those . . . !"

Christina looked deeply uncertain. She still trailed wisps of happiness. Some of her was still in the car with David. She hadn't yet fully entered the domestic nightmare that was Carmen.

"My *pants*!" Carmen howled like a beast. "You *stole* them!"

Christina looked down at the Pants in confusion. "I didn't *steal* them. You left them out on the kitchen counter. . . . I thought —"

"You thought what?" Carmen thundered.

Her mom seemed to shrink. She looked timid now. She gestured at the Pants. She gave Carmen a beseeching look. "I thought maybe you meant them as a . . ."

Carmen glared at her stonily.

"As a . . ." Christina looked pained. "As a peace offering, I guess." She finished quietly.

If Carmen had been kind at all, she would have backed off. This was a tender sort of mistake, potentially sore all around.

"You thought I *wanted* you to wear the Traveling Pants? You seriously thought that?" Carmen's temper was growing so big, she herself was afraid of it. "Are you kidding? I put them out to send to *Tibby*. I would never, never, never —"

"Carmen, enough." Christina held up her hands. "I understand that. I made a mistake."

"Take them off now! *Now*. Now now now!"

Christina turned away. Her cheeks were deep red and her eyes were shiny.

Carmen's shame deepened.

The sick thing was, Christina looked beautiful in the Pants, slender and young. They fit Christina. They loved her and believed in her just as they'd loved Carmen last summer, when Carmen had been worthy of them. This summer they eluded Carmen. Instead, they chose her mother.

Christina had appeared in the doorway moments before, looking free and happy and optimistic as Carmen had never seen her before. She seemed to glide on a kind of magic that Carmen couldn't find. And at that moment, Carmen hated her for it.

Christina reached out her hand, but Carmen refused to take it. Christina held her own hand instead. "Darling, I know you're upset. But . . . but . . ." Tears were jiggling in her eyes as she clasped her hands together. "This . . . relationship with David. It won't change anything."

Carmen clenched her jaw. She'd been through the drill. When your parents were about to ruin your life, they used that line.

Her mother might mean what she said. She might even believe it was true. But it wasn't. It would change everything. It already had.

Tib,

You are not worse than me. I am worse than you. Trust me. We can fight about it more later when you're home.

Here are the Pants. They are technically supposed to go to Lena, but we both had the idea that they would make a great date to your movie premiere. Just give them to Lena after you knock 'em dead, Tibba-dee.

With love from your friend who no longer deserves happiness or nice things,

Carmen

Before walking over to Greta's, Bridget studied herself in the mirror above the bureau. It was kind of a relief not to have to see more than her face, really. She leaned in and inspected the top of her head. There was a solid inch of roots grown in, and they didn't match. Even the dyed parts were fading in patches, giving her hair a weird, skunky look.

She wasn't so crazy about the brown anymore, but she didn't want to risk blowing her cover, either, so she dug a baseball cap out from a pile of dirty clothes and put it on her head. *Voilà.* As a fashion statement, it wasn't much. *Forgive me, Carmen*, she thought, heading out the door.

The attic was starting to take shape now. Bridget had waded through and organized vast loads of books, coats, and magazines and moved everything but the last two of Marly's boxes down to the basement. Now that most of the clutter was gone, she could get a sense of the room itself. It was a classic old-fashioned garret, cramped and sloping, but romantic, too. The ceiling was high in the middle and slanted down to around four feet at the windows. But there were many windows, three on each of the four sides, and they seemed to catch the loveliest light.

It badly needed a paint job, Bridget decided, looking around.

For now, she decided to confront another of Marly's boxes. This, as she had suspected, was where her father came into the picture. There were two papers Marly had written for his class (an A- and a B+. "Fantastic ideas — need to follow through," he'd written on the second). There were many pictures of her with her friends being an adorable and jolly coed. There were no pictures of her in her bed. There were no pictures of her at Shepherd's Hill.

Then there were the wedding pictures, most of them taken on the steps of the Baptist church in town. Bridget studied them carefully, wondering about the furtive quality they had. Her father looked dazed with love, but he tended to hover at the edges of the pictures, his posture stiff. His family wasn't there. He had no colleagues or friends, from what Bridget could determine. It was a wedding, all right, but it wasn't the wedding she would have expected from famous Marly Randolph, a girl who could have been Miss Alabama if she'd wanted to.

Bridget was fairly certain her mother hadn't been pregnant at the time, and yet she'd brought shame upon her groom nonetheless. She'd brought him down in the world. Her father had sacrificed everything to marry her, and Bridget wondered if Marly had disrespected him for it. Maybe Professor Vreeland had been a prize for only as long as she couldn't have him.

At the bottom of this box was the wedding dress. Bridget pulled it out, feeling extra gallons of blood pulsing though her head and her heart. It was so crumpled and faded it was hard to believe it had ever been beautiful. Bridget held it up to her face. Was there any smell of her mother left in it?

She was ready to go downstairs now. She pulled the baseball cap on, even though it was too hot for a hat. She had the image of Greta setting out lunch, and it seemed deeply comforting to her.

"Nice to see you down here a little early," Greta said happily.

Bridget flopped into a kitchen chair. "I'm going to start painting tomorrow, if that's okay."

"You're going to paint it? Yourself? Have you painted before?"

Bridget shook her head. "But I'll figure it out. Don't worry. How hard could it be?"

Greta smiled at her. "You're a good girl and a very hard worker."

It jumped into Bridget's head to say "Thanks, Grandma," and she was surprised at herself.

With a sense of peace, she watched Greta set out their lunch. It had evolved over the summer. Now there were carrots every day, and sometimes sharp cheddar cheese or turkey instead of bologna. Bridget knew Greta watched her very carefully, mentally recording her moods and her preferences. But even as the menu changed, lunch was always at the same time, on the same plates, with the same yellow paper napkins. That was how Greta had been before, too, Bridget realized. That was how it had been in this house long ago.

"My Marly had two children, did you know that?" Greta said as she watched Bridget finishing her sandwich.

Bridget swallowed hard. "You mentioned before that you had a granddaughter."

"Yes, Marly's daughter. Marly had twins. A girl and a boy."

Bridget pulled a thread at the hem of her shorts rather than pretend to look surprised by this information.

"I guess the babies came around two and a half years after they were married."

Bridget nodded, still looking down.

"Pregnancy agreed with Marly. It was a happy time for her. But oh, my, when they arrived." Greta shook her head at the memory. "Twins. Can you imagine? When one needed to eat, the other needed to sleep. When one needed inside, the other needed outside. I moved in with them for the first six months."

Bridget glanced up. "Did you really?"

"Sure," Greta said. Her face was thoughtful. "Only, looking back, I wished I'd done less and taught more. Marly struggled after I left."

No matter how it had gone after that, Bridget felt her first six months on earth must have been comfortable if Greta had been there.

"I adored those children," Greta said, shaking her head. She had tears in her eyes, and Bridget feared for her own eyes. "That little girl. She came into the world with a point of view, I'll tell you."

Bridget considered the deep fraudulence of sitting

there listening to her grandmother talk about her. But she suddenly wanted to know this. It felt good.

"She had a little face you could die for," Greta said, and then she seemed to regret her way of putting it. "She had a real feisty personality, too. She was stubborn and independent, and she could do anything she wanted the first time she tried it. My Lord, her grandfather thought the sun rose and set on that child."

Bridget just listened, hoping it was okay if she didn't nod or even look up. This was what she had wanted, what she had come here for: knowledge at a distance. Only it didn't feel distant anymore.

"I think it was hard on the little boy sometimes. He was quieter and more cautious. He got a little lost, what with the mighty Bee marching around."

Bridget flinched at the mention of her name. She felt sad for Perry. She knew that was how it had been his whole life.

Greta's eyes wandered to the clock on the kitchen wall. "Oh my. Listen to me, talking and talking. You probably want to get back to work, don't you."

Bridget didn't want to at all. She wanted to stay there and listen to Greta. But she made herself stand up. "Yeah, gosh, it's late, huh?"

Bridget paused in the doorway. She didn't want to go back up just now. "I better get some paint," she said.

Greta's eyes lit up. "Yes! How 'bout I run you over to Wal-Mart in the car?"

Bridget liked that idea. "Perfect," she said.

❊   ❊   ❊

Tibby saw a yellow note in her mail slot in the dorm lobby. It told her she had received two packages, and that the RA had them. Tibby didn't relish a visit to Vanessa, with her toys and her moles. Vanessa's room was a favorite target of scorn for Maura. On the other hand, Tibby had a filmmaker's curiosity prodding her to at least get a look at the place.

"Come in," Vanessa called when Tibby knocked.

Tibby swung the door open slowly. Vanessa got up from her desk chair and came to the door.

"Hi. Um . . . Tibby, right? Did you come for your packages?"

"Yeah," Tibby said, trying to get a look around Vanessa.

Vanessa seemed to sense this. "Would you like to come in?" she asked politely.

Vanessa was wearing a Williamston T-shirt and a pair of high-waisted old-lady jeans. She seemed nervous as Tibby followed her into the room. Tibby couldn't help wondering why such a socially awkward person had put herself up for the job of RA.

Vanessa looked for the packages, while Tibby looked at the room. The light wasn't very bright, so objects presented themselves slowly. There were indeed a lot of stuffed animals. All over the shelves and the bed. But as Tibby studied them more closely, she realized they weren't the usual sappy Gund bears and Beanie Babies. They weren't like any stuffed animals she had seen before. In spite of herself, Tibby moved closer to an armadillo hunched in the bookcase.

"Could I look at this?" Tibby asked.

"Sure," Vanessa said.

"God. It's . . . got so many parts," Tibby said, amazed, as she pulled back the layers of thick, pebbly fabric that made the shell.

"I know. It took me forever."

Tibby turned to stare at her in disbelief. "You made this?"

Vanessa nodded. Her face turned pink. She held out Tibby's packages.

Absently Tibby took her packages and put them on the bed. "You *sewed* this?"

Vanessa nodded.

Tibby felt her eyes opening as she looked at all the other creatures around the room—brilliantly colored toucans, koala bears, a two-toed sloth hanging from the closet door. "You didn't make all these," she breathed.

Vanessa nodded.

"Really?"

Vanessa shrugged. She was trying to figure out if Tibby was impressed or if Tibby thought she was psychotic.

"They are . . . unbelievable," Tibby said sincerely. "I mean, they're great. They're so beautiful."

Vanessa smiled, although her arms remained protectively around her middle.

Tibby picked up a vibrant yellow frog with black spots. She wasn't thinking when she heard herself say, "God, my little brother would love this. He would go nuts."

Vanessa loosened her arms. She laughed a little. "Really? How old is he?"

"He's almost three and a half," Tibby said, beginning

163

to remember where she was and why she was there. She returned the armadillo and the frog to their places and picked up her packages.

"Thanks a lot," she said, moving toward the door. Her stomach was churning in an uncomfortable way.

"Oh, you're welcome," Vanessa said. Tibby's praise had changed Vanessa's posture.

"Uh, Tibby," Vanessa said to her back.

Tibby turned her head. "Yeah?"

"Sorry I haven't been by your room or anything. I'm . . . not exactly the greatest RA."

Tibby turned her body too. Looking at Vanessa's earnest face and her loyal T-shirt, Tibby suddenly felt like crying. She couldn't stand Vanessa thinking she was a bad RA, even though she was. "No, you're not. Seriously. You're great," Tibby lied. "If I have any questions, I know where to come," she added lamely.

From her face, Vanessa knew Tibby didn't mean it, although she appreciated the effort. "It covers part of tuition," Vanessa explained.

"I love your animals, I really do," Tibby said as she went out the door.

On her way down the hall, Tibby felt a hollowness under her ribs as she rewound all the snide comments and jokes Maura had made about Vanessa's toys. Maura, the creative artist, who couldn't even finish her script, while Vanessa, the dud, had created a world out of bits of fabric. And Maura was the one Tibby had striven to have as a friend?

Back in her room, Tibby remembered her packages.

One contained the Traveling Pants. Tibby felt too much shame to look at them right then. The other was from home. She opened it to find a batch of foil-covered brownies and three pictures on construction paper. One was a scribble signed with Katherine's name. The second was a scribble signed with Nicky's. The third was a childish self-portrait her mother had drawn with crayons. It showed a frown and a blue tear on her cheek. *We miss you!* it said.

Me too, Tibby thought. Her mouth trembled as she produced a tear to match the one in the picture.

Paul had told Carmen once that you could distinguish a drunk from a drinker, because a drinker could choose to stop and a drunk couldn't.

Carmen was a drunk. She could take or leave alcohol; anger was her mode of self-destruction. She couldn't stop when normal people could.

Her anger the night before had been so big she'd nearly drowned in it. This morning she woke up hungover, in a sweat of remorse. From her bed she listened to her mother making coffee as she always did on Sunday mornings. She heard her mother let herself out of the apartment quietly. Christina would go around the corner to get *The New York Times*. She always did.

Moments after the door clicked shut, the phone rang. Carmen staggered toward the kitchen in a T-shirt and underwear. The machine picked up after the second ring. Carmen's fingers were poised to grab the receiver when she heard the voice recording onto the tape.

"Tina . . . pick up if you're there. . . ."

Carmen shrank back from the phone.

"Tina . . . ? Okay, you're not there. Listen, I was hoping I could pick you up at one and take you over to Mike and Kim's. Then maybe we could go to Great Falls after, if you're in the mood for a hike. Call me if you're free today, okay? Call me as soon as you get home."

David paused. He made a funny humming noise and dropped his voice.

"I love you. I loved you last night. I think about you every minute, Tina." He sort of laughed at himself. "Hadn't mentioned that in a few hours." He cleared his throat. "Call me. Bye."

Carmen felt a strange vacuuming sensation under her ribs, sucking away all that was left of her goodwill, pulling in hostility and fear behind it. There were so many alarming, threatening parts to the message her demons hardly knew where to turn.

Mike and Kim? Couple friends. Couple friends for the happy couple. Her mother had never had couple friends before. She'd had her sister and her cousin and her mother and one or two single-mother friends. Mostly she'd had Carmen.

Carmen had never seen her mother's old life as a consolation prize before. But suddenly, that was how it looked. Now that she had a boyfriend and couple friends. Now that she had the brass ring.

All this time, Carmen had thought her mother had chosen her life. That she'd wanted it. Had she been wishing for something else all along? Had she never had what she wanted? Was Carmen a next-best thing?

I thought we were happy together.

Maybe if she had brothers or sisters and a father around, it wouldn't matter as much. But she and her mother depended on one another in a deep and unspoken way. It was motivated by love and loyalty, but underneath there was fear and loneliness, too, wasn't there? Carmen always came home for dinner. She acted as if it were a natural convenience, but she didn't like her mother to eat alone. What did Christina really feel for Carmen? Was it love? Was it obligation? Was it not having anything better?

Carmen had her friends, and she counted on them, but she never forgot that they had real sisters and brothers. A deeply insecure part of Carmen reminded herself that if there were a fire, they'd have to save their brothers and sisters first. The person who would save Carmen in a fire was Christina, and vice versa. Carmen and her mother could pretend the world was large and varied, but they both knew it came down to the two of them.

Carmen thought back to the night in late June, just about a month ago, when all this trouble had started. The night of her first date with Porter. Carmen was a bluffer, caught in her bluff. She'd made a feint toward breaking an agreement she hadn't realized existed and had never meant to break.

Carmen didn't like change, and she certainly didn't like endings. She kept flowers till they were wilted and sticky and algae grew in the vase water.

I don't want boyfriends, she felt like saying. *I want it back how it was.*

Standing over the machine, which was now blinking crazily, Carmen pressed her thumb on the Play button. She felt herself loathing David as the spontaneity of his emotion dried up in the replay. Had he forgotten that Christina lived with her daughter? That it was embarrassing and inappropriate to leave intimate, practically X-rated messages blaring through the apartment? Did Carmen matter so little that David had forgotten about her completely? Had Christina forgotten her too?

She stumbled to her room and threw herself facedown onto the messy bed. She heard the phone ring again. She didn't move. *Click* went the machine. "Uh . . . Christina? Bruce Brattle here. I'm in the office today and had a brief question. Give me a call, if you could." Long pause followed by a beep.

A few minutes later she heard her mother let herself in. Christina went right for the message machine and hit the Play button. Bruce Brattle's message played. Only that one. Carmen felt her heart pounding a little. She could have corrected the mistake by telling her mom. Instead, she fell asleep.

A little while later, in a dismally unmysterious nap dream, their apartment sizzled and flamed. David valiantly saved Christina as Carmen burned to a crisp.

The centaurs were invited
too, for though wild and
lawless they were none-
theless distant relatives.

—D'Aulaires' Book of

Greek Myths

*S*unday afternoon, Tibby changed into the Traveling Pants before walking to the auditorium in the arts center. Brian wasn't there, and she was relieved. She planned to go out and celebrate after the festival with Maura and Alex. She'd wavered between inviting Brian along and making some excuse to get out of having to bring him.

She put on the Pants without letting herself look too hard or think too much. These were *the Pants*, after all, and she was lucky, very lucky, to have them for the first-ever public showing of one of her films. If things in her life worked out, it would be the first of many. She stood in front of the long mirror, admiring the fit and ignoring the inscriptions. It was hard to figure out how, but her hair actually looked better when she wore the Pants. Even her breasts looked a little bigger—or at least like they existed.

Her heartbeat sped up when she saw the crowd in the

auditorium. Most kids were sitting with their parents. Tibby took a seat by herself in the back with two empty seats next to it. When she saw Alex and Maura in the aisle, she waved them over, feeling slightly guilty about not leaving a seat for Brian. After that she kept her head down. Maybe he wouldn't see her.

First, Professor Graves, the head of the film program, welcomed everybody; then they got rolling. Among the first six movies were a couple of short family dramas, a long interview of a filmmaker's grandmother, an adventure story clearly shot on campus but attempting to look like wilderness, and an embarrassing romantic film.

Alex was fidgeting and making wry comments throughout. Tibby was laughing at them at first, but then she realized Maura was also laughing on the other side, so she stopped. It struck her that Maura was a yeah-girl. Pink glasses or no, she was a follower, an inconsequential person, and Tibby felt herself acting just like her.

The lights went up. Tibby knew her movie was coming in the second of three batches.

"Tibby!" She heard a hissing whisper.

She looked around almost frantically.

"Tibby!"

The voice was coming from a middle row on the left side of the auditorium, and it belonged unmistakably to her mother.

Tibby felt a jolt inside her chest. She forgot about breathing.

Her mom was waving madly. She had a huge smile on

her face. She was obviously excited to be there, and so pleased that she had pulled off this surprise.

And what a surprise. Tibby made herself smile too. She waved. "That's my . . . ," she began numbly. She let her voice peter out. She stood, with the thought that she would somehow go and sit with her mom, but there were no free seats, and the lights were dimming for the next set of movies.

At that moment, Tibby's eyes also fell upon Brian, sitting on the right side, almost equidistant from her mother. He was looking at her like he'd known exactly where she was the whole time. Did he also know her mother was there?

She'd told Brian it was fine if her mother saw her movie, that she didn't care. But from the lurch and sprawl of her stomach, it was seeming like maybe she did care.

Her mother had come all this way for a happy surprise. With a sense of doom in her heart, Tibby waited for the next surprise to come.

Two films came before Tibby's, but she didn't register one thing about either of them.

Hers began slowly, with a close-up of an innocent cherry red lollipop. Then the music kicked up and the lollipop turned evil. The shot widened to reveal it adhered to the back of a well-coiffed brown head. The audience burst into laughter, just as Tibby had hoped they would. But the laughter fell like shards of glass pelting down upon her.

One after another, each of the segments connected with the audience, just the way any filmmaker would dream they would. The laughter rose to near hysteria when the camera followed the back of the elegant pump-shod heel trailing the diaper wipe through the house.

Tibby couldn't make herself turn her head in the direction of her mother's seat until the end, after it was over and a new movie started and, Tibby prayed, began to change the mood. Tibby felt like a pure coward as she stared at the screen ahead.

She could avert her eyes, but she hadn't thought to plug her ears. She heard a snuffle from her left. She wished and hoped she had imagined it. She squeezed her eyes shut. If she could ever in her life have transported herself from one place to another, she would have done it then.

She moved her head ever so slightly to the left and did the rest with her eyeballs. She needed to see her mother, but couldn't face her, even in the dark. Straining her eyeballs to the far corner of her vision, she could see that her mother's head was bent.

Tibby's hands found her face. What had she done?

Alex was snickering at something on the screen. Tibby was lost. She was somewhere else. She didn't look up again until the lights were on and half the people had left.

"Tibby?" Alex was looking at her.

"Yes?"

"You coming?" She was looking into Alex's face, but she wasn't seeing it.

She turned in one direction, and Brian was standing at the end of her row, waiting for her. When she turned in the other direction, she saw that her mother had gone.

❆   ❆   ❆

173

Christina didn't stray more than five feet from the phone. She actually carried it with her when she went to the bathroom. She waited until two in the afternoon to suck up her pride and ask Carmen if anyone had called while she was out that morning.

Carmen shrugged, not meeting her eyes. "The machine picked it up," she said. It wasn't a lie.

"The message from Mr. Brattle?" Christina asked.

Carmen shrugged again.

Christina nodded, her fragile hopes dashed.

It was such pathetic female behavior, Carmen felt the anger churning in her stomach again. "Are you waiting for a call in particular?" Carmen asked.

Christina looked away. "Well, I thought David might . . ." Her voice was faint. Her sentence died off rather than came to a stop.

Mean things filled Carmen's mouth. Somewhere up in a lofty part of her mind, she told herself to go into her room and shut the door. Instead, she opened her mouth.

"Is it impossible for you to go one day without David?" she snapped.

Christina's cheeks turned pink. "Of course not. It's just—"

"You're setting a horrible example, you know. Throwing your entire life away for some guy. Mooning over the phone all day, waiting for him to call."

"Carmen, that's not fair. I'm not—"

"You are!" Carmen insisted. She'd just had that first tantalizing drink, and there was no stopping her now. "You go out every night. You dress like a teenager. You borrow my clothes! You make out in restaurants! It's embarrassing. You're making a huge fool of yourself, don't you know that?"

For days now Christina's happiness had lifted her into a state of benevolence in which she had absorbed Carmen's anger with patience and understanding. Now Carmen could feel her mother sinking back down to earth, and it was satisfying.

Christina's cheeks were no longer sweetly pink; they were red and patchy. Her mouth made a grim line. "That is a nasty thing to say, Carmen. And it isn't true."

"It *is* true! Melanie Foster saw you making out at the Ruby Grill! She's been telling everybody about it! Do you know how that makes me feel?"

"We weren't *making out*," Christina defended herself hotly.

"You were! Do you think I don't know you're sleeping around? Doesn't the church say you're supposed to get married before you do that? Isn't that what you've always told me?"

It was a calculated guess, and by the stricken look on Christina's face, Carmen knew she'd guessed right. It was the equivalent of dropping the H-bomb, and Carmen had done it without preparing for the consequences. She felt nauseated as she stared at Christina. A big part of her wanted her mother to deny it, but she didn't.

Christina looked at the floor and kneaded her hands. "I don't think that is any of your business," she whispered savagely.

"It *is* my business. You're supposed to be my mother,"

Carmen replied. Her mother was now angry enough for both of them.

"I *am* your mother," Christina shot back.

Carmen felt tears flooding her eyes. She wasn't ready to be vulnerable to her mother yet. Instead, she took her very full heart into the privacy of her room, where she could consider what was in it.

"Hey," Brian said from the aisle just beyond where she was standing. He looked sad. He tried to hold Tibby's eyes for an extra moment to figure out what was going on with her.

She dropped her gaze. She didn't want him to see anything.

Brian stood there. He was going to wait for her, of course. Alex and Maura were looking at him, obviously wondering who the loser with the *Star Wars* T-shirt and the bad glasses was.

Tibby took a breath. She needed to say something.

"Uh, this is Brian," she said flatly. Her voice sounded as if it came from a different body than hers.

She pointed to Alex. "This is Alex." She pointed to Maura. "This is Maura."

Brian didn't seem to care about Alex and Maura. He was still gazing solemnly at Tibby with his dark brown eyes. She wished he would go away.

"'Sup," Alex said fleetingly to Brian, turning his back before he'd even finished greeting him. He faced Tibby. "Let's go."

Numbly she nodded and began to follow Alex and Maura out of the auditorium. She wasn't thinking. Naturally Brian followed her.

The four of them somehow ended up in a Mexican restaurant two blocks away. Alex looked annoyed that he hadn't shaken Brian off. Maura made no secret of rolling her eyes in displeasure.

This would have been a good moment for Tibby to explain that Brian was not actually a psychotic stalker but one of her very best friends, who not only hung out at her house all the time but was currently living in her dorm room. She didn't. She couldn't make herself look at Brian, let alone say his name.

They stood awkwardly at the noisy bar. Alex successfully ordered three Dos Equis with his fake ID. He leaned in close to Tibby and clinked his bottle against hers.

"Well, done, Tomko. You stole the show."

Tibby knew he was trying to congratulate her, not to make her cry.

"It was awesome," Maura agreed.

"It wasn't," Brian said, sticking close to Tibby's side. "Her mom was in the audience." Brian seemed to feel that if these were Tibby's friends, they needed to know this. His hand found Tibby's elbow. He was suffering for her.

The bit about her mom didn't seem to register as Alex drank down most of his beer. "You're saying her movie wasn't good? It was freakin' hilarious."

Brian shook his head. "It wasn't." He was honest, after all.

Alex squinted. "What's your problem?"

Brian didn't look at Alex. "I'm worried about Tibby."

"You're *worried* about Tibby?" The derision was so thick in the air Tibby could practically smell it. "Gosh, what a pal. Why don't you go worry about her someplace else?"

Brian looked at Tibby. The look said, *Come on, Tibby, come back to me. We're friends, aren't we?*

But Tibby just stood there gaping, as though someone had taken a machete to her vocal cords.

Alex stepped in closer. He was getting puffed up and martial. "What part of 'Go away' don't you understand?"

Brian saved a last, agonizing look for Tibby; then he left.

Tibby felt tears fill her eyes. What had she done? She cupped her hand on her thigh. Under her fingers was the denim of the Traveling Pants with the careful stitches she'd made at the end of last summer. She looked down and ran her index finger around the outline of the heart she'd sewn in red yarn. Her eyes were too full to read the words she had embroidered below it. She could feel the weight of her body sitting hour after hour on the back porch in the late-summer swelter, her legs falling asleep as she made thousands and thousands of stitches — pulling them out, putting them in — with her stubborn, clumsy fingers. The product of all that toil was a shabby heart and three crooked little words. *Bailey was here.*

Had Bailey been there? Had she? What evidence was there of that?

Tibby's heart felt bereft of her just now.

She put both hands to her cheeks. She needed to steady her head.

Alex was still snarling after Brian. He turned to look irritably at Tibby.

"So, Tibby." His voice was leaded with criticism. "What's with the pants?"

If you scatter thorns,

don't go barefoot.

—Italian proverb

Tibby drove Earl, her beloved Pontiac, due north. When she stopped in Front Royal for gas, she took out her address book. She had never been to Brian's house, strange as that was, but she did have his address. When Nicky turned three, he had insisted upon sending Brian his own invitation for the rodeo party.

It was almost ten thirty when she reached Bethesda. Brian's neighborhood was less than a mile from hers, but the houses were smaller and newer. She snaked around for a while before she found his house. It was a redbrick one-story. She had always felt annoyed by the perfectly pruned bushes and bright flower boxes in the windows of her house, but this plain, shabby place didn't seem preferable. The only light came from a blue TV glow at the side of the house.

Tibby knocked timidly. It was late, and she was a stranger to his family. She waited a few minutes and knocked again.

A man opened the door. He was large and balding. He looked half-asleep. "Yeah?"

"Is, um, Brian here?"

He was annoyed. "No."

"Do you know where he is?"

"No. Brian hasn't been around in a few days."

Tibby gathered this was his stepfather. "Do you think . . . his mom might know?"

His patience was gone. "No. I don't. Anyway, she isn't here."

"Okay," Tibby said. "Sorry to bother you."

She sat in her car and rested her head on the steering wheel. She felt sad for Brian in more ways than she could name.

She drove slowly toward his old hangout, the 7-Eleven on Rogers Boulevard. It was closing up, and he wasn't there. She drove another block to the small park where they sometimes used to hang out after a big afternoon of Dragon Master.

She saw him, a dark outline sitting on the picnic table. His backpack and sleeping bag sat beside him.

She crept a little closer. Unfortunately, Earl was in a noisy mood tonight. Brian looked up and saw her car and her in it. He picked up his pack and his sleeping bag and walked away.

Tibby couldn't go home. She couldn't face her mother. It was too late to burst in on Lena or Carmen. Besides, she hated herself too much to face them.

The heart sewn on the Pants reviled her. It made her cry. She couldn't face it any longer. She stripped off the

Pants and drove to Lena's house. It was perfectly quiet and dark. She folded up the Pants as flat as they could go and stuffed them through the mail slot. Then she turned around and drove back to Williamston, wearing only her shame and her underwear.

Lena lay on the wood floor of her room feeling sorry for herself and generally hating everything and everyone she knew.

If she could have made herself paint, she would have. Painting and drawing always made her feel anchored. But there were times when you felt miserable and you wanted to feel better, and other times when you felt miserable and you figured you would just keep on feeling miserable. Anyway, there was nothing beautiful in the world.

It was hot as only Washington, D.C., in late July is hot. Lena's father didn't believe in central air-conditioning because he was Greek, and her mom loathed the window kind because they were loud. Lena stripped down to her push-up bra (handed down from Carmen, who always bought them too small) and a pair of white boxers. She set up the floor fan so it blew directly on her head.

Lena liked to annoy, irritate, and provoke her mother, but she hated actually being in a fight with her. She hated blowing up at Tibby. She hated the tension between her mom and Christina and Alice. She hated Kostos and his new girlfriend. She hated Effie for telling her about it. (She liked Grandma for not liking Kostos's new girlfriend.)

Lena didn't like fights. She didn't like yelling and

hanging up. She liked silent treatments okay, but not past the third day.

Lena was a creature of regularity. She had eaten peanut butter on whole-wheat bread for the past 307 lunches. She didn't go in for stimulation.

She heard the doorbell. She refused to get it. Let Effie get it.

She waited and listened. Of course Effie answered it. Effie loved doorbells and phone rings. Then Lena heard Effie screech excitedly. Lena listened harder. She tried to figure out who it could be. Effie didn't usually screech at the UPS man, but you never knew. Or maybe it was one of her friends with a new haircut or something. That could elicit a screech from Effie.

Lena concentrated on the sounds. She strained to hear the visitor, but she couldn't make out a voice. It didn't help that Effie talked five times louder than normal people.

Now they were coming up the stairs. The footsteps didn't have the rapid-fire artillery sound of Effie and one of her friends. The second set of footsteps was slower and heavier. Was it a boy? Was Effie bringing a boy upstairs in the middle of the afternoon?

She heard a voice. It *was* a boy! Effie was going to take a boy to her bedroom and very possibly make out with him!

Suddenly Lena realized the two sets of footsteps hadn't taken the turn for Effie's bedroom as expected. They were coming in the direction of Lena's bedroom. With a burst of panic it occurred to Lena that her door was open. She was mostly naked and a boy was coming toward her room and her door was open! Well, it wasn't like she could have seen this coming. She could count the number of times a boy had come up those stairs on one hand. Her parents were strict that way.

Lena was frozen on the floor. The footsteps were close. If she leaped up to shut the door, they would see her. If she stayed where she was, they would see her. If she got up and grabbed her bathrobe . . .

"Lena?"

At the sound in her sister's voice—excitement bordering on hysteria—Lena jumped to her feet.

"Lena!"

There was Effie. There indeed was a boy. A tall, familiar, and excessively good-looking one.

Effie had thrown her hand over her mouth at the sight of what Lena was and wasn't wearing.

The boy stood there looking captivated and amused. He didn't avert his eyes as quickly as he should have.

Lena's head was fuzzy. Her heart whizzed like a Matchbox racer. Her throat swelled painfully with emotion. She felt heat rising from every part of her body.

"Kostos," she said faintly. Then she slammed the door in his face.

Bridget had memorized Greta's schedule. Monday evenings she played bingo at church. Wednesdays she played bridge with her neighbors across the street. Today was Thursday, the day Greta went to the Safeway to do her weekly shopping and splurge on a shell steak. On the third Thursday of every month, her son Pervis came from Huntsville to have dinner, and Greta bought two shell steaks. Bridget volunteered to tag along. The real draw for Bridget was the cold of the meat aisle. She'd become a girl of simple pleasures.

"What's your son like?" Bridget asked, lazily watching the signs flash by on the interstate.

"Quiet. Not so social," Greta said.

"What's he do in Huntsville?"

"Custodial services at the U.S. Space and Rocket Center." She looked at Bridget in confidence. "That's a fancy way of saying janitor. He cleans and buffs the floors."

"Oh." She remembered her uncle Pervis always in his bedroom, always at the window looking through his telescope. Once, when she'd been older, he had come to Washington, D.C., and stayed with them overnight. It was the only time she remembered him coming. He'd set up his telescope, got it all set and trained, and let her look through it. Pervis saw a thousand familiar pictures in the sky, and Bridget saw chaos.

"His father and I saved up our money and sent him to space camp there the summer he was nine. I don't think he ever wanted to leave. He's happy with it."

"Did he ever get married?" she asked.

"No. He's always been real shy with girls. I don't see him getting married. He's got his ham radio friends. That's about as social as it gets for him."

Bridget nodded. Pervis had realized his dream of working at the Space Center, yet he spent his days looking down.

Thinking of Pervis made her think of Perry, his name-sake, who was like him in many ways, minus the ham radio. Bridget had finally spoken to Perry for a few minutes on the phone the night before. He'd been curious about Greta, but guarded. He didn't want to hear anything about Marly.

At the Safeway, Greta marched around purposefully with her cart and her coupons, while Bridget drifted through the refrigerated and frozen aisles, letting her mind go to places it had never gone before.

She wondered about Perry and she wondered about her father. Tragedy brought some families together, maybe, but not hers. Her father never talked about what had happened. He never talked about the things that might lead to talking about what had happened. There were so many things they couldn't talk about, they had stopped trying to talk about much of anything.

She pictured her father, when he wasn't at school, sitting in his den, wearing his earphones tuned to NPR. He never played the radio to the whole room, even when he was alone.

Perry spent his time in front of the computer. He played elaborate fantasy games on the Internet. He spent more time interacting with strangers than with people he knew. Bridget sometimes forgot she lived in the same house with him, let alone that they were twins.

It was sad. She knew it was. She wondered if maybe she could have held on to them better, Perry and her dad. Maybe if she'd tried hard enough she could have kept them feeling like a family and kept her home feeling like a home. Instead, they seemed to float out from under the roof, off into the stratosphere, farther and farther apart, orbiting nothing.

Lena strode around her room, her face burning. Kostos was here. Kostos was here in her house. Kostos, in three dimensions. Living, breathing Kostos.

Was it real? Was she having a psychotic break? It wasn't *that* hot, was it?

She had dreamed it. She had dreamed him. Her knees swayed with the disappointment of that idea. God, how she wanted him to be real.

He looked the same. He looked much better.

He'd seen her in her bra! *Oh my.*

Nobody in the world besides her mom, her sister, and her three best friends ever saw her without her clothes on. She was a modest person. She was! She didn't even like fitting rooms unless they had doors that closed all the way. Kostos had seen her twice!

Kostos was downstairs in Lena's house! Effie had brought him downstairs. They were in the kitchen. That is, if he really existed and this whole thing wasn't a dream, they were in the kitchen.

He had come to see her! All this way! What did that mean?

But wait! He had a girlfriend! What did *that* mean?

Lena was walking in such a tight circle she was making herself dizzy. She straightened out her path and sent herself to the door.

Oh! Get dressed. Oh, yeah.

The Traveling Pants were sitting on her desk chair, waiting patiently. Did they know about this? Had they seen this coming? Lena eyed them suspiciously before she pulled them on. What exactly were those Pants up to? Were they going to make her miserable before they made her happy? *Oh, please, no.*

She pulled a white T-shirt over her head. She took a quick peek in the mirror. Her face was shiny with sweat. Her hair was dirty. She had a stye in her eye. *Oy.*

What if Kostos remembered her as beautiful and when he saw her now he thought, *God, what happened? And here I traveled all this way?* Her face had launched at least one ship, and now the ship was going to turn right back around.

What if he wasn't even waiting for her in the kitchen? What if he was leaving town in a hurry, thinking, *Wow, how things change.* He was probably waiting for the bus at Friendship Station.

In desperation Lena drew on some lip liner. It was orange. Her hand was shaking too much to stay in the lines. It looked horrible. She ran into her bathroom and washed it off. She washed the rest of her face too, so it wasn't so shiny. She pulled her dirty hair back into a knot.

Fine. If he thought she'd gone ugly, fine. If that was what he cared about, then too bad. Besides, he had another girlfriend!

Lena looked at herself in the mirror despondently. Grandma thought she was prettier than Kostos's new girlfriend. What did Grandma know? Grandma thought

Sophia Loren was the hottest thing going. It didn't matter what Grandma said; Lena was certainly *not* prettier than Kostos's new girlfriend!

Lena made herself stop pacing. She forced herself to take a breath, possibly her first in the last ten minutes.

Calm. Calm down. She needed to quiet her mind. *Shut up!* she screamed at it.

Ahhh. Okay.

Kostos was downstairs. She would walk downstairs. She would say hello. That was what she would do.

Deep breath. Okay. Calm.

Lena stumbled at the top of the stairs and grabbed the railing before she fell down the whole flight. More breaths. She walked into the kitchen.

He was sitting at the table. He looked up at her. He was even more . . . how he was before.

"Hi," he said. He gave her a small, questioning smile.

Was her entire body shaking or did it just seem that way? Her bare feet were sweating profusely. What if she slipped and fell in a puddle of her own foot sweat!

He looked at her. She looked at him. She imagined a cloud of romance washing over her and embracing her in its grace and flattering light, giving her good ideas for things to say. Any moment now.

Come on! He was a boy, she was a girl. He was a boy with a different girlfriend, but still. Wasn't fate supposed to take over sometime around now?

She stood. She stared.

Even Effie looked worried on her behalf.

"Sit down," she ordered Lena.

Lena obeyed. She was safer off her feet.

Effie passed her a glass of water. Kostos already had one.

Lena didn't dare touch the glass in case her hand shook.

"Kostos is working in New York for a month this summer. Isn't that amazing?" Effie said.

Lena's heart went out to her sister. Effie knew how to take care of her sometimes.

Lena nodded, trying to process this information. She didn't trust her vocal cords with the job of saying anything yet.

"An old school friend of my father's runs an advertising agency there," Kostos said. He was answering Effie, but his eyes stayed on Lena. "He offered me this internship months ago. My grandfather's health is much better, so I thought I'd give it a try."

There were too many thoughts for Lena to contain in her head. She wished she had a separate head for each of the thoughts. First, there was Kostos's father. Kostos had never spoken of him before this. He was so forthright and brave about it, it gave Lena an aching feeling.

Then there was the thing about being in New York. Why hadn't he told her? Had he been planning it before they had broken up? Had any thought of her figured into his plans?

"I've always wanted to see Washington," he went on. "I grew up on *Smithsonian* magazine." He smiled more to himself than to them. "Grandma thought it would connect me to my American heritage."

So he hadn't come to America to see Lena, obviously. That was disappointing. He hadn't come to Washington to see Lena. But he had come to this house to see her. He'd at least done that, hadn't he? Or had he stumbled over their doorstep on his way to the subway? Was his girlfriend going to pop out of the pantry or anything?

"I hope it's okay, just dropping in like this," he said. "It turns out you live right near the place I'm staying."

Figures, Lena thought bitterly.

"I'm sorry if I caught you at a . . . bad time." He said that to Lena, and his eyes had a mischievous look. Even a sexy look, she would have thought if she hadn't known that he didn't care about her anymore.

"Where are you staying?" Effie asked.

"With another family friend. You know how Greeks are—a port in every storm. Do you know the Sirtises in Chevy Chase?"

"Yeah. They're friends of our parents too," Effie said.

"They've made it their mission to show me everything in D.C. and introduce me to every Greek family in Washington, Maryland, and Virginia."

Effie nodded. "How long are you here?"

"Just till Sunday," he said.

Lena wanted to throw a plate at his head. She felt as though she might cry. Why was he acting as if they didn't even know each other? As if they weren't even friends?

Why hadn't he even called her to say he was coming? Why had she stopped mattering to him?

Lena felt tears sting her eyes. They had kissed each other. Kostos had told her he loved her. She had never, ever felt about anyone, *anyone*, the way she felt about him.

You broke up with him, a combination Effie-Carmen voice in her head reminded her.

But that didn't mean you were allowed to stop loving me, she felt like saying to him.

Was she so deeply forgettable?

She felt like running up to her room and pulling all his letters from their shoe bag and shoving them in his face. *See?* she'd shout. *I'm not just nobody!*

Kostos stood up. "I should get going. I'm due at the National Gallery before it closes."

Lena realized she hadn't yet said a word.

"Well, great to see you," Effie said. She looked plaintively at Lena, as if to say, *Just how big of a loser are you, anyway?*

The two girls trailed him to the front door. "Take care," he said. He was looking at Lena.

She looked at him in pure agony. She felt that her eyes were blinking at him from deep, deep inside her head. They'd spent months apart, longing for each other, wishing fervently for a letter or a phone call or a snapshot, and now he was here, close enough for her to kiss, so heartrendingly handsome, and he was just going to go and leave and never see her again?

193

He turned. He walked out the door. He headed down the walk. He was really going. He looked back at her once.

She ran after him. She put her hand in his. She let her tears fall; she didn't care if he saw. "Don't go," she said. "Please."

She didn't really do that. She ran up to her room and cried.

Please give me a second

grace.

—Nick Drake

Tibby couldn't face another hour in her room. There had been almost twenty-four unbearable ones since she'd returned from D.C. late the night before. She hated this room. She hated everything she had thought and felt and done inside it. She couldn't make herself get into her bed. There was no safe place for her to be, least of all her own mind, where her conscience had overthrown the normal government. It ranted at her and harangued her and would *not* shut up no matter how cruelly she threatened it.

In desperation, she got into her car and drove to Washington. She didn't even know specifically where she was headed until she turned up at the Giant on MacArthur Boulevard.

She found herself at midnight standing in the checkout line with a pathetic-looking fistful of orange carnations. But then her conscience shot that down too. The flowers would die, and anyway, neither of them had cared much about flowers. Then she had an inspiration. There was one thing both of them had loved.

Tibby went to the cereal aisle and found a bright yellow box of Cap'n Crunch's Crunch Berries.

She parked at the bottom of the cemetery and scrambled up the paths and along the little sculpted hills with her Giant bag in her hand. The ground was soft and her shoes were digging into the soil. It gave her a bad feeling. She stopped to take them off. Better to tread barefoot and lightly over the grass.

Bailey's gravestone had arrived since she'd last been there. It looked like a gravestone.

Tibby leaned the yellow cereal box against the gray marble. No, the colors looked too lurid for a graveyard. She opened the box and took the bag out. There, that looked better. She stuffed the empty box back into her plastic bag.

She was a bit worried about something as she surveyed the stone. She took a marker out of her bag and on the back of the stone, very, very small, she printed MIMI in smart, boxy letters. She didn't want Bailey to be alone in there, or Mimi to go entirely unmarked.

She lay down on the grass. Her clothes were getting drenched, but she didn't care. Half blades of recently mown grass coated her bare, wet feet. She turned over so her cheek was resting against the ground. "Hi," she whispered.

Her tears were soaking into the earth. She had a feeling of wanting the rest of her to soak in along with them.

Is it any nicer up there? she wanted to ask.

How had Tibby let herself get so far away? Where had she been? Her whole life since Bailey had died now seemed to her like the distant wanderings of an amnesiac, full of confusion and forgetting.

She reached out her arm and touched the cold stone with three of her fingertips.

Remind me, she needed to ask. *I don't seem to know how to be.*

Her ear was pressed to the ground along with her cheek. She listened.

"Lenny, you broke up with him," Bee said kindly, after listening patiently through Lena's avalanche of woe, even though it was midnight.

"But I wasn't the one who forgot about him," Lena moaned into the phone.

Bee was quiet for a moment. "Len," she said as gently as she possibly could. "Breaking up with someone is kind of like forgetting about them. It's saying you don't want to be with them anymore."

"But maybe I didn't mean it that way," Lena said tearfully.

"But maybe that's how it sounded to him," Bee said.

"Well, he didn't have to go and get a new girlfriend," Lena replied accusingly.

Bee stifled her sigh. "You *broke up* with him. I saw your letter. He is allowed to get a girlfriend after that. It is fair." Her voice softened again. "I know you are so sad, and I am sad for you, but you need to think about how this might seem in his eyes."

"What should I *do*?" Lena asked. She had to do something. She felt so desperate she couldn't even stand to be in her own skin. She would rather have clubbed herself over the head with her history binder than feel the things she was feeling.

This was why she had broken up with him. So she wouldn't have to go through this. This wishing and wanting and not having. Why had it turned out so wrong?

"Lena?"

"Yes."

"You still there?"

"Yes."

"You know what you need to do?"

"No," she lied.

"Think about it for a minute."

Lena thought. She did know. But she couldn't admit it, because then she might actually have to do it.

"I can't," she said miserably.

"Okay," said Bee.

"Mom." Tibby touched her mother's shoulder. "Mom?"

Alice's eyes opened. She was disoriented. It was three o'clock in the morning. She sat up in bed.

Before Tibby's wondering eyes, her mother instinctively put her hands on Tibby's sad face. Alice's eyes were full of worry that Tibby wasn't where she was supposed to be. Alice remembered that she loved Tibby before she remembered how mad she was at her.

Roughly Tibby threw her arms around her. Her sobs

were dry and quiet. *Take me back*, she wanted to say. *Let me be your girl again.*

On the night of the fight, Carmen sat for many hours in her darkened room. In one of those hours, she overheard a whispered, strained conversation from inside her mother's room. Carmen knew Christina was talking to David. She had poured gasoline all around her mother's tender relationship, and the missed phone call was the lit match. Carmen listened in ugly, guilty satisfaction as agonized, overextended Christina broke up with confused, resistant David. She overheard the feeling of it clearly, even without hearing all the actual words.

Later that same night, when Carmen went to get a glass of orange juice, she couldn't help glancing into her mother's room. Carmen looked away quickly, but she'd seen Christina's tear-streaked face and puffy eyes.

The next day, Monday, her mother came straight home from work and roasted a chicken. She and Carmen ate in near silence.

Tuesday night Christina claimed a headache and stayed in her room. Carmen stole into the kitchen for some ice cream and noticed one of the pints of Ben & Jerry's was already gone.

Wednesday night Carmen went over to Tibby's, feeling guilty about leaving her mother at home all alone. When she returned, Carmen heard the laugh track of a *Friends* rerun through her mother's bedroom wall.

David hadn't called, and it seemed Christina hadn't

called him again. From everything Carmen could tell, it was really over.

Carmen had wanted to ruin it. And so she had.

Oh, Bee.

Remember last summer, how furious I was with my dad and Lydia and how my anger got so big I tried to bring the whole place down with me? Remember that?

Well, did you know there are two kinds of people in the world? There are the kind who learn from their mistakes and the kind who don't. Guess which kind I am?

I know you are always finding ways to love me in spite of how horrible I am. I hope I haven't run out of chances.

With love and agony,
Carmen

On Saturday, Bridget went for a run in the morning before the soccer game. She'd gotten up to four miles. Slow ones, but still. When she arrived at the field, she was sweaty and sticky, but happy in the way only running could make her happy.

She took her usual spot on the sidelines. Billy looked for her. He looked relieved to see her there. She noticed he swung close by her in the first quarter, in case she had anything to say. She just waved.

By the end of the half, Burgess was down by one. Billy ambled over. "What do you think?" he said.

She was enjoying this. "I think your midfield is a disaster," she said.

Billy looked alarmed. "Yeah?"

"Oh, yeah."

"Why?"

"If Corey can't pass the ball, tell him to take up tennis."

Billy disappeared for a moment and came back with Corey. He sort of shoved Corey at Bridget. "Listen to her," Billy instructed.

"Corey."

"Yeah."

"Pass. Pass the ball. You handle all right, but you can't shoot worth a damn."

Indignation settled over Corey's face.

Billy looked grave. "She's right," he pronounced.

The whistle blew, and Billy hauled Corey back into the game. She noticed right away that Corey started passing.

That was something Bridget loved about boys. They took insults well.

Burgess won it 2–1, and there was the usual cheering on the field after the final whistle. Bridget cheered and screamed right along with them. All the high school kids bunched up to go out afterward. Corey was already making out with his girlfriend by the goalpost. Billy came over to her. "You want to come out?"

Bridget considered this. It was nice that he'd asked, but he hadn't asked in a way that made her want to go. He'd asked in a way that let her know he was grateful.

Grateful and interested were a world apart. "No. Thanks, though," she said.

Instead, she hiked out to Interstate 65. A bunch of the high school kids passed her on the road. They were clumped together in a convertible, and she walked alone on the shoulder. She knew how it looked to them and she didn't care. Some girls couldn't stand being alone. Bridget was different. She went to movies, restaurants, even parties by herself. She loved her three friends above all other things, but she'd rather be alone than cling to people she didn't care about.

When she got to the Wal-Mart she bought a bunch of things, most importantly a soccer ball. She hitched a ride back, hopped out at the courthouse, and found her feet swerving her past the soccer field again. It was dark out now, but there were a few strong lights illuminating three patches of grass.

With a swarm of emotions in her chest, she took the ball out of its box and smelled it. She had tears in her eyes. She dropped it on the ground. She loved it clean and shiny, but she loved it dusty, too.

She had quit soccer back in November because she hadn't wanted people counting on her anymore. She'd just wanted to sleep. For the entire autumn and winter, she had watched her former teammates and pretty much everyone involved in athletics at school stare at her in the halls as if she'd personally amputated her legs.

But she loved soccer. She loved it in every one of her muscles. She'd missed it deeply and painfully. Her body needed to be in motion. She was a voracious person.

She had dreamed about connecting her foot to a ball again. Kick. There she went. It rolled softly. She kicked it again. A puff of dust rose from the ground. Her heart was galloping madly. She ran to keep up with it. Kicking, running, kicking. She let the blurring hexagons and pentagons hypnotize her. This was nice, just this. She didn't need any games or coaches or cheering onlookers or college scouts. She just needed this.

"She hasn't gotten out of bed in three days," Carmen said, sipping her latte. "I feel horrible. I want to be there for her, but she won't even look at me."

Tibby was listening, but she wasn't listening in the way Carmen liked best. She wasn't nodding and egging her on. She was sitting very quietly, shredding her croissant between her fingers.

Finally she looked up. "Carma?"

"Yeah?"

"Did you tell your mom yet?"

Carmen pulled the lid off her coffee. "Tell her what?"

"Tell her about David calling on Sunday?"

Carmen was surprised. She had already confessed her guilt on this one. "No."

"Do you think . . . you're going to?"

"Tell her?"

"Yes."

Carmen cast her eyes toward the big menu board, wanting to change the subject.

Tibby was looking straight at her. "Hey, Carma?"

"Uh-huh."

Carmen was considering the price difference between a tall, a large, and a magnifico latte. And anyway, why didn't anybody call anything small anymore? When you ordered a latte, if you asked for a small the cashier looked at you as though you were retarded. "You mean *tall*?" she'd say patronizingly. Small *is a relative term!* Carmen felt like screaming at them.

"Carma?"

"Uh-huh."

Tibby's face was so unusually earnest that Carmen knew she had to pay attention. "Maybe you should tell her. It won't fix everything, but it might make her feel better."

"Who feel better?" Carmen snapped suspiciously.

"Her. You. Both," Tibby said carefully.

Carmen's mouth opened before she could stop it. "Like you're the expert on mother-daughter relations," she spat.

Tibby looked down at the stringy pile that had been her croissant. Her features seemed to shrink in her face. "I'm not. At all. Obviously."

"I'm sorry, Tib," Carmen said reflexively, putting her hands over her face. Tibby had already been feeling down. Her expression was fragile and her features looked impossibly delicate in her freckly face. Carmen hated herself for making Tibby sadder.

"That's okay." Tibby stood up. "You're right." She

swept up the mess on the table. "I have to go. I told my mom I'd pick Nicky up at swimming."

Carmen stood up too. She wished this conversation had turned out differently. "When are you going back to Williamston?"

Tibby shrugged. "A couple days."

"Call me later, okay?"

Tibby nodded.

"Please don't be mad at me," Carmen begged.

"I'm not." Tibby offered up a smile. It was weak, but it wasn't fake. "Seriously. I'm not."

Carmen nodded, relieved.

"But Carma?"

"Uh-huh?"

"You should talk to your mom."

Carmen felt like crying as she watched Tibby walk out the door and across the parking lot. She knew a worse friend would have made her feel better.

Power corrupts. Absolute

power is kind of neat.

—John Lehman

Carmen was a disaster. Tibby was a disaster. Lena was an even bigger disaster. Carmen considered this as she strode toward the Burger King on Wisconsin Avenue. The only current nondisaster was Bee, who ordinarily took the cake in disasters. A strange summer it was shaping up to be.

Carmen had the day off from work, so she'd spent Lena's lunch hour sitting and sweltering with her in the parking lot behind the store. Well, Carmen had done most of the sitting, while Lena had done the pacing and obsessing.

Carmen opened the door, enjoying the wave of cold, corporate air. As her eyes adjusted, she squinted at a blond girl standing at the counter. Maybe it was knowing Kostos was in town, but Carmen couldn't shake the feeling of seeing flashes of people she thought she knew. On sidewalks, in the lobby of her building, outside Lena's store.

Carmen walked toward the counter, studying the back of the blond girl. She had cutoffs and a perm, and she was counting out her change. *No way*, Carmen said to herself. It couldn't be.

And yet, as Carmen ordered french fries, she couldn't stop looking over at the girl. It couldn't be who she imagined it might be, because the girl Carmen was thinking of didn't have a perm, and she would never have worn shorts like that. And also she lived in South Carolina.

Still, Carmen waited impatiently for the girl to turn around. The girl was taking so long to count out her change, it might really be her, Carmen considered.

Finally, the girl did turn, and she looked straight at Carmen. After a moment of surprise, her face lit up.

"Oh, my God," Carmen muttered.

The girl hurried over, carrying her soda, a duffel bag slung over her shoulder. "Carmen!"

Carmen stood there frozen. Apparently Kostos wasn't the only ghost from last summer to have returned. "Krista?"

Krista looked both excited and shy. "I can't believe I ran into you?"

"What are you doing here?"

"I was hoping to find you," Krista replied. She felt around in the front pocket of her shorts and with some effort yanked out a crumpled piece of paper. "I tried your place a few minutes ago, but nobody answered."

On the paper Krista had written Carmen's address and phone number.

"Wow . . . really? Well . . ." Carmen wanted to say *why?* without it sounding impolite. "Are you here with . . . uh . . . friends?" Carmen was mesmerized by the eyeliner

209

and the shorts and the small red tank top. It had to be Krista, but Carmen didn't quite believe it was Krista.

"No. Just me."

"Oh," Carmen said. The only thing that had stayed the same, that convinced Carmen this girl was actually Krista and not an imposter, was the gold add-a-bead necklace.

Carmen quickly paid for her french fries. "Do you . . . want to sit down for a minute?" she asked, leading the way to a table.

No matter that she was a fugitive, Krista probably couldn't forget her manners if she tried. She stood beside her chair until Carmen was seated.

"Um, is your mom in town?" Carmen asked. It would give the mystery a whole other dimension if Lydia and possibly her dad were in town without even having called Carmen.

Krista's face darkened slightly. "No." She cleared her throat. "I am here to get away from her."

Carmen's felt her eyebrows shoot upward. "You are? Why?"

Krista looked around in case someone might hear. "She's been tickin' me off is why."

Carmen was stunned, and she didn't try to hide it.

"Does she know you're here?" Carmen asked slowly, as if she were talking to Jesse Morgan.

"No." Krista had a fearful yet triumphant look.

"Krista." Carmen was staring at her seriously now. "Is everything okay? You seem really . . . different."

Krista fidgeted with the paper from her straw. "I've been wanting to do my own thing this year, and my mom makes a fuss about everything."

Carmen nodded dumbly.

"I remembered you running off to Washington last summer without telling a soul. That's what gave me the idea."

Carmen put her hands in her lap so Krista wouldn't notice her picking the skin around her thumbnail. "But I live in Washington."

Krista nodded, a look of self-doubt creeping into her eyes. "That's why I came here? I hoped maybe I could stay with you a little while?"

Carmen thought she might explode. "You want to stay with my mom and me?" She wondered if Krista had stopped to consider that Christina was her stepfather's ex-wife.

Krista nodded. "If that's all right? Sorry not to call first." She dropped her head slightly. "I should have called."

"No, no. That's okay. Don't worry about it." Carmen surprised herself by touching Krista's wrist reassuringly. "You can stay with us for a few days."

Krista pointed to her earlobe. It looked red and puffy. "I double-pierced my ears and my mother freaked. That was part of the fight that made me come here."

Carmen absently felt for the two holes in her own earlobe. "Krista, have you talked to Paul?"

Krista's blue eyes were round inside the ring of eyeliner. She shook her head.

"Does anybody know you're here?"

"No. And please don't tell them?" she answered seriously. Krista was still an uptalker, and it undercut the potency of her rebellion.

Carmen swallowed. How could she not tell Paul? She

stood. "We should maybe get going," she said. She picked up the bag full of french fries she'd bought as a treat for her mother and motioned for Krista to follow.

Her apartment building was just two blocks away. Going up in the elevator with Krista, Carmen wondered what her wounded mother would say when she introduced her to the daughter of her ex-husband's wife and mentioned that she might be staying awhile.

Alarmin' Carmen,

You will never never never ever ever ever run out of chances. Don't you know that?

You're right. There are two kinds of people in the world. The kind who divide the world into two kinds of people and the kind who don't.

Love always and no matter what,
Bee

When Tibby was eleven, the year Bridget's mother had died, she had had the secret idea that her family could adopt Bridget. In her eleven-year-old way, Tibby had sensed that Mr. Vreeland had grown too isolated to take care of his daughter anymore. Bee's brother, Perry, barely left his room, content with his computer games.

Bee was so fidgety and eager, and her house was still and empty. Tibby had ached for her friend.

In Tibby's eleven-year-old heart she had known she was a sister to Lena and Carmen and Bee, but she'd longed to be a sister officially, too. She had reasoned that Carmen only lived with one parent and Lena already had a sister, so that meant hers was the family for Bee. She'd made a painstaking drawing of how her room would look with two beds and two dressers and two desks.

Tibby remembered how far and wide she'd allowed her imagination to rove. She'd made plans to share her allowance. She'd benevolently determined that Bee shouldn't have to do any chores for the first year, and after that they could trade off. She'd imagined her parents, especially her father, cheering Bee on at her soccer games. She'd wondered whether Bee would ever call herself Bee Rollins, and whether a stranger would ever see Tibby and Bee eating at a restaurant with their parents and think that they looked alike.

When Tibby was thirteen, her mother had gotten pregnant, and she had indeed become an official sister. She became an official sister again when she was fifteen. Tibby had always felt that this was a case of God listening to her prayers and taking them a bit too literally.

For some reason, Tibby had brought the old drawing of her bedroom to Williamston with her. In fact, the first thing she did when she unlocked the door of 6B4 was to prop up the drawing above her dresser, in front of the mirror. She squinted at the tiny rectangle she'd drawn to represent Mimi's cage. She remembered drawing it at an equal distance from the two beds, so that Bee could enjoy Mimi too and wouldn't feel envious.

She wondered what Alex would think if he saw this drawing. What would he think if she told him that she'd been profoundly attached to her guinea pig until it had died when she was nearly sixteen years old?

What would Bailey think of Alex?

She knew what Bailey would think of Alex. If she tried, she could see through Bailey's eyes, and it was like holding a mirror up to the world. Bailey would know Alex was a poser and she wouldn't think about him at all. There were too many other genuine characters out there, people Bailey would want to think about.

This made Tibby remember Vanessa. She unpacked another of the items she had brought from home. It was a see-through bag full of Gummi creatures—snakes, monkeys, salamanders, turtles, fish. Nicky had given it to her. Tibby guessed there was roughly one sugary creature for every cruel thing Maura had said about Vanessa, every nonfunny thing Tibby had dutifully laughed along with.

Carefully Tibby tied a green ribbon around the top. She used the blade from the scissors on her desk to make the ends curl up. She attached a little note. *Thanks for being a great RA*, she wrote in neat, anonymous cursive. She left it outside Vanessa's room. She knocked on the door and then whisked herself away before Vanessa could see her.

It was such a dorky thing to do, but at least Tibby was being the kind of dork she could feel good about.

❁   ❁   ❁

"Paul, pick up the phone," Carmen commanded from behind a closed door in her bedroom. She probably wouldn't have bellowed into the answering machine like that if she'd been calling him at home—at her dad and stepmother's house in Charleston. But Paul was staying at U Penn for most of the summer, taking extra classes and playing soccer. "Hey, Paul's roommate. Hey, you. Pick up the phone. *Please?*"

No answer. Why weren't people in college dormitories ever home?

She hung up and signed online.

Paul. Hey! Call me right away. Right now!

She pushed the Send button.

She tiptoed to the door and opened it quietly. Krista was still asleep.

Running away seemed to agree with Krista. When Carmen had been on the run, she'd slept fitfully and in short bursts. She'd had constant stomach pains. Krista seemed full of appetite. Carmen had offered her a french fry from the bag she'd intended for her mother, and Krista had gratefully eaten the whole bag. Then she'd fallen asleep within five minutes of hitting the pull-out couch. She hadn't stirred in over two hours.

Carmen was halfway through *CosmoGIRL!* when the phone finally sounded. She pounced within a quarter of a ring.

"Hello?"

"Carmen?" Even in an emergency, Paul's voice came slowly.

"Paul. *Paul!*" she whispered. "Do you know who is sleeping on my fold-out couch at this very moment?"

Paul was silent. He was absolutely the wrong person to play guessing games with.

"No," he finally said.

It was too absurd a bit of information to just dump without a buildup, but what choice did she have? "Krista!"

That took a moment to settle on him. "Why?"

"She ran away!"

"Why?" Paul didn't sound quite surprised enough.

"She's not getting along with your mother. They had a fight. I don't know. She got her ears pierced or something." Carmen paused. "Have you . . . seen your sister lately?"

"In April."

"She's really . . . different than last summer. Don't you think?"

"How?"

"Oh, I don't know . . . makeup, different hair, different clothes. You know."

"She's trying to be like you."

Carmen's lungs seemed to shrivel. There wasn't enough air to make words.

Leave it to Paul. He said one word for every thousand of hers, but he did make them count.

Carmen wasn't sure which implication to respond to. When she got some air into her lungs, she went for the obvious. "Are you saying I dress like a slut?"

"No." Paul often sounded baffled by the things she read into his words.

"W-well," she spluttered. Maybe a different tack was better. "Why do you think she's trying to be like me?"

"She admires you."

"No way! She does?" Carmen said it louder than she'd meant to. She heard stirring in the living room.

"Yes."

"Why?" Carmen couldn't help asking, even though she knew Paul was a terrible person to fish compliments from.

He paused at length. "I don't know."

Great. Thanks. "Well, what should I do?" Carmen whispered. She heard footsteps. She had to get off. Carmen couldn't let Krista know she had betrayed her at the first possible opportunity.

"I can't tell her I told you!" Carmen added. "I promised not to tell anybody."

"Let her be with you awhile," Paul said. "I'll come soon."

"She's awake. Gotta go. Bye." Carmen hung up just as Krista knocked on her door.

"Hi," Krista said faintly, the weave of the blanket imprinted on her cheek. Whatever trace of bravado had brought her there was wearing off.

Carmen suddenly felt tender toward Krista. Maybe it was just that she was a big, fat sucker for flattery.

Because now that she took a moment to look, Carmen could see that Krista's new do was a truly sad approximation of Carmen's own wavy hair. Where Carmen's hair was full and dark, Krista's was fair and scant. Krista's hair was pretty left alone, but it couldn't stand up to a perm. Krista's cutoffs were very much like a pair Carmen had worn last summer in Charleston, but the effect of them on Krista's blue-white stick legs was radically different. The black eyeliner Carmen often wore blended into her dark lashes, but it made Krista look vaguely like a drug addict.

"May I?" Krista asked, hesitating at the door.

A very polite drug addict.

"Of course. Come in." Carmen waved her in the door. "You sleep okay?"

Krista nodded. "Thanks. Do you happen to know the time?" she asked.

Carmen turned to her clock radio. "Five thirty. My mom will be home in a little while."

Krista nodded. She looked tentative in her postnap disorientation. "Do you think this will be okay with her?"

"'This' meaning you?"

Krista nodded. Her eyes got big the way they used to last summer whenever Carmen cursed.

"Yeah. Don't worry." Carmen led her into the kitchen and poured a glass of orange juice for each of them. "So . . . hey. Do you feel at all like maybe . . . calling your mom?"

"I'd rather not." Krista shook her head. "She'll be furious at me."

"She's probably long past furious. She's probably really worried. You know what I mean? You could just tell her that you're safe and everything."

Krista looked partway convinced. Carmen remembered

her being malleable. "Maybe I will . . . call her tomorrow?"

Carmen nodded. She could understand that. If you were going to make a stand, you had to hold out twenty-four hours, at least.

Krista drank her juice in silence for a while.

"So you and your mom had a big fight, huh?" Carmen asked, keeping her voice gentle.

Krista nodded. "We fight a lot lately. She says I'm rude. She hates everything I wear. She can't stand it when I raise my voice." Krista swiped a frazzled blond strand behind her ear. Carmen was amazed to hear the hard little fiber of anger in Krista's voice. "She wants everything quiet and perfect in her house. I don't feel like being quiet and perfect anymore."

Carmen knew she had trailed poison through Lydia's orderly little world last summer, but she hadn't known Krista was eating it. "I don't blame you," Carmen said.

Krista touched the rim of her orange-juice glass. Clearly she longed to confide in Carmen. "If I act the way she wants me to act, I'm just invisible." Her voice was plaintive. "If I act the way I want, she says I'm ruining her life."

Krista appeared to be searching Carmen's face for some kind of wisdom. "What would you do?"

Carmen considered this position of responsibility into which she had been thrust.

What would she do? What would *she*, Carmen, do?

Whine, resist, complain. Throw rocks through the window of her father and stepmother's house. Run away like a coward. Torment her mother. Act like a selfish brat. Destroy Christina's happiness.

Carmen opened her mouth to try to give some advice.
She closed it again.

There was a word for this. It started with an *h*. It not
only indicated you were a horrible waste of a person but
also somehow seemed to indicate that you were fat.

What was it?

Oh, yeah. Hypocrite.

Nothing takes the taste

out of peanut butter quite

like unrequited love.

—Charlie Brown

Tibby laid the stack of CDs on the counter. "It wasn't any of these," she said. "The one I'm looking for, it wasn't just piano. It had other instruments too."

The man nodded. He was in his forties, she guessed. He wore Hush Puppies on his feet and had the haircut of a person who didn't care about his hair.

"Piano and other instruments?" he asked her.

"Yes."

"It was a concerto."

Tibby's eyes lit up. "Yes. I think you're right."

"You're sure it's Beethoven."

"I think so."

"You think so." He looked as though he needed a cup of coffee.

"Pretty much totally sure," she added quickly.

"Okay, well, if it's Beethoven, there are five of them. Probably the best known is the *Emperor* Concerto," he explained patiently.

Tibby was grateful. This man had already spent a good deal of time on her problem. Luckily there wasn't much doing in the classical section at ten forty-five in the morning.

"Can I listen to it?"

"I have a listening copy of it here somewhere. It might take me a few minutes to find. Do you want to come back later?" He looked hopeful.

She didn't want to come back. She needed it now. "Can I wait? I really, really need it." She had nine days and so, so much work to do.

She watched him search too slowly. "Can I help you look?"

Reluctantly he allowed her to come behind the counter and search through a box.

"Here," he said at last, triumphantly holding up a CD.

"Yay!" she called. She grabbed it and hurried over to the listening place.

She knew after just a few seconds. "This is it!" she practically shouted at him.

"All right!" he said, nearly as excited as she was.

She honestly felt like hugging him. "Thank you. Thank you so, so much."

"You're welcome," he said happily. "It's rare I have an emergency in this job."

Back in her dorm room, she faced the computer. In one hand was the DVD with all the precious video she had copied from her equipment at home. In the other was the *Emperor* piano concerto.

She stuck the CD in the slot and stared at the blank screen. She let it play over and around her. She didn't move. She couldn't do it yet. She put her hand on the DVD and took it away again.

This was hard. She hadn't looked at any of it since last summer. She wasn't ready, she had told herself. But maybe she would never be ready. Maybe she just had to make herself do it.

She took the DVD out of its plastic case. She put it down on her desk. The music swooped and soared. Her heart was beating fast.

There was a knock on her door. Her head snapped up. She turned the music down. She cleared her throat. "Hello?" It came out rusty.

The door pushed open. It was Alex.

"Hey," he said. His face was more tentative than usual. "You're back. Where've you been?"

She kicked the wall under her desk. "I just had to go home for a while and take care of a couple things."

He nodded. He gestured toward her computer. "You working on the movie?"

She considered him. "Not the one you're thinking of. Not the one about my mom."

"No?"

"I'm not doing it anymore." She had wanted to throw the movie down the sewer, but she had forced herself to keep it around as punishment.

"What are you going to do for your term project?"

"I'm doing a new movie."

"You're *starting* a new one? Now?"

"Yeah."

"Huh. You think you can do it in a few days?"

"I hope so."

He acted so aloof all the time, but he obviously took this pretty seriously. She was beginning to see how it was with him. He could mock and smirk all he liked, but he also wanted to get into Brown. He was a fake risk-taker, a phony rebel. It took one to know one.

"What's it about?"

She looked protectively at her DVD. She couldn't let Alex into this. This was a lot harder and more dangerous than taking cheap, nasty shots at her mother.

"I don't even know yet."

She turned back to her desk. He turned to leave.

"What are you listening to?"

For a moment she seriously considered disavowing the music she had spent more than an hour trying to find. Pretending she had tuned the radio to the wrong station.

"It's Beethoven," she said instead. "It's called the *Emperor* Concerto."

He looked at her a little strangely. He turned to go again. Her heart was beating fast. "Hey, Alex?" she said.

"Yeah?"

"You know that guy Brian? Who didn't like my movie?"

Alex nodded.

"He's one of my best friends in the world. He practically lives at my house."

Alex looked confused. And then uncomfortable.

225

"You might have mentioned that before," he said stiffly.

Tibby nodded. "Yeah, I should have." A reckless impulse was crawling up her ribs as if they were a ladder, making its way toward her mouth. "And you know what else?"

He shook his head very slightly. He didn't want to know what else.

"That movie I made was awful. It was mean and shallow and stupid."

Alex wanted to leave her room. He wasn't the kind of person who tolerated confrontations well.

"And you know what else?"

He walked toward the door. He thought she was insane.

"Vanessa the RA is more of an artist than Maura or you or I will ever be!" she shouted after him. She wasn't sure if he heard that last bit, and she didn't care. She wasn't saying it for his benefit anyway.

Lena walked around feeling as though she'd stuck her finger in an electrical socket and left it there. She experienced continual shivers and jolts, followed by the sensation that her entire body was encased in dryer lint. He was here. He was here! What if she never saw him again?

At breakfast she'd been so preoccupied she'd buttered her mother's toast, forgetting the cold war they'd been having since she'd discovered Eugene.

At work her eyes were constantly darting to look out the window. Kostos was staying nearby. He could walk by anytime. The entire Washington, D.C., metropolitan area was a potential meeting place. Maybe she would see him in the next five minutes. Maybe she would never see him again. She was desperately afraid of both possibilities at the same time.

She walked all the way home from work in a near trance, imagining that every bus that passed contained Kostos looking out the window at her.

When she walked in the door at home, she felt that something was strange. Effie was setting the table. Effie was setting too many places at the table.

When Effie saw Lena she nearly exploded. "Kostos is coming over for dinner," she erupted breathlessly.

Shivers, jolts, and dryer lint. Lena put her hand to her head. It felt as if it didn't balance on her neck anymore. "What?"

"Yeah. Mom invited him."

"How? Why?"

"She talked to Mrs. Sirtis. Mrs. Sirtis told her Kostos was in town. Mom couldn't believe we didn't know and we hadn't invited him, seeing as he's practically family, practically Valia and Bapi's grandson."

Lena stood there blinking. She had been bypassed. She was not important to anyone. Kostos was everyone's friend but hers.

Lena was not only mad and jealous of Kostos's new girlfriend, Lena was also mad at everyone in the Kaligaris family, and all the Sirtises as well, even the ones she'd never met.

"Do you think Mom is trying to torture me?" Lena asked.

"Honestly? I don't even think she thought about you."

Okay. That didn't help.

Effie observed the stricken look on Lena's face. "I mean, she knows you and Kostos liked each other last summer. She knows you wrote some letters. She probably figures you lost track of each other. Have you ever talked to her about it?"

"No."

"So there you go," Effie said.

Lena fumed. Since when did you have to tell your mother everything for her to know?

"When's he coming?" Lena asked.

"Seven thirty," Effie said sympathetically. She felt sorry for Lena.

Lena felt sorry for herself that her younger sister felt sorry for her. She looked at her watch. She had fifty minutes. She would go up to her room and take a shower and get dressed, and when she came down she would be a different person.

Alternatively, she would lie down in her bed and fall asleep till morning and probably no one would even notice.

Carmen couldn't help feeling sad when she saw her mother in the door later that evening. She was a post-pumpkin Cinderella. The magic was gone. Three weeks ago Christina had stood in the same doorway wearing the Traveling Pants. Back on that night she had towered and shone like a woman who was loved.

Tonight she looked distinctly underloved. She wore her hair and her shoes and her expression for no one. Her whole body seemed angled toward the floor.

"Hi, Mama," Carmen said, coming out of the kitchen with Krista behind her. She gestured to Krista. With her eyeliner smudged from sleep, Krista looked even more peculiar. "This is Krista. She is actually, uh, kind of Dad's stepdaughter." Carmen tried to keep it light.

Christina raised her head and blinked. A few weeks ago she'd been too happy to be fazed by anything. Now she was too unhappy. She nodded. "Hi, Krista." She saved her look of extreme confusion for Carmen.

"Krista is, um, taking a little break from home, and we were hoping she could stay here for a couple days." She shot her mom a look that said she knew it was weird and could they discuss it later. She pointed to the messy bed that had already transformed the small living room. "You know, on the couch?"

"Well, I guess that would be all right." Christina's bafflement didn't appear to harden into judgment of any sort. "If it's all right with her mom."

"Thank you," Krista murmured. "Thank you so much, Mrs. . . ." She trailed off. She looked somewhat desperately to Carmen for help.

"Mrs. Lowell," Mrs. Lowell supplied.

The awkwardness was at last dawning on Krista. Her mother was also Mrs. Lowell. Krista's entire upper body, from shoulders to scalp, turned pink. "Sorry."

Dinner was one of the least comfortable meals

Carmen could remember. Krista tried politely to make pleasant conversation, but all roads led to Al. Christina was a good sport about it, but it was obvious she just wanted to go to bed.

"Do you want to go out for ice cream?" Carmen asked her mom as they cleaned up. "We were thinking of going to Häagen-Dazs."

Christina sighed. "You two go. I'm exhausted." She almost looked apologetic, which made Carmen feel horrible. Christina hadn't left the house for days except to go to work. But she wasn't mad at Carmen. She was just sad. She had surrendered to her fate. It was as if she had no business being happy.

Why did you let me ruin everything? Carmen found herself wanting to ask her mother. She had the perverse wish that the ugly consequences of her tirades would magically dissolve within a few hours. She wished her victims would just snap right back like cartoon characters after they got their heads flattened by a frying pan. Instead, the wreckage lived on, far longer than her anger.

Krista was looking for something in her duffel bag. She walked to the door in a pair of blue plastic slides exactly like a pair sitting in Carmen's closet. Krista looked eagerly at Carmen. The tips of her ears stuck through her sad, wrinkly hair. Carmen felt like an agent of destruction.

Why do you want to be like me? Carmen found herself wanting to ask Krista.

Carmen had always wanted to be important. But she didn't want to be this important.

❅   ❅   ❅

230

Lena was clean. Her hair was washed. She smelled fine.

When Kostos walked in the door she tried to keep her head from falling off.

She watched him, as though in a dream, as he greeted her father. She watched him kiss her mother on both cheeks. She watched him hug Effie. She watched him not hug her but shake her hand instead. As he was shaking it, she felt that her hand was several hundred degrees below zero.

She watched him speak Greek to her parents, maybe even tell a joke, because her parents both laughed and beamed at him like he was a superhero and a comedian all rolled into one.

Lena wished she could speak Greek. She suddenly felt like a dolphin that couldn't swim.

They sat in the living room. Her dad offered him wine. Kostos was a man, practically. He was dazzling. He was a parent's dream.

Lena's dad offered her apple juice. She felt like a scrawny fifth grader in comparison. As if she hadn't even hit puberty. It was a good thing she'd broken up with Kostos, because she'd saved herself the misery of discovering that she wasn't nearly good enough for him. Well, actually, she hadn't saved herself that misery, had she?

Lena tried to remember things to like about herself. She tried to remember reasons why Kostos might have liked her. She couldn't think of one. Maybe she should just go upstairs.

At dinner, Lena sat next to him.

He told a funny story about Bapi Kaligaris, when Grandma had tried to get him to wear new eelskin shoes in favor of his preferred white ones. "This are good, honest shoes!" Kostos bellowed in a perfect imitation of Bapi. "Are you trying to turn me into a dandy?" Lena's father looked so joyful and homesick Lena half expected him to burst into tears.

Kostos was everything she remembered him to be. Why had she had so little faith in him? So little faith in her memory? Why had she been so impatient?

When Lena was eating her lamb chop, she felt a shoe brush against the sole of her bare foot. She nearly choked on her food. A tingle ran right up her leg and out the top of her scalp. Her entire body was on alert. Every nerve ending was reporting to her brain in one tangled traffic jam.

Had he meant to do that? Her heart roared along. Could he be trying to tell her something? To send a tiny message?

She didn't dare turn her head to look at him. She couldn't even make herself finish chewing the bite in her mouth. Did he know she was feeling hopeless? Did he want to give her one small pinprick of hope?

You *broke up with* him, the Carmen-Effie-Bee combo pointed out once again.

But I didn't stop loving him!

Okay.

It was out. At last it had been acknowledged. She'd finally chosen, and she'd chosen B. She resumed chewing.

She did love him. She loved him, and he didn't love her anymore. That was the hard, cold truth. She would have relocated to Alaska to avoid admitting that, but now it was out. It was done. It was horrible, but it felt better to be honest.

The nerves in the sole of her foot reached out to him. The slightest touch would mean the earth to her. It came. The gentlest graze. She looked down.

It wasn't Kostos's foot. It was Effie's.

There are two tragedies

in life.

One is not to get your

heart's desire.

The other is to get it.

—George Bernard Shaw

It took Lena hours to fall asleep, and once she did, she had a dream that made her wake up again.

The dream had the ratty, two-bit quality of an old-fashioned science filmstrip. She heard the whir of the film flying through the projector and the fan that kept the light cool. The film showed two greatly magnified cells moving through a roughly drawn diagram of the human body. One cell was traveling from the brain, and the other from the heart. The cells met at about the clavicle. They bounce bounce bounced together until both membranes gave way at once and they joined.

In the dream, Lena raised her hand and heard herself saying to Mr. Briggs, her ninth-grade biology teacher, "That can't happen, can it?"

Then she woke up.

When she woke up she went to the bathroom, because she really had to pee. And while she was peeing, she got tired of herself. She got tired of not being able to say what she wanted or do what she wanted or even want what she wanted. She was tired, yes, but she couldn't sleep.

She sat on her windowsill for a long time and looked at the three-quarter moon. It was the same moon shining on Bee and Carmen and Tibby and Kostos and Bapi and all the people she loved, near and far.

No, she wasn't going to be sleeping anymore tonight. She put on the Traveling Pants under her nightgown and put her denim jacket on over that. Before she could think better of it she went downstairs and out the door. She closed it very carefully behind her.

It was about a mile to the Sirtises', and Lena walked it with a reckless feeling in her heart. She had already come to terms with the worst possible thing. It couldn't get any worse.

But she owed it to herself to see if it could possibly get better.

She had been to the Sirtises' house enough times to know where the guest bedroom was. But as she sneaked around the side of the house, she was suddenly afraid that they had a burglar alarm and that she was going to set it off. She imagined sirens wailing and dogs barking and Kostos watching the cops drag Lena off wearing handcuffs over the sleeves of her nightgown. Maybe she hadn't come to terms with the worst possible thing.

It was lucky the guest bedroom was on the first floor, because she was bad at climbing and had terrible aim.

The lights were off in the room. Naturally. It was nearly three in the morning. She climbed through the bushes that lined the side of the house. She felt very stupid. She knocked softly on the window. She knocked again. What if she woke the whole house? How would she explain herself? The whole Greek community would be whispering about Lena the sexual predator.

She felt him stirring before she actually saw him at the window. Now her heart felt like an unmanned AK-47, wheeling around in her rib cage and blasting everything in range. Kostos saw her and opened the sash.

If the sight of Lena in her nightgown and jeans knocking on his window at three in the morning gave him the feeling of a waking nightmare, he didn't let on. He did look surprised, though.

"Can you come out?" These were the first words she'd spoken to him since he'd arrived. She was proud that she'd had enough breath to send them to his ears.

He nodded. "Wait. I'll be there," he said.

She pulled herself out of the bushes, losing a little of her nightgown in the process.

His white T-shirt looked blue in the moonlight as he came toward her. He had pulled a pair of jeans over his boxer shorts. "Come with me," he said.

She followed him into the backyard, to a corner shielded by tall, old trees. He sat down and she sat down too. Her jean jacket was hot from all the walking. She took it off. She perched on her knees first, then sank down on the damp grass to sit cross-legged.

The summer sky was magical to her as she looked up at it. She felt heedless and not so afraid.

He was watching her face very carefully. He was waiting

for her to say something. She was the one who'd pulled him out of his bed in the middle of the night.

"I just wanted to talk to you," she said in a voice a little louder than a whisper.

"Okay," he said.

It took a while to get the words up and out. "I missed you," she said. She looked in his eyes. She just wanted to be honest with him.

He looked in her eyes right back. He didn't look away.

"I wish I hadn't broken off our letters," she said. "I did it because I was afraid of missing you and wanting you all the time. I felt so stretched out. I wanted to feel like my life belonged just to me again."

He nodded. "I can understand that," he said.

"I know you don't feel the same way about me anymore," Lena said bravely. "I know you have a girlfriend now and everything." She picked a blade of grass and rubbed it between her fingers. "I don't expect anything from you. I just wanted to be honest, because I wasn't before."

"Oh, Lena." Kostos's expression was strained. He sat back in the grass and put his hands over his face.

Lena found herself staring at his hands instead of his eyes. She cast her own eyes down at the grass. Maybe he didn't want to talk to her anymore.

At last he pulled his hands away. "Don't you know anything?" he said. He said it like a groan.

Lena's cheeks turned warm. There was a sob in her throat. She had expected him to be sympathetic to her, no matter what. Now she felt her courage slipping. "I don't," she said humbly, her head bowed. She could hear the tears in her voice.

He pulled himself up and turned to her. His body was facing hers straight on, no more than a foot away. To her amazement, he took one of her hands in both of his. He looked pained by the tragedy in her face. "Lena, please don't be sad. Don't ever be sad because you think I don't love you." His gaze was steady on her.

Her tears were perched on her lids, and she wasn't sure which way they were going to go.

"I never stopped," he said. "Don't you know that?"

"You didn't write me anymore. You got a new girlfriend."

He released her hand. She wished he would keep it. "I didn't get a new girlfriend! What are you talking about? I went out with a girl a few times when I was feeling miserable about you."

"You came here all the way from Greece without even telling me."

He semi-laughed — more at himself than at her. "Why do you think I came here?"

She was afraid to answer. The tears slopped over her lids and ran in big rivulets down her face. "I don't know."

He reached out to her. He put a finger on her wrist. He let it float up to touch a tear. "Not because I want a career in advertising," he said.

On one level her mind was spinning madly, and on another it was focused and calm. The smile she put forth threatened to warp at any second. "Not because of the Smithsonian?"

He laughed. She found herself wishing he would touch her again. Anywhere. On her hair. On her ear. On her toenail.

"Not because of that," he said.

"Why didn't you say anything?" she asked.

"What could I have said?"

"You could have been happy to see me or told me you still cared about me," she suggested.

He laughed his rueful laugh again. "Lena, I know how you are."

Lena wished she knew. "How am I?"

"If I come close, you run away. If I stay still then maybe, slowly, you might come."

Was she like that?

"And Lena?"

"Yes?"

"I am happy to see you and I still care about you," he said.

He was kidding, but still she took it to heart. "And I had lost all hope," she said.

He put his hands over hers and held them against his chest. "Don't ever lose hope," he said.

She reached for him slowly, rising to her knees and finding his mouth with hers. She kissed him gently. He groaned a very quiet groan. He put his arms around her and kissed her deeply. He fell backward and pulled her onto the grass on top of him.

She laughed and then they kissed some more. They rolled in the grass and kissed and kissed and kissed until a boy on a bike threw the newspaper up the walk and scared them apart.

The sun was lighting the sky from the bottom as Kostos pulled her to standing from the grass. "I'll walk you home," he said.

He was barefoot and had bits of grass stuck all over his shirt. His hair was sticking up on one side. She could only imagine how she must look. She giggled most of the way. He held her hand.

Just before they reached her house, he stopped and kissed her more. He let her go. She didn't want to go.

"Beautiful Lena," he said, touching her collarbone. "I'll come for you tomorrow."

"I love you," she told him bravely.

"I love you," he said. "I never stopped."

He pushed her a little toward her door.

She didn't want to go. She didn't want to be anyplace without him. It was hard to make herself walk away.

She turned around for a last look.

"I never will," he promised her.

Bridget stood back and looked at the attic with a sense of accomplishment. She'd applied two coats of cream-colored paint. She'd painted the ceiling matte white and the trim semigloss. She'd painted the wide-planked floor a beautiful green, the color she remembered the Gulf of California being on sunny days last summer.

As an extra surprise for Greta, she'd set up a pretty white iron bed frame that had been in storage. She'd found a reasonable mattress. She'd sanded an antique bureau and painted it with the same cream-colored paint she'd used for the trim. On a trip to Wal-Mart she'd bought cheap—but still nice—white cotton eyelet bedding and simple white lace curtains.

The final touch was a big armful of purple hydrangeas she'd gathered in the backyard while Greta was out. She found a glass pitcher and set them on the bureau on a piece of blue fabric.

Other than the one box left in the corner of the room, it was perfect.

She thundered downstairs. "Greta! Hey!"

Greta was vacuuming. She hit the Power button with her foot. "What is it, hon?"

"You ready?" Bridget asked, making no effort to hide her excitement.

"For what?" said Greta, playing coy.

"You want to see your attic?"

"Are you finished already?" Greta asked that like wasn't Bridget the cleverest girl in the whole world.

"I'll follow," Bridget ordered.

Grandma took the two flights slowly. Bridget noticed the cottage-cheesy texture under her skin and the stringy purple veins that spread over her calves.

"Ta-da," Bridget crowed, leaning past Greta to open the door at the top of the stairs with a flourish.

Grandma gasped. As if she were in a movie, she threw her hand over her wide-open mouth. She studied the room for a long time, every single part. "Oh, honey," she said. When she turned around, Bridget could see there were tears in her eyes. "It is *so* beautiful."

Bridget couldn't ever remember feeling as proud. "It looks good, doesn't it?"

"You made a little home up here, didn't you?"

Bridget nodded. Without thinking about it quite like that, she really had.

Greta smiled. "I didn't peg you for the domestic type, I'll admit."

"Me either!" Bridget answered, her eyebrows high on her forehead. "You should see my room at home." She got quiet. She hadn't meant to bring up anything about home.

Grandma let it go. "You worked your tail off on this job, honey, and I am so grateful to you."

Bridget shuffled modestly. "No problem."

"And I already have somebody in mind to move in."

Bridget's face fell, and she didn't try to hide it. She hadn't actually imagined somebody moving in here and throwing her out. Was Greta all done with her? Was there no more work for her here? Was this really it?

"You do?" she said, trying not to cry.

"Yes. You."

"Me?"

Grandma laughed. "Of course. You'd rather be here than in that falling-down boardinghouse on Royal Street, wouldn't you?"

"Yes," Bridget said, her heart lifting high.

"So it's done. Go get your bags."

❊ ❊ ❊

Carmen discovered a strange scene when she walked into her kitchen the next morning. Her mother and her father's stepdaughter were sitting across from each other at the small round table, chewing companionably on poached eggs.

"Morning," Carmen said groggily. She'd been half hoping she'd dreamed the whole Krista episode.

"Would you like a poached egg?" Christina asked.

Carmen shook her head. "I hate poached eggs."

Krista ceased chewing the very bite in her mouth. She had a look of yearning on her face, as if she wished it were she who had thought to hate poached eggs.

Carmen backed up in a hurry. "I don't hate them, actually. I like them, actually. Brain food. I'm just not in the mood for them." It was a tricky business, being somebody's role model. It was a lot of pressure, especially in the morning.

"Are you baby-sitting today?" Christina asked her.

Carmen got out the sweet Cheerios and a bowl. "Nuh-uh. The Morgans left for Rehoboth yesterday afternoon. I don't work again till Tuesday."

Her mother nodded vaguely. Christina hadn't appeared to listen to her own question, let alone Carmen's answer.

Christina got up to pour more coffee, and Carmen took sudden note of the skirt she was wearing. It had gray and white pleats, and her mother had owned it since before Carmen was in nursery school. There were first-string outfits and there were second-string outfits, but this skirt belonged on the bench. Forever.

"Are you wearing that to work?" Carmen asked,

forgetting to hide her disbelief. How long had it been since either of them had done laundry?

Her mother was easily hurt these days, so Carmen shouldn't have been surprised to see her disappear into her room.

A few minutes later, Carmen looked up from her cereal to see Krista gazing motionlessly at her half-eaten poached egg, and Christina wearing yesterday's pants.

It was pathetic. It was horrible. Carmen hated herself and hated them for listening to her.

"Hey, I have an idea," she said in an overloud voice to the two of them. "From now on, nobody listen to anything I say."

Lena lay in her bed until the middle of the next day, just her and her bursting heart, thinking about everything that had happened. She wanted to keep herself to herself, as she was often inclined to do. But she also wanted to share the news, so she was glad when the phone rang and it was Bee.

"Guess what?" Lena blurted out immediately.

"What?"

"I did know."

"You did know what?"

"I did know what I needed to do."

"About Kostos?"

"Yes. And you know what else?"

"What?"

"I did what I needed to do."

Bridget screamed. "You did?"

"I did."

"Tell me."

Lena told her everything. It was hard to give such a private, visceral experience to the spoken word, but she also had the reassuring sense that she was locking it down.

Bee screamed again when she was done.

"Lenny, I am so proud of you!"

Lena smiled. "I'm proud of me too."

Tibberon: C, have you talked to Lena yet? She sounded so giggly I thought I was talking to Effie. I'm happy for her. Kind of scary, though, too. I want her to still be Lenny. One Effie is enough over there.

Carmabelle: I talked to her. It's amazing. The Love Pants are at it again. Except for me. Is there something wrong with me, Tib? I mean, besides all the regular things?

What is that you express

in your eyes?

It seems to me more than

all the words I have read

in my life.

—Walt Whitman

Sometimes you just had to face it. You had to march right into the ugly middle, Tibby told herself. Otherwise you ended up flat against the wall, creeping fearfully around the edge your whole life.

That was what she told herself, and she was sticking with it. She put the disk into her computer.

She studied the files. She couldn't remember what was what. She was a good labeler, but Bailey was not, and Bailey had been her PA and supposed organizational whiz. Then again, Bailey had been twelve. Tibby picked one and double-clicked. She had to start someplace.

An image materialized on her screen. It was her setup shot from the day at the 7-Eleven. It was from their first day of filming last summer—Tibby remembered it so distinctly. It was the day she'd met Brian.

The picture moved from the counter display of Slim Jims to the man working the register. Just as she remembered, he slapped his hands over his face, shouting, "No camera! No camera!" Tibby felt the smile on her face.

Then the shot changed and Tibby gasped. There it was. Tibby felt as though every nerve in her body were on alert. It was Bailey's face, close up. She felt the surge of emotion smack her like a sandbag across the head. Fat tears floated in front of her eyes. Without thinking, Tibby's finger hit the Pause key. The resolution diminished, but the image was even more striking. Tibby leaned in so close the tip of her nose touched the screen. She drew back. She was almost scared the face would disappear, but it didn't.

Bailey looked over her shoulder at Tibby. She was laughing. She was right there. Right there.

Tibby hadn't seen her since the last night of her life.

She had imagined Bailey's face at least a million times between then and now, but the further she got from the real Bailey, the less distinct it became. She was glad for the real face again, for Bailey's eyes.

Beethoven was rollicking along. Bailey was laughing.

Tibby let the feelings wash over her. She could sit here and cry for as long as she liked. She could crawl under the desk. She could run around in the parking lot. She could live big. She could make herself to do things that were hard. She could.

For once, Tibby was right smack in the middle, and she could see a lot better from here.

Her mother was at work and Krista was asleep and the Morgans were at the beach and Bee was in Alabama and Lena was at the store and Tibby was in Virginia and Carmen was sitting in her closet.

Her closet was so full of crap it was a walk-in in name only. Carmen loved shopping, but she hated throwing anything away. She loved beginnings, but she hated endings. She loved order, but she hated cleaning.

Most of all, she loved dolls. She had a collection that could only belong to a solitary female child of guilt-ridden parents.

She loved dolls, but she wasn't good at taking care of them, she decided as she pulled out the three cardboard boxes of them that lived under her hanging clothes. Throughout her childhood they had been dear to her. She had played with them long after normal girls had stopped. But her efforts at washing and grooming and dressing and improving them, her many eager makeovers, had left them looking like veterans of a long and grueling war.

Angelica, with the brown hair and the mole, had a crew cut from the time Carmen had tried to crimp her plastic hair with a curling iron. Rosemarie, the redhead, had two black eyes from the time Carmen had applied eye makeup with a Sharpie. Rogette, her favorite doll of color, wore a hideous half-stitched rag from the time Carmen had taken up sewing in imitation of her aunt Rosa. Yes, Carmen had loved them, but they couldn't have looked worse if she had set out to mangle them.

"Carmen?"

Carmen jumped. She dropped Rogette. She squinted in the darkness of her room.

"Sorry to surprise you."

She picked up Rogette and stood. "Oh, my God. Paul. Hi."

"Hi." He had one of those large, outdoorsy backpacks over his shoulders.

"How did you get in?" she asked.

"Krista."

Carmen winced. She chewed on her thumb. "She's awake? Is she all right? Is she mad at me?"

"She's eating Frosted Flakes."

That seemed to answer all three questions. Carmen was still holding Rogette. She held her up. "Meet Rogette," she said.

"Okay."

"I was cleaning out my closet."

He nodded.

"I'm pretty much a social whirlwind. You know, things to do, people to see."

It took him a long time to register that she was kidding.

"Did you tell your mom?" Carmen asked.

"She knew," Paul said.

"Everything's all right? You think Krista is okay?"

He nodded. He didn't look worried.

"So . . . how's school?" she asked.

"Good."

She'd imagined college would make Paul more relaxed and less polite, but from the way he stood in the door of her room, she doubted it had. She pictured him as the sole sober pledge of Delta Kappa Epsilon.

"Summer school fun? Soccer? Good?"

He nodded. Paul was to chitchat what Carmen was to self-restraint. Silence descended.

"You?" he asked.

Carmen sighed and took in a lot of air to start her answer. "Oh, it's kind of a mess." She waved her hands around. "I ruined my mother's life."

Paul looked at Carmen the way he often looked at Carmen. As if she were the star of a Discovery Channel special.

Krista appeared at the door behind Paul. She was holding Carmen's copy of *CosmoGIRL!* She flapped it a few times. She didn't seem in the least annoyed that Paul was there. "I'm going out to get us milk shakes."

"Okay." Carmen waved. "You need money?"

"No. I got."

Paul looked amused. Krista was teaching herself to talk like Carmen too.

Carmen pointed to her bed. "Sit." She pulled herself up onto her desk, sitting and swinging her feet in the air.

Paul did as he was told. Awkwardly he moved a pile of clothes out of the way. He didn't take to sitting on a girl's bed as easily as some guys did. He sat there, feet on the ground, shoulders square. She felt proud of how handsome he was, tall and strong, with his sweetly long, dark eyelashes fringing his navy-blue eyes. He never acted like he was handsome.

She wasn't going to wait for Paul to restart the conversation. She'd be waiting till next week. "Paul, remember the guy David I e-mailed you about? The guy who liked my mom?"

He nodded.

"Well, he really liked her. Like, loved her. And she was falling for him, too." She looked up at him. "Unbelievable, right?"

Paul shrugged.

"Okay, well." Carmen pulled her heels up onto the desk with her and hugged her knees. "This is the part of the story where Carmen is bad."

Paul looked patient. He knew of several such stories.

"I just got crazy. I can't explain. My mom was out all the time. She was dressing like a fourteen-year-old. She even borrowed the . . . Never mind. Anyway, I felt like she had all this happiness . . . and I had nothing."

Paul nodded more.

"And I just . . . I yelled at her. I told her I hated her. I said all these mean things. I ruined it for her. She broke it off."

Paul's face was earnest. His eyes were squinched up in concentration, like he was trying his hardest to understand the inscrutable Carmen.

How good it was having a guy like Paul. He had witnessed her at her absolute worst last summer, and still he hung in with her. Granted, he didn't say much, but over the past year he had become her true, devoted friend. He never ignored an e-mail, never forgot to call her back. He had real things to worry about. His father was such a severe alcoholic he had been in and out of rehab since Paul was eight years old. Before Carmen's father had married Paul's mother last summer, Paul had taken care of his mother and sister as though he were the head of the household. And yet, no matter what nonsense Carmen rattled on about, he always listened like it mattered. He never groaned or looked horrified or told her to shut up.

"You were jealous," he said finally.

"I was. I was jealous. And selfish and small."

Big tears were suddenly shivering in Carmen's eyes. They warped the face of poor Rogette, discarded on the floor. Carmen was bad at loving. She loved too hard.

"I didn't want her to be happy without me." Carmen's voice came out wobbly.

Making very little noise, Paul appeared beside her, sitting next to her on the desk. "She would never be happy without you."

Carmen had meant to say that she didn't want her mom to be happy without Carmen getting to be happy too. But as Paul's words bumped around in her brain, she wondered if maybe he'd understood something she hadn't.

Had she been jealous of her mother? Or had she been jealous of David?

Paul linked his arm with hers. Carmen cried. It wasn't much, maybe, but it felt like everything.

Kostos did come for her, but not when she expected. Lena wished for and wanted him through breakfast, lunch, and dinner, but he didn't come until she was already in bed. She heard the acorn against her window.

Her heart rising up nearly out of her chest, she went to the window and saw him there. She waved and rushed down the stairs and out the back door as fast as she could. She practically threw herself at him. He pretended to fall backward. He staggered a few giant steps and pulled her down with him.

"Shhhh," he told her as she was laughing.

They found the most private place they could find in her yard. It was at the side of the house under the thick-leaved magnolia tree. If her parents found out, not even the dazzling Kostos could save her.

She was in her nightgown. He was more properly dressed.

"I've dreamed about you all day," she told him.

"I've dreamed about you for a year," he told her.

They started out slow, kissing. That was all they needed for a long, long time, until she put her hands inside his shirt. He let her explore his chest and his arms and his back, but at last he pulled away. "I have to go," he said miserably.

"Why?"

He kissed her. "Because I'm a gentleman. I can't trust myself to be one too much longer."

"Maybe I don't want you to trust yourself," she said boldly, letting her hormones do the talking.

"Oh, Lena." He sounded as though he were partly under-water. He wasn't looking at her as though he wanted to go anywhere.

He kissed her more and then broke away. "There are a few things I want to do with you *very badly*."

She nodded.

"You haven't done . . . these things before, have you?" he asked.

She shook her head. Suddenly she was worried he thought she was inept.

"All the more reason," he said. "We have to be slow. Make it count."

She was touched by his honor. She knew he was right. "I want to do those things too. Sometime."

He held her and squeezed her so hard she had to stifle a shout. "We have time. We'll do all of those things millions of times, and I will be the happiest person in the world."

They kissed and kissed more until finally she had to let him go. She wanted to gobble up her whole future in this one night.

"I have to leave tomorrow morning," he told her.

Her eyes instantly filled with tears.

"I'll come back, though. Don't worry. How could I stay away? I'll come back next weekend. Would that be all right?"

"I don't know if I can wait," she said, her throat aching.

He smiled and held her for one last minute. "Any place at any time. If you are thinking of me, you can be sure that I am thinking of you."

Billy practically accosted Bridget on her way to the hardware store, where she was going to buy parts to fix Greta's refrigerator door. She was now paying her seventy-five dollars a week to Greta and was busy vanquishing every disobedient thing on the property—the weeds in the lawn, the wobbly coffee table, the peeling paint at the back of the house. Bridget was in her running clothes, her hair was stuffed into a scarf, and her mood was giddy because she'd been thinking about Lena.

"You didn't come to practice on Thursday," he said.

Bridget just stared at him. "And?"

"Usually you come."

"I do have one or two other things to think about," she said.

Billy looked offended. "Like what?"

She prepared to look offended right back, but then he laughed. His laugh was just as choky and full as it had been when he was seven. She loved the sound of it. She laughed too.

"Hey, can I buy you a milk shake or something?" he asked her.

He wasn't flirting, but he was genuinely friendly. "Okay."

They crossed the street and sat down at an outside table in the shade. He ordered a mint-chip shake and she got a lemonade.

"You know what?"

"What?" she asked.

"You look familiar."

"Oh, yeah?"

"Yeah. Where are you from?"

"Washington, D.C.," she answered.

"Why'd you come all the way down here?"

"I used to come here when I was a little kid," she explained, wanting him to ask more.

But he didn't ask more. He didn't even listen to the last part of what she said, because at that moment, two girls stopped by on their way down the sidewalk. One was a busty brunette and the other a small blonde wearing very small, very low pants. Bridget recognized the girls from the soccer field. They smiled and flirted with Billy while Bridget retied her shoes.

"Sorry about that," Billy said when they were gone. "I had a crush on that girl for a year."

Bridget felt sad. She remembered when she herself had been the girl boys had crushes on, not the one they talked to about them. "Which one?" she asked.

"Lisa, the blonde," he said. "I'm a sucker for blondes," he added.

Instinctively she touched her skunky hair packed in its bandana. The drinks came.

"So how do you know so much about soccer?" he asked.

"I used to play," she said. She held the straw between her teeth.

"Were you any good?" he asked.

"I was all right," she said around the straw.

He nodded. "You'll be at the game Saturday, right?"

She shrugged, just to punish him.

"You gotta be there!" He looked worried. "The whole team will freak if you're not there!"

She smiled, enjoying herself. He didn't have a crush on her, but this wasn't so bad. "Oh, all right."

"Krista's taking her mom to brunch at Roxie's," Carmen explained to her mother over toaster waffles. Both Al and Lydia had arrived the evening before to make peace with Krista and take her home.

Christina smiled. It was a ghost of a smile, really, but

downright mirthful compared to her expression of the last few weeks. Roxie's, notable for its clientele of drag queens, stood at the edge of Adams Morgan. Krista had heard about it from Tibby with wide, fascinated eyes. Carmen was actually pretty pleased with her protégée. Krista was going down, but not without a fight.

"Al too?"

"No, it's a mother-daughter day. Krista's going home with them tomorrow."

Her mother nodded thoughtfully. "I like Krista."

"She's sweet. She's all right." Carmen tore off half a waffle and stuffed it in her mouth. "Are you coming tonight?" she asked after she'd chewed and swallowed.

Her mother's face settled back into its look of distant forbearance. "I guess I am."

As every couple had an identity in marriage, they also had one in divorce. Carmen's parents practiced "amicable divorce." This meant that when Al and Lydia arranged to have dinner at a restaurant with Carmen, Al was bound to invite Christina to come along to meet his newer-model wife, and Christina was bound to accept.

"You okay about meeting Lydia?"

Christina considered this, sucking on her empty fork. "Yes."

"Yes?" Her mother was stoic. Her mother was brave. Carmen was maybe adopted.

Christina looked like she was about to say more, but she stopped herself. "Yes."

These weeks, they stayed on the surface together.

Carmen wanted a million things from her mother, but she was afraid to press. She deserved nothing.

She had certainly eaten and slept, although she couldn't remember exactly what or when.

Tibby had lost track of time and space and even going to the bathroom. There was a lot of video to go through, especially after she had called Mrs. Graffman and asked for a few tapes from their collection. She needed to be absolutely scrupulous about saving all her original material, and every stage of her edit took deep concentration.

In the course of her work, she'd discovered pretty quickly that the stuff she'd shot for her actual documentary last summer was worthless. The beautiful things were hanging around the edges. They were the outtakes and the overhangs—Bailey setting up shots or breaking them down, Bailey's careful tinkering with the boom.

Tibby also loved the parts when Bailey's eye was behind the camera. Bailey had a remarkably patient style. Unlike Tibby, she wasn't in a hurry to muscle everything into the shape of a story. She didn't goad her subjects into saying what she wanted them to say.

The one part that Tibby had purposely filmed that was any good was her interview with Bailey. Bailey sat in the chair by the window, as luminous as an angel, the Traveling Pants bagging at her feet. There was even a shot of lumpy, sleeping Mimi in the mix. Tibby was mesmerized by Bailey's brave, straight-on face, her peeking-out soul, no matter how many times she watched.

Today she was working on the soundtrack. It was easy, really, because she was just going to play Beethoven straight through. But as she listened, the music wasn't having exactly the effect she wanted.

She put her head back. She was dizzy. She'd been up for a lot of hours. The end-of-summer festival was less than four days away.

The quality she loved about the music involved Brian whistling to it. Somehow, in her sleep-deprived mania, this struck her as art. It wasn't Kafka and explosions at Pizza Hut. It was the rise and fall of Brian's whistle.

He made the world to be a

grassy road

Before her wandering feet.

—W. B. Yeats

It had been a summer of awkward meals. Carmen sat between Lydia and Krista. Christina sat between Al and Paul.

Carmen so dreaded the long, miserable silences they were sure to endure, she'd actually prepared a few topics for discussion:

Summer movies
Sequels—a good idea or inherently problematic?
Popcorn—what exactly is that buttery mess? (Make room for Christina to cite stunning calorie facts)

Sunscreen (Throw a bone to the mothers.)
SPF—what's it all really mean?
Worst sunburn ever? (Appear to leave up for grabs. Let Al win with oft-told story of sailing in the Bahamas.)

Ozone. (Allow all to be in agreement over liking it. Not liking holes in it.)

Air travel—has it gotten worse? (Allow adults to go on and on as needed.)

(If situation grows desperate.) Israel/Palestine.

But strangely, the paper stayed in her pocket. She listened quietly as the conversation made its own brave start: Lydia described Roxie's and surprised Carmen by being able to laugh about it. Lydia laughing made Christina laugh too. It was a small and rosy miracle.

Then Krista told about getting lost for three hours and twenty-two minutes on the D.C. subway. That immediately launched Al into a long, educational summary of the various colors and lines and junctions of the Washington, D.C., mass transit system. He even whipped out his map for illustration.

Then somehow or other, that led to the story of how Al and Christina got lost the night they brought brand-new baby Carmen home from the hospital. Carmen knew the story well, and she usually hated hearing it because the punch lines were always Carmen crying or Carmen spitting up. But tonight she listened raptly as her parents traded back and forth narrating the different parts of the story, being funny and amicable. Lydia laughed and winced appreciatively. Al held Lydia's hand on top of the table, to let her know it was okay, he loved her better now.

Al ordered the wine in a funny Italian accent. Krista fiddled with her beads and whispered something nice to her mother. Lydia insisted Christina try a bite of her "divine" corn-and-lobster salad.

Carmen felt flushed and warm with pleasure as she looked around at the animated faces. This was her family, weird as it was. She'd gone from a dysfunctional three to a completely haywire six.

Paul looked at her. *It's all good*, he seemed to say.

She smiled. And the real bonanza was, she'd gotten Paul in the deal. Paul, who was the kindest, most patient person she knew.

She thought back to last summer, the day she'd met Lydia and Krista and Paul for the first time. She'd been furious at her father. She'd thought it was an ending, but it had turned out to be a beginning.

She looked at her mother, bearing up gracefully. Al and Lydia were a couple; Christina was alone. Christina always bore up gracefully. As a single mother with a full-time job. As a person with a broken heart.

Her mother deserved a beginning too.

At 9:15 the phone rang, and Lena pounced on it. The phone was her worst enemy and her best friend, but she never knew which until she answered it.

"Hello?" she said, barely disguising her eagerness.

"Hi."

It was her best friend.

"Kostos." How she loved his name. She loved just saying it. "Where are you?"

"At the subway station."

Her stomach commenced the spin cycle. She forced herself to pause, slow it down. "In . . . which . . . city?"

"In your city."

"No." *Please, please.* "Really?" Her voice sounded squeaky.

"Yes. Can you come and get me?"

"Yes. Yes. Right away. Just let me, um . . . lie to my parents."

He laughed. "Wisconsin Avenue side."

"Bye."

It was almost too good that she still had the Traveling Pants. She pulled them on and lied hastily to her mother about going for ice cream with Carmen. She flew out the door and into her car, blessing her parents for letting her use it whenever she liked.

He was there waiting for her, a silhouette standing solidly on both feet. He wasn't a dream or a hoax. She buzzed down the passenger-side window so he could see that it was her. He was hardly in the car when he kissed her big and full on her mouth and cradled the back of her head in his hands. "I couldn't stay away," he told her breathlessly. "I took the train right after work."

He kissed her more and some more until finally she remembered she was at the wheel of a car on a major thoroughfare. She looked up, delirious, trying to bring the streaming streetlights into focus. "Where should we go?"

His face was vivid, locked onto hers. He didn't care.

"Do you think we should do something besides kiss?" she asked. "I mean, should we keep some semblance of a date? Are you hungry or anything?" Her body was most eager for the making out.

He laughed. "I am hungry. I do want to take you out. But, no, I don't really want to do anything where I can't touch you for more than a few minutes."

Love inspired her. "I think I have an idea."

She drove to the A&P. She supervised the buying of raw cookie dough and a quart of cold two-percent milk from the refrigerated aisle, a box of strawberry Pop-Tarts with pink icing from the cereal aisle. They found a lot of ways to touch each other—his hands on her waist, her hip pressed to the side of his, his lips, briefly, on her neck—even there under the squinting grocery store lights.

She tried to drive as carefully as possible, speeding along the forests of Rock Creek Parkway, even though he kissed her elbow and touched her hair. She drove along the Potomac River, and the glowing marble faces of the monuments rose up around them like an ancient city. The road was nearly empty but for them. The glittering water and the pale arched bridges were so beautiful they were struck silent.

For once it was a simple matter to park. They carried their bounty in a brown paper bag to the wide white stone steps and gazed up reverently at Mr. Lincoln, floodlit and enthroned in his marble temple.

"This is the most beautiful time to see the monuments,

but nobody ever comes," Lena explained, gesturing at the emptiness around them.

Some people might have thought that the solemn gaze of a great president might cool a person's passion, but Lena disagreed. They ate and they kissed, deeper and more involved each time. She pinched off pieces of cookie dough and he gazed at her in her green tank top. He considered her shoulders, her neck, her mouth as though in a rapture. Her beauty through his eyes made her take a kind of pleasure in it she'd never felt before.

Was she making him as happy as he was making her? Was that even possible? But then again, could she feel this good, this close, if he weren't feeling at least some of it too?

It seemed a fitting transition to go from the Great Emancipator to the very stars themselves, but you couldn't see them when you were too near the lights. So they wandered off the landscaped paths to a dark, private clearing, where they lay on their backs, overlapping one ankle each. It was exceedingly thoughtful of the rest of the world to leave them completely alone.

The warm air was sweet tonight. The thick summer leaves were sweet. Tonight, even the garbage overflowing the rim of the can was sweet.

Some nights the stars winked and teased coldly from a great distance. Other nights they seemed to smolder and urge one on in a personal way. Tonight was the second kind of night. Lena felt grateful that it was summer, and that when they were together they had no ceiling pressing these feelings down.

First just their ankles touched. Then forearms and hands. Then, boldly, Lena found herself, her whole body on top of his, curving into all his parts and places. "Is this too fast?" she asked him.

"No." He said it forcefully, as though afraid she might stop. "No and yes. Too fast and too slow." His chest moved as he laughed. "But please don't stop."

She let her hands float over his stomach. "Do you think you could take a short break from being a gentleman and start again tomorrow?"

Gently he rolled her over so that he was on top of her, but was suspending most of his weight on his hands. He buried his head in her neck. "Maybe. A little." It was muffled in her earlobe. An exalted little shiver shot down her backbone.

Relishing her present and her very near future, she watched him bend over her stomach and kiss her private skin. Slowly lifting up her shirt to reveal tiny bits of her at a time, he lavished kisses over her belly button and upward to her ribs. In pure, delicate disbelief at this outer, unimagined possibility of pleasure, she felt him open her bra and sweep the light cotton of her shirt over her head. He looked at her with all the veneration he'd had when he'd seen so much of her in the olive grove last summer. But then she'd belonged only to herself, and she'd wildly covered her body with her hands. Tonight she belonged to him, and she wanted nothing more than for him to see her.

Without waiting she pulled his shirt off too. She pressed her naked self against his naked self.

Memory is funny, and it does tell lies. But tonight, the look of bare Kostos in the moonlight was no less beautiful than the bare Kostos she had seen in the pond in Santorini and had imagined all those times since. Her spirit flooded her body from end to end and tip to tip, and she thought of a line from a song she loved.

All your life, you were only waiting for this moment to be free.

Carmen liked the idea of baking cookies with Jesse and Joe. As she'd cheerfully grabbed the butterscotch chips and rainbow sprinkles from the grocery store shelves on her way to work, it had seemed to her the kind of project a really fine baby-sitter would do.

But now, when faced with the actual spectacle, it seemed less fun.

"Jesse, honey, lightly. Just a little tap," she begged him.

Jesse nodded and smashed the egg against the side of the metal bowl. Hundreds of tiny shell bits slid down into the batter. He looked up at her for approval.

"Well, maybe a little gentler would be good. Maybe I'll do the next—"

It was too late. Jesse was already battering egg number two against the rim.

"Ahhhhhhh!" Joe was reaching toward the sprinkles and howling.

"Joe, I know you want another sprinkle. But I don't think Mommy—"

Babies were flailing and incompetent most of the time, but then once in a while, they blew your mind with pure precision. Carmen watched in disbelief as Joe leaned forward, shot out his hand, connected with the small tub of sprinkles two feet away, closed in on a handful, and knocked the tub so dramatically off the counter that sprinkles rained down.

"Oh, my God," Carmen muttered.

"Stir, right?" Jesse asked excitedly, satisfied that the eggs had been crushed to oblivion.

"Well, maybe we should try to—"

She put Joe down on the floor so she could fish some of the shells out of the dough. But Joe tried to pull himself up to standing with the help of a kitchen chair, and the sprinkles rotated under his feet like a hundred ball bearings. His fall was fast and loud.

"Oh, Joe," Carmen groaned. She swept him up and hopped around the room to avoid the sprinkles. "Want to play with my cell phone?" she offered. She didn't care if he called Singapore.

"Here." She stuffed him into his high chair, grabbed the broom from its hook, and began sweeping up the sprinkles.

"Stir, right?" Jesse called again from his perch on the counter.

"Um . . . yes," Carmen said wearily. They wore you down so fast. She'd only been here for fifteen minutes.

She heard Mrs. Morgan coming down the stairs. Carmen leaped toward Joe, attempting to wipe all evidence of sprinkles from his mouth and hands.

Mrs. Morgan appeared at the door to the kitchen in a

suit. Carmen was amazed at how elegant she looked. "Wow," she said. "You look fantastic."

"Thanks," Mrs. Morgan said. "I have a meeting at the bank."

"Mama! Mama!" Joe screamed. He threw Carmen's cell phone across the room and put his arms out toward his mother.

Don't do it, Carmen warned in her head. But inevitably, the forces of the universe sucked Mrs. Morgan toward her baby. She picked him up.

"Mommy! Look at this!" Jesse shouted.

"Are you making *cookies*?" Mrs. Morgan asked, with as much enthusiasm as if he had won the Nobel Peace Prize.

"Yes!" Jesse shouted delightedly. "Taste it! Taste it!"

Mrs. Morgan peered into the bowl.

"Please, Mommy? I made it."

As Mrs. Morgan hesitated, Carmen watched Joe bury his head in his mother's armpit. Carmen had seen this coming. A thin trail of snot stretched right across the lapel of Mrs. Morgan's black suit, exactly as though a slug had slid across the fabric. Mrs. Morgan didn't notice, and Carmen didn't have the heart to tell her.

Carmen's memory suddenly supplied images of her own mother's work clothes—the gabardine skirt on which Carmen had gotten a bloody nose, the tweed blazer on which she had spilled blue nail polish.

"Mommy, it's yummy!" Jesse urged the spoon toward his mother's mouth.

Mrs. Morgan kept her eager smile intact as she examined the bits of shell slithering through the yolk. "It will be even more delicious after it's cooked," she remarked.

"Please?" Jesse wheedled. "I made it!"

Mrs. Morgan leaned forward and took the tiniest taste. She nodded encouragingly. "Oh, Jesse, it's wonderful. I can't wait to taste the cookies!"

Carmen watched Mrs. Morgan in disbelief. Would she, Carmen, have been willing to taste that mess? Would *her* mother? As quickly as the question had flashed into Carmen's mind, the answer followed it. Yes, Christina would have tried the dough. She would, and she had.

In that moment, Carmen understood how it was for mothers. Mrs. Morgan didn't taste it because she wanted to. She did it because she loved him. And for some reason, Carmen found this thought mysteriously comforting.

Lennyk162: Carmen! Where are you! What's up with your cell phone? I've been trying to call you all day! I want to talk to you SO MUCH.
Carmabelle: Cell out of order. Be right over.

Tibby called Brian at home. She almost never did that. The answering machine picked up. It was one of those unpersonalized computer-generated messages that came with the machine. It reminded her of buying a picture frame and leaving in the picture that came from the store instead of supplying your own.

She cleared her throat. "Uh, I hope this is the right

273

number. . . . Brian, it's Tibby. Will you call me at Williamston? I really want to talk to you."

She hung up. She tapped her thumb against the edge of her desk. Why should he call her after the way she'd treated him? If she were him, she wouldn't call herself. Or if she did, it would only be to tell herself that she was an asshole.

She dialed the number again. The message played again. "Brian? It's Tibby again. Uh . . . one thing . . . well, really the main thing I wanted to say is that I'm really sorry. More than sorry. I am ashamed. I . . . ." Tibby looked out the window and suddenly realized that she was laying her guts out to an answering machine that didn't even have a personalized message. She was crazy. She hadn't been sleeping enough. What if she was dialing the wrong number? What if Brian's mom and his stepdad picked up the messages? She slammed the phone down.

But wait a minute. What was she thinking? Was she too cowardly to see her apology through, after the way she'd treated Brian? She was just going to hang up in the middle of it? Did she really care more about what his mom and stepdad thought than about being a decent friend?

Tibby looked down at her feet. She was wearing elephant slippers. She was also wearing plaid pajama bottoms and a bathing suit because all her clothes were dirty. She was also wearing a towel tied around her middle because they'd turned up the air-conditioning too strong in the dorm. She hadn't showered or gone outside in several days. What dignity, exactly, was she trying to preserve here?

Tibby dialed the number again. "Brian? It's, uh, Tibby again. What I wanted to say is that I am sorry. I'm so sorry I can't find any words that could cover it. I want to get the chance to apologize to you in person. And also I wanted to tell you that I am, um, screening a movie—a new one, not the old one—on Saturday at three at the auditorium here. I know you won't want to come." She stopped to catch her breath. She was running her mouth like a lunatic. "I probably wouldn't if I were you. But just in case you do, it would mean a lot to me." She hung up. Was this too weird? Was she going to earn herself a restraining order from the whole family?

She dialed the number again. "And sorry to call so many times," she said in a rush, and quickly put down the phone.

There is no remedy for

love but to love more.

—Henry David Thoreau

F riday night Bridget ran almost seven miles, all the way to the bend in the river where Billy's old house sat. Maybe he still lived there.

Her body was changing, she could feel it. She wasn't totally back to normal, but she was most of the way there. Her legs and her stomach were getting muscular and strong again. Her hair was blond again. Running by herself, she took off her baseball cap, which felt like a relief. She let her hair breathe in the warm evening air.

She stopped by Greta's to pick up her ball and went straight to the soccer field. It had become a ritual for her, kicking around by herself at night in the three patches of light.

"Gilda!"

She turned around and saw Billy coming toward her. He was probably on his way to a party where all the girls enjoyed crushes from all the boys.

"Hi," she said, out of breath, glad she'd remembered to put her baseball cap back on her head.

"I thought you didn't play anymore."

"I started again."

"Oh." He looked at her. He looked at the ball. He loved soccer as much as she did. "You want to play?"

She smiled. "Sure."

There was nothing like a handsome opponent to get Bridget's adrenaline pumping. She found her pace, keeping the ball in front of her. She zagged left, one-touched it, then shot. She heard Billy's moan of disbelief behind her. "Lucky shot," he said, and they started again.

It was as though she were back on the Honey Bees again. Bridget had always had an exploding capacity to be as good as she wanted to be, and tonight it enabled her to get around Billy five times in a row.

Panting, he sat down in the middle of the field. He put his hands over his face. "What the hell!" he bellowed into the night air.

Bridget tried not to look smug. She sat down next to him. "You're wearing jeans. Don't take it too hard."

He lowered his hands and stared at her. He had the spooked look back from a few weeks ago. He squinted at her. "Who are you?"

She shrugged. "What do you mean?"

"Are you, like, Mia Hamm in disguise or something?"

She smiled and shook her head.

"I'm the best guy on our team!" he shouted at her in frustration.

She shrugged again. What could she say? She had a long career of pruning boys' egos on the soccer field.

"You remind me of this girl I used to know," he mused, more to the grass than to her.

"Yeah?"

"Her name was Bee, and she was my best friend till I was seven. She used to kick my ass also. So I should be okay with this."

His eyes were animated and sweet. She liked that he was a good sport under his pride. She wanted to tell him who she was. She was sick of the whole game. She was sick of stuffing her hair into a baseball cap.

She noticed he was looking at her legs. She might not be a beauty, but she knew her legs were getting nice again. They were toned and tan from running for five weeks straight, not to mention her nightly soccer workout. He didn't look spooked and he didn't look grateful. In fact, he looked a bit awkward. He cleared his throat. "I, uh, better get going. You'll be there tomorrow at five, right? It's the second-to-last game before the tournament, you know."

She was going to slap his shoulder, but the gesture didn't come off pal-ish as she'd meant. She sort of brushed it instead. Her fingers tingled where she'd touched him. He looked at his shoulder and back at her. Now he looked confused.

"I'll be there," she promised.

When she let herself quietly in the door, she saw the flickering blue light of the television in the living room. She tiptoed in to say good night to Greta, but she was already asleep in the armchair, her head lolling. In front of her was perched a tray on a stand with the remnants of her dinner. Friday was her TV night. It made Bridget sad to look at her. Her life was so small, and so simple, and so completely unremarkable. Could Bridget ever fit into a life that small?

And then she couldn't help thinking of Marly. Marly's life had never been small or simple. With Marly, you woke up to a different world every day. Every hour had been remarkable, good or bad. Did living big mean ending up like her?

Standing there in the living room, where Marly had preened with a thousand dates and Greta snoozed in front of the television, Bridget wondered whether it came down to the claustrophobic choice between dying beautiful or living ugly.

Tibberon: Lenny, I'm happy for you and Kostos. But please don't tell me you did it. Can't handle that right now.

Lennyk162: Didn't, Tib. Don't be scared. But I can't lie. I wanted to. It may be soon.

It was late. Carmen had spent all afternoon and evening at Lena's. Her head was full of love and passion—Lena's love and passion—and it was thrilling but threatening, too. It was one more thing to separate them from their common childhood.

By the time Carmen got home, her thoughts stretched out, forward and backward, in a full and sentimental way. It made her miss her mother and yearn for her, even though Christina was lying in the next room.

Carmen pulled on a sleeping T-shirt and brushed her

teeth, and then she crawled into her mother's bed. It was still, even when they were at odds, the softest place in the universe. Christina rolled over and propped her head on her elbow. Usually on nights like this, she would rub Carmen's back, but tonight Carmen didn't wriggle in quite that close. She didn't deserve it yet.

"Mama?"

"Yes?"

Carmen sniffed a little. "I need to tell you something."

"Okay." Christina had probably known this was coming sometime.

"Remember the Sunday when you were still with David and you thought he didn't call all day?"

Christina thought back. "Yes," she said.

"Well, he did call. I rewound his message and a new one recorded over it by mistake. I should have told you the truth, but I didn't."

From the look on Christina's face, there was anger, but it wasn't right up close. "That was a shabby thing to do, Carmen."

"I know it was, and I'm so sorry. I'm sorry for that, and I'm sorry for the awful things I said. I'm sorry I made you so unhappy."

Christina nodded.

"I'm sorry I ruined it for you and David. I wish I hadn't." Carmen's eyes filled up. "I don't know why I did it."

Christina still didn't say anything. She had a knack for waiting out Carmen's lies.

"Okay, I do know why I did it. I was scared it would be the end of you and me."

Her mother reached over and touched her hair. "You made mistakes. But you aren't the only one," Christina said slowly. "I did too. I let it go too fast. I got carried away." Christina's eyes were fixed tightly and intently on Carmen's face. "But listen to me, *nena*. There could never be an end of you and me."

Carmen felt a tear dribble down her elbow and soak into the mattress. "Can I ask you a question?"

"Of course."

"Have you wanted to meet a David for a long time? This whole time of just being us, have you been lonely?"

"Oh, no. No." She petted Carmen's head like she had when Carmen was a child. "I've been so happy being your mother."

Carmen felt her chin quivering. "Really?"

"More than anything else."

"Oh." Carmen smiled shakily. "I've been happy being your daughter."

They both rolled onto their backs and looked up at the ceiling.

"Mama, what do you want?"

Christina thought for a while. "Falling in love is a wonderful feeling. But it was scary how it took me over. I don't know if I want that."

"Hmmm . . ." Carmen considered the cracks in the plaster molding.

"What about you, sweet? What do you want?"

"Well." Carmen lifted her arms in the air and locked her elbows. She examined her hands up there. "Let's see. I want you to leave me alone, but not ignore me. I want you to miss me when I go away to college, but not be sad. I want you to stay exactly the same, but not be lonely or alone. I want to do the leaving, and not have you ever leave me. That's not really fair, is it?"

Christina shrugged. "You're the daughter. I'm the mother. It's not meant to be fair." She laughed. "I don't recall you changing any diapers."

Carmen laughed too.

"Oh, and one other thing." Carmen rolled back onto her side, facing her mom. "I want you to be happy."

She let her words sink down upon them. After a while she wriggled in close enough for her mom to rub her back.

Bee,

I send you the Pants full of love and strangeness. I'm living in another world here. I know you'll understand, Bee, because you live here too. I don't just mean doing major things with a guy, although I understand a lot more about that now. I mean putting yourself out there in the way of overwhelming happiness and knowing you're also putting yourself in the way of terrible harm. I'm scared to be this happy. I'm scared to be this extreme.

But you are here with me, Bee. I always wished I were as brave as you.

Love,
Lena

If the missing and wanting had been hard before, it was nearly unbearable now. It felt to Lena like the multitude of her thoughts and dreams and fantasies about Kostos weighed down the hours and made them go extra slowly.

She was living outside herself, living for when they could be together. That was what she had wanted so badly to avoid. But Lena realized now, maybe that was just how much love cost.

When he'd called her on Monday, she had literally caressed the phone. She would rather have listened to him breathe for an hour than hang up.

When he'd called Tuesday, she had giggled for an hour and a half, causing herself to wonder whether the real Lena was perhaps locked up in a closet somewhere with duct tape binding her mouth.

He hadn't called Wednesday, and when he called on Friday, he didn't sound right. His voice had a flatness she hardly recognized. "I'm afraid I may not be able to come this weekend."

She felt suddenly dizzy. "Why not?"

"I—I may have to go back."

"To go back where?"

"To Greece," he said.

She gasped. "Is your bapi okay?"

He was silent for a minute. "Yes, I think he's fine."

"Then why? What?" She was too intense. She was hurling herself at him like a cat on a cockroach. She wished she could hold back.

"Some other business at home that came up," he said

slowly. "I'll explain it when I know what's going on." He didn't want her to ask any more.

"Is it bad? Will everything be okay?"

"I hope so."

Her brain was fervently concocting possible explanations that wouldn't be devastating to her.

"I have to hang up," he said. "I wish I didn't."

Don't go! she wanted to scream at him.

"I love you, Lena."

"Bye," she said inevitably.

He couldn't go back to Greece! She would die! When would she ever see him again? The one thing getting her through up to now had been the thought that she only had to wait until Friday.

She hated this. The uncertainty. The powerlessness. She felt as though he had blown a gaping hole in the expected path of her life. The sidewalk now ended just a few yards ahead.

Effie stood in the doorway of her room. She had on her running shoes. "Are you okay?" she asked.

Lena shook her head. She closed her eyes hard to keep the tears inside.

Effie appeared at her side. "What is it?"

Lena shrugged. She gathered up her voice from somewhere near her ankles. "I think that being loved by Kostos is even harder than not being loved by him."

"Your grandchildren used to come visit here, didn't they?" Bridget asked Grandma from under her hat at breakfast.

Grandma chewed her toast. "Oh, yes. Every summer until they were almost seven. And I used to go up north to see them for six weeks every winter until they were five."

"Why did you stop?" Bridget asked tentatively.

"Because Marly asked me not to come."

"Why, do you think?"

Greta sighed. "Things were starting to go downhill by then. I don't think she wanted anybody looking too closely at her life, especially not me. I had too many opinions about the children, and neither she nor Franz wanted to hear them."

Bridget nodded. "That's sad."

"Oh, honey." Greta swayed in her seat. "You can't know how sad. Marly loved her children, but she had a hard time. She used to go to bed after she fixed them lunch, and by the time they were eight or nine, I suspect she went back to sleep after breakfast. She'd get overwhelmed halfway through sorting the laundry and leave it on the machine for days until Franz got around to it."

Bridget pressed her palm to her cheek. The kitchen darkened as the sky outside grew overcast. She remembered her mother lying in bed through the afternoons and evenings. She remembered her mother getting upset and frustrated by the buckles of Bridget's sandals or the tangles in her hair. Bridget had learned to be careful about spills and recycle her clothes, because they took a long time to come back from the wash.

"Why did . . . they stop coming? The kids, I mean."

Grandma rested her elbows on the table heavily. "To tell you honestly, I think it was because I was having bitter disagreements with Franz. I knew Marly was in trouble, and I worried about her all the time. Franz didn't want to see the things I was seeing. I told him Marly needed the help of a doctor, and he said no. I told him Marly needed medication, and he disagreed. I think he was mad at me, so he took the kids away. He told me to stop calling. To leave Marly alone. I couldn't do it."

Bridget noticed that Greta's lips quivered. She patted her old lady hands fixedly.

"And I was right to worry. I was right to, because — "

Bridget stood up so fast she almost knocked her chair backward. "I've got to do something upstairs. Sorry, Greta. I just remembered. I better go."

She went up the steps without looking back. In the attic the first thing she saw was the box, the one she'd been putting off. In her dreams she was Pandora. She imagined that the box was a yawning black hole between her and her childhood, and that once she opened its flaps, she would fall into it and die.

Bridget lay in bed and listened to the storm brewing outside. She fell asleep for a while, and when she woke up, she was looking at the box again. The sky was darkening. She could practically feel the barometer plunging.

She watched the wind flutter the eyelet curtains. The gray sky seemed to turn the floor gray in its image. She loved this room. She felt more at home here than in any place she'd ever been. But still there was that box. She peered out the window at the nervous landscape.

She went over to the box and opened it. Now was a good time to get it over with. She wanted to prove to herself that it wasn't really so scary. And if she didn't do it now, when would she do it? She had to get to the end of this story.

The top layer was mostly pictures of the happy young family. Marly and Franz with their two blond babies. In the car, at the zoo. All the usual stuff. More absorbing to her were the ones with her grandparents. Bridget squinting in the sun on her grandfather's shoulders, grinning big next to Greta, her mouth orange and sticky from a Popsicle. She smiled at the sight of the Honey Bees' team picture. There she was with her boy haircut and her arm clamped around Billy Kline. The middle of the box was packed with her and Perry's various art projects, and a pile of Perry's disintegrating comic books. She threw a lot of that stuff away.

Under that were photographs Marly must have sent to her mother in the years after they'd stopped coming to Alabama. Bridget's and Perry's stiff-looking school pictures from third through fifth grades. There was a hilariously dorky picture of the Septembers from the summer after fourth grade. Tibby was still missing several teeth. Bridget sported the mother lode of braces, with little rubber bands stretching across the front. Carmen had her awful, floppy version of the Jennifer Aniston hairdo. Lena looked normal, but that was Lena.

The last picture was the sad one. From the date on the back, Bridget knew it had been four months before her mother died. Bridget guessed her mother had sent it to Greta to prove to her that she was doing just fine, but if you looked at it for even a minute, the illusion fell heartbreakingly apart. Marly's limbs were too thin. Her skin looked as though it hadn't seen daylight in weeks. Her pose on a park bench looked totally artificial, like she'd been set up at the Sears photo studio. Her smile seemed fragile and atrophied, as though she hadn't moved her mouth into that shape for many months.

Bridget loved the Marly who glittered and preened, but this was the woman she remembered.

Bridget got up. She was fitful. Her legs needed her to walk around. The sky was as dark as if it were night. She flicked on her light, but it didn't respond. The storm had knocked the power out.

Bridget went down the stairs to check on Greta. To her surprise, she found her huddled in the corner of the kitchen with a flashlight.

"Are you all right?" Bridget asked.

Greta looked shiny with sweat. "My sugar's up. I'm having trouble doing the injection in the dark like this."

Without thinking, Bridget strode over to help. "I'll hold the flashlight for you," she offered.

As she held it, she watched breathlessly as Greta readied the needle and poked it into her skin. Suddenly Bridget's beam of light was tilting and scooting all around the room. Her hand was shaking so hard she dropped the flashlight and it banged across the floor. Her whole body was shaking. "I'm sorry," she cried. "I'll get it." Instead, she lost her footing and fell onto her knees in the middle of the room.

"Honey, it's okay. I got it," Greta said soothingly, but it seemed to Bridget that she was saying it from a great distance.

Bridget tried to get up, but her head was all wrong, her eyes were all wrong. She couldn't focus on anything. She felt panicked, like she had to keep moving. She burst through the side door and out into the yard. She heard Grandma's voice calling behind her, but she couldn't focus on it. She kept walking.

She walked through the needling rain for blocks down to the river and then walked alongside it, on her familiar path. Walking didn't feel fast enough, so she started running. The river was up, lapping against its sides. She felt tears dribbling from her eyes, mixing with and disappearing in the rain. The rain was so heavy, and suddenly she pictured her raincoat bunched under her seat on the Triangle bus, traveling the country, leaving her out here alone.

She ran and ran, and when she couldn't run anymore, she fell on the ground and let it catch her. She lay on the wet, muddy bank and let the memories overtake her, because she couldn't help it anymore.

There was her mother with the needle in her skin, white-blue skin. There was the hair, long and yellow, fanned out on the floor. There was her mother's face that didn't move even with the screaming, all the screaming. It was Bridget's screaming. She was screaming and her mother's face stayed still, no matter how Bridget shook her. And she screamed and screamed until somebody came and took her away.

That was how the story went. That was how it really ended.

A pigeon is the same

thing as a dove.

Did you know that?

—Bridget Vreeland

Sometime before sunrise, Bridget picked herself up and walked back home. She let herself in the side door and numbly walked up the steps to the bathroom. She took a long, blasting hot shower, wrapped herself in a towel, took a comb from her shelf, and walked down to the kitchen. She poured a big glass of water and sat at the table in the dark.

She was tired. She was dazed. She felt like she had died.

She heard footsteps on the stairs and then heard Grandma come into the kitchen behind her. Grandma sat down across from her at the table. She didn't say anything.

After a while, Greta took the comb from the table and stood up. She walked behind Bridget and began combing out her wet hair, gently and slowly, pulling all the knots out from the bottom like a pro. Bridget let her head relax into her grandmother's chest, and she let herself remember the many times Greta had done this before, always slowly, always patiently.

Bridget closed her eyes and let herself remember other things in this kitchen. Grandma fixing her bowls of cereal when she was supposed to be asleep, spooning in the cough syrup when Bridget had bronchitis, teaching her gin rummy and looking the other way when she cheated.

By the time Bridget's hair was entirely combed and smooth, the sun had risen, casting light on the silky gold strands. Greta kissed her on top of the head.

"You know who I am, don't you?" Bridget said in a fragile voice.

She felt Greta's nod against her scalp.

"You've known for a long time?"

Another nod.

"The whole time?" Bridget asked.

"Not the first day," Greta answered, protecting Bee from feeling sad that her scheme had failed entirely.

Bridget nodded.

"You're my honey Bee. How could I not know?"

Bridget considered that. It made sense. "Even with my hair different?"

"You are you, however your hair is."

"But you didn't say anything."

Greta lifted her shoulders and dropped them. "I figured I'd take your lead."

Bridget nodded again. It was remarkable and true. Greta sensed what Bridget needed. She had always done that.

Crawling back in bed, with her raw skin and her smooth hair, Bridget had a feeling of comfort spreading through her insides. She'd let in the memories of a mother who couldn't seem to love her, but in the same flood had rushed in memories of the mother who could.

Through the middle of August, Lena got up in the morning and went to bed at night. Sometimes she went to work in between. She ate once in a while too. She saw Carmen, and she listened to Carmen talk. She had a few stiff conversations with Tibby. The time Bee called she hadn't been home. Lena was the kind of person who liked to share good news. Bad news she kept for herself.

Kostos had gone back to Greece. He hadn't explained why. When she had asked if she'd done anything wrong, he'd gotten upset. For the first time in days his voice had lost its flatness.

"No, Lena. Of course not. Whatever happens, you didn't do anything wrong." His voice had been thick with emotion. "You are the best thing that ever happened in my life. Never think you did anything wrong."

Somehow, she wasn't reassured by that.

He had promised he would write all the time and call when he could. She knew he wouldn't be calling much. It cost a fortune and would put a burden on his grandparents. Their house in Oia wasn't even set up for e-mail.

It was back to the letters. The delay of gratification seemed like torture beyond anything even Kafka could have dreamed up.

I don't know if I can do this, she thought on many occasions. But what was the alternative? Fall out of love with him? Impossible. Stop caring? Stop wishing she could be with him? She'd tried that once. She was too far gone to try it again.

"Lena, are you all right?" her mother asked her one morning at breakfast.

No! I'm not! "I'm fine," she said.

"You look so thin. I wish you would tell me what's going on with you."

Lena also wished it. But it wasn't going to happen. For a long time, especially since the Eugene debacle, they'd orbited each other at a wide distance. It wasn't like her mother could suddenly hug her and make everything better.

Carmabelle: Tib. Saw Brian riding bike today. Almost ran over him. Looks amazing. Is handsome. Not kidding.

Tibberon: Are kidding. Or mistaken.

Carmabelle: Am not.

Tibberon: Are too.

Bridget needed a run. A long, fast one. For days she'd been hanging close to the house, padding around in Greta's slippers and letting Grandma make her lemonade and rub her back. She'd gone a long time without a mother.

Usually when she slept twelve hours at night it meant she was falling apart, but these nights, with her quiet dreams, she felt as if she were remaking herself, putting herself together.

She washed her hair vigorously, four times in a row, watching the last of the faint brown dye go down the drain. Then she put on her running shoes.

The air was a little cooler than usual, and her breath settled into an easy rhythm right away. Her body felt light and wonderful, as if she'd cast off a very heavy, very dark blanket.

The river was still extra full from the day and night of storms. Her feet slipped a little on the muddy parts of the path, but she slowed down without breaking her stride. She could have run a million miles today, but she decided to turn back once she was five miles out. The trees were so lush and thick they drooped heavily over the river's edge. Big-leafed magnolias towered to the sky. A thick coat of moss seemed to cover every boulder and rock.

"Hey!"

"Hey!" the voice shouted out a second time before she realized it was directed at her.

She slowed down and made a half turn.

It was Billy. He was waving to her from farther up the grassy bank. It made sense. She could see his house from here if she stood on her tiptoes.

He came toward her. He looked confused by her appearance.

She touched her head, remembering she hadn't covered it. What was the point anymore?

"You look . . . different," he said, eyeing her carefully. "Did you dye your hair?"

"No, I . . . kind of . . . undyed it."

He looked surprised.

"I mean, this is how it usually is."

There was something stirring in his eyes. He was grasping for something.

"You do know me, Billy," she said.

"I do, don't I?"

"My name isn't Gilda."

"No."

"No."

He was racking his brain, she could tell he was.

"It's not Mia Hamm, either."

He laughed. He studied her a little longer. "You're Bee," he said finally.

"I am," she said.

He smiled, amazed, happy, bewildered. "Thank God there aren't *two* girls in Burgess who can kick my ass all over the soccer field."

"Just one," she said.

He pointed to his forehead. "I *knew* I knew you."

"I knew I knew you."

"Yeah, well, I wasn't going under an alias, was I?"

"No. Besides, you look exactly the same."

"You look . . ." He considered her. "The same too," he decided.

"Funny how that is," she said, feeling giddy.

They started walking together along the river.

He was grabbing looks at her as they went. "Why were you using the fake name?" he asked finally.

It was a reasonable question. She wasn't sure what the answer was anymore. "My mom died, did you know that?" So it wasn't an answer, but it was information she wanted him to have.

He nodded. "We had a memorial service for her here.

I remember thinking maybe you would come."

"I didn't know about it. Or I would've."

He nodded again. She was leaving open a lot of questions, she knew, but people didn't press you when your mother was dead.

"I thought about you a lot," he said. She knew by his eyes that he meant it. "I felt sorry a lot. About your mom, I mean."

"I know," she said quickly.

He touched her hand lightly as they walked. They had only ever talked about soccer before this, and yet he was able to be serious with her now, to absorb who and what she was.

"I wanted to come here and see this place again," she explained after some silence. "I wanted to see Greta and find out about my mom, but I . . . I didn't want any . . . commitments. I guess."

He seemed to find this rational, although she couldn't be sure.

"I don't feel that way anymore," she added.

She liked how carefully he looked at her, but she was ready to change gears now.

"So how'd y'all fare against Decatur?" she asked. Now that she was herself again, it was funny to hear her voice relaxing into the old accent.

"We lost."

"Oh. Too bad. I figured you got rained out Saturday."

"We played Sunday," he said. "Lost three-one. The guys say it's because you weren't there."

Bridget smiled. She liked that idea.

"I told them I'd ask you to be our coach, officially."

"How about I'll do it unofficially?"

He settled for that. "No more missing games, Coach," he said. "And you've got to come to practice, too. We've got the final tournament next weekend."

"I promise," she said.

At the end of the path, they aimed themselves in their different directions. Billy grabbed her hand as she was walking away. He squeezed it once, not hard, and let it go.

"Glad you're back, Bee."

Tibby had to leave the dorm. It had been three days since she'd seen the sunlight, and she'd eaten every flake and grain from every miniature cereal box she'd pilfered from the cafeteria—dry, after she'd run out of milk. She didn't need to shower, necessarily, or do her laundry, or comb her hair, but she did need to eat.

She was wandering through the lobby of her dorm, arguing with herself about a couple of her edits, when she plowed straight into Brian.

"Brian!" she shouted when she realized it was indeed him and not her tricky imagination.

He smiled. He got close enough to hug her and then lost his nerve, so she reached out and hugged him.

"I'm so, so glad to see you," she said.

"I got your messages," he said.

She winced slightly.

"All of them," he added.

"Sorry about that."

"No problem."

Happily she studied his face. "Hey. Where are your glasses?" And as the question left her lips, she realized that Carmen had a point. If Tibby forced herself to be objective, she could see that Brian looked perfectly presentable. She had a terrible thought. "You didn't get contacts, did you?" What if Brian, of all people, had suddenly turned vain? What would that mean for the world?

Brian looked at her as if she were crazy. "No. They broke." He shrugged. "I can't see."

Tibby laughed. She was so relieved that he was her friend again.

"Can you come to the cafeteria with me? I'll sneak you in?"

"Sure," he said.

At the entrance to the building, Tibby saw Maura. Some cowardly part of herself wanted to hide, to pretend she hadn't actually seen her. They hadn't spoken in over a week. Tibby felt certain Alex had told her all about Tibby's harangue.

Maura was decked out in a leather skirt. Tibby was still wearing her plaid pajama bottoms. Her tank top was splotched with ink. Brian glanced at Tibby cautiously. Maura looked down, obviously preferring the charade where they acted as though they hadn't seen each other.

Tibby spat in the face of her cowardly self. "Hey, Maura," she said. "I didn't properly introduce you to my friend Brian. Maura, this is Brian. Did I mention that he's my friend?"

Maura looked cornered. She glanced around at the

people streaming through the lobby. She didn't want to be seen talking to the girl wearing pajamas. Tibby found herself wishing, perversely, that Brian looked as much like a doofus as she did, rather than perfectly presentable.

Maura acknowledged them with a tight, unpleasant smile and sidestepped Tibby to get to the elevators.

Later, in the cafeteria, Tibby wanted to introduce Brian to everyone she knew, but unfortunately, that came down to Vanessa. Vanessa agreed to sit at their table and promised to show Brian her animals when they got back to the dorm.

"He's cute," Vanessa whispered to Tibby as Brian went to get them orange juice.

The first letter took eight days to come, and Lena knew by the feel of it in her hands that it wasn't going to make her happy. It was light and thin, and Kostos's normally expansive handwriting looked oddly compressed.

Dearest Lena,

It is hard for me to write you with this message. I am in a situation here that is troubling me. I want to wait to explain it to you until I know how it will be resolved. I'm sorry for the suspense. I know it isn't easy on you.

Please bear with me for a bit longer.

Kostos

Under his cold sign-off he'd written something else at a different time, she guessed, because the ink had dried a slightly different color, and the writing was much looser, almost drunken.

I love you, Lena, he had scrawled at the bottom. *I couldn't stop if I tried.*

She studied it, feeling a strange sense of detachment. What could it be? She'd spent so many hours trying to calculate and guess, and she hadn't come up with one hypothesis that made any sense.

He said he loved her. Though she generally did a poor job of holding and trusting that notion, she did believe him. But why did he say he couldn't stop if he tried? It sounded like he was trying. Why was he trying? What could possibly have come up that made him want to stop loving her?

Was his bapi sick again? That would be devastating, but it wouldn't have to split them apart. If he needed to stay in Oia, then fine. She would find a way to be there next summer. Maybe even for the Christmas holidays.

Lena felt like a pebble falling down a well. She dropped through the air with nothing to hold her. She knew the ending, when it came, would be painful. But even suspense became monotonous after too long.

She was waiting, waiting. Falling.

The next letter was worse.

Dear Lena,

I cannot continue to feel committed to you. Nor do I want you to feel committed to me any longer. I am sorry. Someday, I will explain it all to you and I hope you'll forgive me.

Kostos

The bottom had arrived. She crashed against it, but it brought no sense of closure or understanding. She just lay there at the bottom looking up. She knew there must be a very tiny circle of light up there somewhere, but just now she couldn't see it.

Pools of Sorrow, Waves of joy

—John Lennon and

Paul McCartney

"Hello, is this David?"

"Yes. Can I ask who this is?"

"It's Carmen Lowell. You know, Christina's daughter?"

He paused. "Hi, Carmen. What can I do for you?" He sounded guarded—all business. He knew that Carmen hadn't exactly played Cupid between him and Christina.

"I'd like to ask you a big favor."

"Okay . . ."

His "okay" had the ring of "in your dreams."

"I'd like you to pick my mother up tonight at seven and take her to Toscana. The reservation is under Christina."

"Are you her social secretary?" he asked. He was allowed to be a little bitter. Besides, she frankly appreciated that he wasn't talking down to her.

"No," Carmen snapped back. "But I did my share of messing things up between the two of you. I feel it's my responsibility to fix it if I can."

He paused again. "Seriously?" He was afraid to believe her.

"Seriously."

"Does your mom want to see me?" His voice reached up high and plaintive on the last word. He wasn't all business anymore.

"Are you insane? Of course she does." Carmen hadn't actually checked that fact with her mother yet. "Do you want to see her?"

David breathed out. "Yeah, I do."

"She's missed you." Carmen couldn't believe what was coming out of her mouth, but fostering love was turning out to be a lot more fun than ruining it.

"I miss her."

"Good. Well, you two have fun."

"Good."

"And David?"

"Yeah?"

"Sorry."

"Okay, Carmen."

Tibberon: Have you talked to Lena? I'm worried about her.

Carmabelle: I've been calling and e-mailing for two days. I'm worried too.

Lena was sitting by herself in the back of the store under a rack of hanging blouses. She knew she needed to look industrious, but she couldn't do it today. She hugged her knees. She was losing her mind in stages. The first stage was doing weird things, and the second was not caring anymore.

Today she had spoken to Tibby and Carmen twice each. She found herself feeling angry with them for not being able to say things that could make her feel better. But she was beginning to realize there weren't any things that could make her feel better.

She felt the stubble on her calves. She picked the thick nail on her baby toe until it almost came off. The pain was the only thing in this place that fit her.

A woman walked through with a bunch of clothes flopped over her arm. Lena saw her from the back as she chose a fitting room. *You shop. I'll just be here.*

She listened to the lady fumble and thump around in the tiny torture chamber with the curtain that didn't fully close. It was as good as anything else to listen to. Lena closed her eyes and bowed her head.

She heard a throat clear. "Excuse me?" The voice was timid. "Do you think this looks all right?"

Lena looked up. She had lost track of the lady, but now here she was, standing in the middle of the carpet. Her feet were bare and flat. She wore a gray washed-silk dress that sagged and swayed over her small, bony frame. The woman's face was shadowed, and her skin looked as thin as cellophane. Only the blue veins in her neck and hands seemed vivid. But the color of the dress matched almost identically the shade of her large, lovely eyes. It didn't look good, but it probably looked better than anything else in the shop would have.

Lena stopped looking at the lady's dress and looked at her face. Until now, Lena hadn't been able to put her finger on the particular look of so many women who shopped here. Truthfully, she hadn't tried very hard to put her finger on it. But now she saw it so clearly. It was need. It was hope. It was a plea for some small signal that they were worthwhile.

This woman's need was raw. Suddenly Lena knew who she was. She was Mrs. Graffman. She was Bailey's mother. Mrs. Graffman didn't know Lena, but Lena knew about her. She had lost her daughter, her only child. She didn't have anyone to be a mother to anymore. Lena knew nothing about loss compared to her.

Lena looked at Mrs. Graffman's face. She saw what it needed and she didn't look away. Lena rose to her feet. "That dress . . . I think it makes you look . . . beautiful." The words came out as light as the air, truer than any lie Lena had ever told.

When Bridget got home from running one afternoon, there was a package waiting for her. She ripped it open instantly, standing at the kitchen table.

The Pants! They'd come back to her. With a clanging in her chest, she tore up the stairs, stripped off her running clothes, and jumped into the shower. You weren't allowed to wash the Pants. She wasn't crazy enough to try them on just after she'd run ten miles on an August day in Alabama.

She dried herself, put on underwear, and took up the Pants. *Please fit*, she begged them. She pulled them up and closed them in one fluid motion. *Ahhhhh.* They felt so good. She did a victory lap around the attic. She ran downstairs and outside and did a victory lap around the house. "Yay!" she shouted to the sky, because it felt so good to feel good again.

She put her hands on her thighs, soaking in the connection to Carmen and Lena and Tibby, and loving them so much. "It's okay!" she wanted to shout loudly enough for them to hear. "I'm going to be all right now!"

Greta cast her a bemused look as Bridget shot past her, back up to the third floor.

The contents of the last box were still piled in the corner. Bridget was ready to put it all away and be done with it now. She grabbed the box to repack it, but as she did, she stalled. There was a yellowed square left in the bottom that she hadn't noticed before. Her euphoria dimmed as she reached in after the paper. It was the back of a photograph, she realized as she put her fingers on it. She promised herself she would be okay, whatever it was.

The picture showed a girl, about sixteen, sitting on the steps of Burgess High. She was beautiful to behold with her giant smile and her yellow curtain of hair. Bridget's first thought was that it was her mother. She just assumed it. But as she looked closer, she wondered. The picture looked too old to be of her mother. And besides, the character of the face was different. . . .

Bridget thundered back downstairs.

"Grandma! Hey!" she shouted.

"Out here," Grandma called from the yard. She was hosing down the little garden that hugged the back of the house.

310

Bridget thrust the picture in her face. "Who's this?"

Greta looked at it. "Me," she said.

"That's you?"

"Sure."

Bridget studied it again. "You were beautiful, Grandma."

"Is that so surprising?" Greta asked, trying to look offended but not seeming to care very much.

"No. Well. A little."

Grandma hosed Bridget's foot. Bridget hopped around laughing.

When Bridget settled down she came back to the picture. "You had the hair."

Grandma cocked her head. "Where do you think you got it from, missy?" she asked playfully.

Bridget's answer was serious. "I always thought I got it from Marly. I always thought it meant I was like her."

Greta transitioned easily into Bridget's new mood. "You are like her in some ways—in some wonderful ways."

"Like how?"

"You're intense like she was. You're brave. You have her beauty, no doubt about that."

"You think so?" Bridget longed for reassurance on this point more than she ever had before.

"Of course you do. Whatever color you want to make your hair."

Bridget liked that for an answer.

Greta turned off the hose and tossed it into the flower bed. "You're very different from her too."

"Like how?" Bridget asked again.

Greta thought. "I'll tell you an example. The way you came into this house and remade that attic. You pulled it apart and worked day after day to put it back together. It made my heart grow to see your patience and your hard work, Bee. Your mother, God bless her in heaven, couldn't pay attention to any one thing for longer than an hour or two."

Bridget remembered that about her mother, how quickly she had become impatient. With a book, with a radio station, with her children. "She gave up too easily. Didn't she?" Bridget asked.

Greta looked at Bee like she was going to cry. "She did, honey. But you won't."

"Grandma, can I keep this picture?" she asked. Of all the thousands of things she had sifted through in the attic, this one looked like hope. This was the one she wanted to keep.

Carmabelle: Len. Please answer me? Please? I'm coming over.
Lennyk162: Not right now. I'll call you later, okay?

Distantly, from the bottom of the well, Lena heard the knock on the door. It came twice more before it occurred to her that it was her door and she was supposed to answer it.

She coughed up her voice. "Who is it?"

"Lenny, it's me. May I come in?"

Carmen's voice was so lovely and familiar, and yet it belonged to the world above.

"Not . . . right . . . now," she managed to say.

"Lenny, please? I really need to talk to you."

Lena closed her eyes. "Maybe later."

The door opened anyway. Carmen walked straight over to the bed where Lena was huddled.

"Oh, Lenny."

Lena made herself sit up, though her bones seemed to slump and cave. She began to cover her eyes with her hands, but then Carmen was right there. There was no hiding. Carmen put her arms around Lena and held her.

Lena let her heavy head fall into Carmen's neck, giving way to the inexpressible mercy of her friend's warm skin.

"Lenny." Carmen hummed and held, and Lena cried.

Lena cried and shook. She cried, and Carmen cried for her.

After a while Lena realized she wasn't at the bottom of the well, but here, with Carmen.

"Mark him! Rusty, go!" Bridget screamed from the sidelines. She paced the length of the field in the Traveling Pants, barking orders and ranting encouragement like any good coach. Her hair was free and incandescent, but her players didn't care. They wanted her for her mind. Or her strategy, more specifically. At the half, eleven guys crowded around her, wide-eyed and attentive, as if she were an oracle.

Greta sat a few yards behind her in a beach chair, smiling and shaking her head, alternately studying the game and her crossword puzzle.

"Jesus, Corey, stop mooning around the goal. Rusty, don't get so far ahead of Billy. You're useless when you're offsides; I don't care if you are fast. And also, their right midfielder is dead on his feet and has no viable sub. That's where you work 'em." She rearranged her lineup a little and sent them back onto the field.

Eight minutes into the second half, Mooresville's over-worked midfielder took to the sidelines and got subbed by the backup goalie, who was at least forty pounds over-weight. Bridget knew it was in the bag at that point.

Billy threw his arms around her after the win and lifted her off the ground. "All right, Coach!" he shouted. They all swarmed around her happily, shouting and yelling and celebrating.

"Let's not get cocky," she said. Then she realized how much she hated it when coaches said that. "Screw that," she said, laughing. "Get cocky all you want. We're gonna flatten Athens at four."

Burgess didn't flatten Athens at four, but they did beat them, securing a berth in the final the next day.

It turned out that the final pitted them against Tuscumbia, all the way from Muscle Shoals. Bridget woke up early and put on the Pants for another spin. She brought her clipboard down to breakfast and detailed her complex strategy to Grandma, who tried very hard to look interested but kept sneaking peeks at an article in *Ladies' Home Journal.*

Billy appeared at the screen door, white-faced, at nine. "We're dead," he said.

"What?"

"Corey Parks took off for Corpus Christi with his girl-friend last night."

"No!"

"Yes. She threatened she'd break up with him if he didn't drive her."

Bridget grimaced. "Oh, no." She shook her head. "I never trusted Corey. Not since he faked the knee injury so he could go to King's Dominion."

"Bee, we were six," Billy said.

Bridget didn't back down. "Well, you know. The more things change . . ."

At the field half an hour later, with the two sides assembled and two towns present to cheer and harangue, the situation didn't look any better. Burgess was no deeper a team than Mooresville. Bridget surveyed her bench unhappily. Their one reliable sub had left for Auburn two days earlier. Seth Molina had shin splints and refused to wear his game shirt. Rason Murphy had such bad asthma Bridget worried that if she put him on the field on a sultry day like today, he would up and die. She would do better to suit up Greta and throw her into the game.

She and Billy paced together, considering their options. There weren't any options.

They looked toward their sorry bench. "This is hopeless," Billy said.

The whistle blew to start the game. Bridget stood frozen on the sidelines as her team filed onto the field — all ten of them.

Tuscumbia went up by four and stayed there, possibly out of pity, till the half was called. Most of the fans were booing or departing by that point.

Bridget had nothing to say to her team at the half. They had the wrong number of players; subtle strategy wasn't really going to make a dent.

"This is humiliating," Rusty opined.

The team trudged back onto the field. The ref was ready with the whistle. Billy was mouthing something to Bridget.

"Huh?" she shouted at him, moving closer.

He mouthed it again. He was waving his hands around like mad.

"What? I can't hear you."

"Honey Bees!" he blasted at her. "I'm saying 'Honey Bees.'"

Finally she got it. He was waving her into the game.

Bridget laughed. Without thinking she ran onto the field beside him.

Everybody looked confused as she stood there in her jeans and running shoes in the middle of the field.

"She's our sub!" Billy shouted to the ref, Marty Ginn, who also happened to own the Burgess Fine Pharmacy. "Rason has asthma," Billy added, knowing perfectly well that Marty had spent eighteen years filling prescriptions for Rason's inhalers.

Marty nodded. He looked to Tuscumbia's captain. "All right with you?" he asked.

Tuscumbia's captain seemed to find the whole thing entertaining. The game was already a farce, so who cared if there was a girl wearing long pants in the middle of it? He shrugged and nodded, as if to say, *What next?*

The whistle started the half.

Bridget began running slowly up the field, just getting

her legs under her. She followed the action around at a distance until she felt the adrenaline building and her eyes and her mind and her feet getting that harmonious feeling that lifted her playing up and up. Then she got down to business. She easily stole the ball from a Tuscumbia forward and began to dribble at speed, a touch and three paces, a touch and three paces.

Nine months away from competitive soccer hadn't made Bridget worse, it turned out. Also, she was wearing the Traveling Pants. They were the wrong shape and texture for competitive sports, granted, but they made her happy. And Greta had yanked herself off her duff and was tearing along the sidelines, shouting for Bridget like a maniac. That didn't hurt.

Bridget rose and rose until she was up in the clouds. She could afford to be generous. She assisted Rusty. She assisted Gary Lee. She assisted Billy twice. She set up the plays and doled them out like Christmas presents until the game was tied, the shouts of protest from the opposing team grew deafening, and the last minute began ticking away. Then she took the last goal for herself. She'd never said she was Mother Teresa.

Carma,

I know you needed these especially, so here they are, as fast as I could get them to you. Please note the grass from the soccer field

I left for you in the back pocket. A tuft of the sweet homeland for your enjoyment.

The Pants worked their magic. I'm so happy, Carma. I'm not going to tell you all about it now or even on the phone, because I want to tell you in person. I'm coming home soon. I found everything I needed here.

Love,
Bee

Let me feel now what

sharp distress I may.

—Charles Dickens

"Outta bed."

Christina squinted at Carmen in irritation. "No."

"Yes."

"No."

"*Mamaaaa.*"

"Why?"

"Because . . ." Carmen tapped a little drumroll on her mom's bureau. "You are going out tonight."

"No, I'm not."

"Yes, you are."

"Carmen, I am not going out with your father and Lydia again."

"I know you're not. Anyway, they're gone. You're going out with David." *Ha.*

Christina sat up. Her cheeks were pink at the very mention of his name. She tried to look suspicious and mad. "Since when?"

"Since I called him and set it up." Carmen opened her

mother's closet and began surveying the shoe options.

"You didn't."

"Did so."

"Carmen Lucille! This is not your business!"

"He misses you, Mom. You miss him. It's so obvious. You're sad. Just go. Be happy."

Christina piled pillows onto her lap. "Maybe it's not that easy."

Carmen pointed to the bathroom. "Maybe it is."

Christina hesitated. Carmen could close her eyes and plug her ears, and still she would know how much her mom wanted to go. But Christina was trying to be rational and responsible, and Carmen appreciated that.

"I'm not telling you to lose your head, Mama. I'm not even telling you to take up where you left off with him. I'm just saying, go out to dinner with the guy who loves you."

Her mother swung her feet over the edge. This was working.

"You never have to go out with him again if you don't want." Carmen knew the chances of that were zero, but hey.

Her mother started toward the shower.

"Wait." Carmen rushed back to her room. She took the Traveling Pants from the top of her bureau and shook them out gently. She rushed back to her mother.

"Here."

Christina's eyes got swimmy. She pressed her lips together. "What?" Christina said in a whisper, even though she knew what it meant.

"These are for you to wear."

"Oh, *mi nena.*" Christina grabbed Carmen and pressed her close. Carmen realized she could lift her chin and rest it on the top of her mother's head. That was sad, a little.

When her mom pulled away, Carmen felt tears on her neck.

"I can't take them. If I'm going to try again, I have to be a grown-up this time."

"Okay." Carmen understood that.

"But Carmen?"

"Yeah?"

Her mother's mouth wobbled and tipped. "It means the world to me that you offered."

Carmen nodded. She picked up her mother's hand and pressed a kiss onto her knuckles. "Go, Mama. Shower. Get dressed. Hurry!"

Carmen strode back to her own room. "I'll get the camera all ready for when David gets here!" she called over her shoulder.

Carmabelle: Tib. I'll bring the Pants when I come to the screening. Can't wait to see you.

Tibby knew she was a true-blue believer in the Pants, because otherwise she could not have put them on today, considering what had happened the last time she had worn them. For her, the Pants were about putting in bad, lame-o stitches and pulling them out again, judging people and being able to change her mind. She could surprise herself, that was what Bailey had said.

She touched the embroidered heart as she walked into the auditorium. Her own heart felt as if it were beating just beneath her skin. Her bones no longer felt hard and protective.

For some reason, when she saw the cluster of people waiting for her in a row of seats at the back of the auditorium, she had the strangest sensation that she had died. The world was over, and all the people she had hurt and disappointed had come back to give her a second chance.

Her mother and father were there. Brian was there. Lena and Carmen, Mr. and Mrs. Graffman. Even Vanessa. *I want to deserve all of you,* she thought.

Her movie came first. It started with Bailey in the window and sunlight pouring all around and Beethoven. The picture switched to Wallman's and Duncan Howe and to Margaret at the Pavillion movie theater and to Brian at the 7-Eleven. She'd interspersed these segments with bits from the home movies she'd gotten from the Graffmans. Bailey taking her first steps as a baby, Bailey running after a butterfly in her backyard, and—this was a hard part—Bailey as a feisty six-year-old with a baseball cap and no hair underneath. The last segment was the interview. Bailey talking and looking, seeming to take as much from the camera as she gave to it.

The end was the still picture from the 7-Eleven. The one with her looking over her shoulder at Tibby and laughing. The image dissolved slightly as it hung there, and it turned to black and white. It stayed on the screen as the music played on.

Brian, sitting next to her, reached out and took her hand. She squeezed his in return. She realized he was whistling along with the music, but so quietly she was probably the only one who could hear it.

At last the music finished and Bailey's face flickered off. The darkness felt empty without it.

Mrs. Graffman leaned her head against her husband's chest. Tibby's mom reached for Tibby's hand on one side and Carmen's on the other. Lena held her head. All of them cried freely.

Outside in the bright sunlight, Tibby's parents hugged her. Her mother told her she was proud. Carmen and Lena squeezed her and praised her again and again. Brian had tears in his eyes. Tibby was surprised when Alex came over. She steeled herself for his comment, though she was well beyond taking it to heart.

"Well done," he said. His eyes were uncertain; it came out almost like a question. He studied her as though she were a stranger. Which, in a way, she was. He was flattened against the wall, and she could see all around.

If you are Greek, you know that it is traditionally considered an insult to the ancient gods to think you know when things can't get any worse. If you make this mistake, then the gods will prove you wrong.

One week to the day after Lena received the apocalyptic letter from Kostos, Grandma called from Oia and told Lena's father that Bapi had had a stroke. He was in the hospital in Fira, and he wasn't doing well.

Lena's father, being a lawyer and an American now, demanded to talk to Bapi's doctors and shouted a lot and wanted to have Bapi airlifted to the research hospital in Athens. The reply came that Bapi was too fragile to be moved.

Lena only had time to leave messages for Tibby and Carmen about what had happened and to call Basia's and quit a week early. She was packing her suitcase in a daze along with the rest of her family when she remembered the Traveling Pants. She was supposed to get them that day! It was midafternoon and they still hadn't arrived. Who had had them last? They'd been moving around so fast lately, Lena couldn't remember. The flight to New York was leaving in two hours! In spite of the crises around her, this became the most urgent source of her worry. How could she go to Greece without them?

As the rest of her family scurried around the house, she waited by the front door, hoping for a glimpse of a delivery truck. She dragged her feet in the last minutes before her departure.

"Lena, come on!" her mother was screaming at her from the car as she paused on the sidewalk, still hoping the Pants would somehow magically appear in time.

They didn't, and she took it as a bad omen.

Lena and her family stood by on the flight to New York, and the following morning on a direct flight to Athens. On the 747 rumbling eastward over the Atlantic Ocean, Lena spent most of the time looking at the seatback in front of her. But a lot of scenes played out on the blue polyester. Bapi and his wrinkly elbows poking out the window on the night of the festival of the Assumption last August. Bapi eating Cheerios in his white tasseled shoes. Bapi looking long and hard at her paintings, taking them as seriously as anyone ever had. It seemed funny, maybe, to find your soul mate in an eighty-two-year-old Greek man, but that was what had happened to Lena last summer.

Lena's father wrote in a notebook. Effie slept against his left shoulder. Lena's mother sat grimly beside her.

At one point, between the first movie and the second, they caught each other in a grim look and then proceeded to stare at each other grimly.

I wish we could help each other, Lena thought. *I wish that you trusted me enough to tell me important things and that I trusted you.* Then she found herself wishing that her mother could be her soul mate and not Bapi, who was probably dying. Then Lena started to cry. She curled up in her seat with her back to her mother and let her shoulders shake and her breath forget all the usual patterns. She blew her nose loudly into a cocktail napkin. She was crying for herself and Bapi and Kostos and her grandma and her father and the Traveling Pants that hadn't come in time, and then for herself some more.

And yet, when the captain ordered the flight attendants to prepare for arrival, and Lena saw the ancient and beautiful terrain of her grandmotherland below, she felt a thrill in the bottom of her stomach. Somewhere inside, her irrepressible, naïve heart was leaping with eagerness to see Kostos again, even under these wretched circumstances.

Bee,

I wish there was a better way to find you, 'cause I want to talk to you right away. So badly. I just found out Lena's bapi had a stroke. They all left for Greece yesterday. After everything she's been through, I feel so horrible. I want to make sure you know.

Love,

Tibby

Lena had reasonably begun to believe that what you least wanted to happen was certainly the thing that would happen.

When they pulled up in the rental car after a long climb up the cliffs of Santorini to the village of Oia and saw Grandma standing outside her egg-yolk front door, her belief was confirmed.

Grandma wore black from head to toe, and the lines on her face all seemed to point straight down. Lena heard a small cry leave her chest. Her father leaped out of the car and hugged his mother. Lena saw Grandma nodding and crying. They all knew what it meant.

Effie put her arm around Lena's shoulders. Lena's tears were on call, ready for duty. She had cried so much in recent days, she actually felt thirsty. Lena's hair mixed with Effie's hair as they held each other and cried. Then they all took turns hugging Grandma. When Grandma saw Lena she let out a moan and seemed to collapse on her shoulders. "Beautiful Lena," she said, sobbing into her neck. "Vat has happened to us?"

The funeral was to take place the following morning. Lena woke up and watched the Caldera at dawn, dark gray and pink. The window of her bedroom, now shared with Effie, brought the memories of last summer so close around her she felt as if she could hold them. She remembered sketching Kostos in charcoal from this very spot.

With a thrum of anticipation and anxiety at seeing Kostos, Lena took extra pains with her appearance. She wore a beautiful sheer black blouse over a camisole borrowed from Effie. She wore pearls in her earlobes. She blow-dried her hair and wore it down around her shoulders, a rare occurrence. She put on the slightest bit of eyeliner and mascara. She knew that even a little makeup set off her celery-colored eyes dramatically, which was why she almost never wore it.

Lena always downplayed her looks. She wore simple, uninteresting clothes. She hardly ever wore makeup or jewelry and wore her black hair back in a knot or a sloppy ponytail. From when she was a little girl, her mother had always told Lena her beauty was a gift, but as gifts went, Lena compared it to the Trojan horse.

Her beauty made her feel self-conscious and exposed. It brought her the kind of attention she hated. The very obviousness of it made her feel cheated. Effie, with her big nose, was allowed to be passionate, quirky, whole-hearted, and free. Lena, with her small nose, got to be pretty. Lena spent too much of her life making sure none of the people she trusted cared about how she looked, and avoiding the people who did.

And yet, today, she was polishing up the gift. Today, her hollowness over Bapi, her aching eagerness for Kostos made her desperate, willing to try any power available to her.

"Oh, my God," Effie said upon seeing her descend the stairs. "What have you done with Lena?"

"Duct tape in the closet," Lena answered.

Effie admired Lena in seeming awe for a few minutes. "Kostos is going to eat his poor heart out," she declared.

And thus, feeling guilty and small, Lena had her private soul read like a poster by her little sister, Effie.

Tibby looked down at the linoleum floor and remembered how plain and depressing her dorm room had seemed the day she'd moved into it two months ago. Now the floor was covered with dirty clothes she was tossing haphazardly into a large Hefty bag. On her bed she laid out all the videocassettes she had gathered and used in making her movie. On her desk was her iBook, which had worked so hard with her this summer. The computer had been a bribe, but she'd come to love it anyway. On her bureau was her eleven-year-old drawing of her bedroom, which had kept her company in a funny way. There was also the certificate announcing that her movie had won highest honors from the film department, and the note of congratulations from Bagley, her screenwriting teacher. On her nightstand was the purple poison dart frog Vanessa had made expressly for Nicky. Each of these things gave her pleasure as she tucked them, one by one, into her suitcase.

The last thing she packed was a picture she'd taped to the door. It was a picture of Bailey in the hospital not too long before she died. Mrs. Graffman had given it to Tibby when she'd come for the movie screening.

It was hard for Tibby to look at. Even as she cherished it, she wanted to press it safely between two books on a high shelf and leave it there forever. But she promised herself she wouldn't do that. She promised herself she would hang it on the wall of her room, no matter where she was. Because Bailey had understood what was real, and when Tibby saw Bailey's face, she couldn't hide from it.

Love is a snowmobile racing

across the tundra and then

suddenly it flips over,

pinning you underneath. At

night, the ice weasels come.

—Matt Groening

The mass for Bapi was held in the plain and lovely whitewashed church Lena had visited many times last summer. The service was all in Greek, naturally, including her father's eulogy, which left Lena to her own memories and meditations of Bapi.

She held Grandma's hand tightly and yearned for a glimpse of Kostos. He would be terribly sad, she knew that much. While she had only had the chance to love Bapi for one summer, Kostos had known him almost all his life. Lena had observed the subtle ways Kostos looked out for Bapi as he grew older and more feeble—hauling the garbage, replacing the roof tiles—while still making Bapi feel manly and respected.

Lena wanted to share this with Kostos. He was one of the very few people who knew what Bapi meant to her. No matter what it was that had come between them, they could be close today, couldn't they?

Toward the end of the service, Lena caught sight of

him at last. He was across the aisle from her family, on the far side, wearing a dark suit, and mostly obscured by his grandfather. Was Kostos looking for her, too? Here they were, in a small church on this tiny island on such a day. How could he not?

Lena and her family were the last members of the solemn recession. They followed the priest through the big doors and into the churchyard, where the entire congregation had gathered to pay respects, one by one, to Grandma the widow. How strange it would be, Lena mused numbly, to wake up for thousands of days as a wife, and this one day to wake up as a widow.

It wasn't until that moment that Lena got a clear view of Kostos, and he, presumably, of her. She was struck by the stiffness of his posture. Usually the air around him seemed to buzz with his animation, but today it seemed perfectly still. His eyebrows were drawn down so far she could hardly see his eyes.

For some reason, Lena had failed to notice at first gaze the woman standing next to Kostos with her hand clamped on his elbow. She looked to be in her early twenties. Her hair was highlighted blond and her skin was yellowish against the black of her suit. Lena didn't remember ever having seen her before.

This began a dull pounding inside Lena's chest. She knew somehow that the woman wasn't part of his family or a close family friend. She could just tell. Lena stood there, hoping Kostos might wave or beckon her over, or notice her in any way, but he didn't. She waited alongside her grandma, kissing and shaking hands, and nodding to a lot of heartfelt sentiments she couldn't specifically understand.

Though his grandparents were among the first to hug and kiss Valia, Kostos waited until almost the very end. The sky had clouded over darkly and the churchyard had emptied by the time he approached, with the blond woman still at his side.

Awkwardly Kostos hugged Grandma, but they said nothing to each other. The blond woman timidly pecked Grandma on the cheek. Lena stared at this unfamiliar woman, and she stared back at Lena. Lena waited for some sort of greeting or introduction, but it didn't come. Grandma's mouth made a straight line across her face. Lena felt confused, and slightly panicked at the strangeness on all sides.

The priest, who had hovered kindly throughout the proceedings, seemed to sense the social breakdown. He knew enough English to want to facilitate.

"Kostos, you must know Valia's son and daughter-in-law from America." He gestured toward Lena's parents standing a few feet away. "And Valia's granddaughter?" He gestured from Kostos to Lena and back again. "Lena, do you know Kostos and his new bride?"

Bride.

The word flew around Lena's ears like a mosquito, diving and threatening before it bit her. And then it bit her.

She looked at Kostos, and finally, he looked at her. His face was all different. As his eyes met hers, knowing and seeing her at last, her vision began to fuzz at the edges.

Lena sank down to the ground. She put her forehead to her knees. She was vaguely aware of her mother's worried hands on her back. Dimly she felt Kostos's alarm as he broke his stiff posture to reach for her. Lena's basic human instinct made her hang on to consciousness, even though it would have been a blessed relief to let it go.

The bedroom was not big enough to contain her anguish. The house was not big enough. Lena wondered, as she stepped quietly out of the house and started up the darkening road, whether the sky would be able to hold it.

She walked barefoot up the dusty road, not sure of her destination until she got up to the top, to the wide, flat expanse that spread from cliff to cliff. Numbly she set herself in the direction of the little olive grove. It was a place she and Kostos had shared, but she felt sure he had since abandoned it, as he had abandoned everything that was theirs, including her. There were many pointy, spiny things sticking into the bottoms of her tender, suburban feet, but that was okay with her.

When she got to the grove, she hovered by the little olives as though they were her long-lost children. She stepped over the rocks and sat by the side of the pond, much diminished since last summer. The whole island was drier and yellower than it had been then.

This was the place where it had all started. It seemed ceremonial to wash her sore feet and make her good-byes here too.

She thought she'd be finishing it alone, but she heard the crackle of footsteps behind her. Her heart leaped, but not because she thought it was a criminal or a wild boar. She knew who it would be.

He sat next to her, rolled up his funeral pants, and put his feet in the water next to hers.

"You're married," she said, flat and numb.

She clamped her jaw before she allowed herself to look at him. He was obviously pained and embarrassed and sorry and blah blah blah. So what.

"She's pregnant," he said.

Lena had been prepared to be remote and unmoved, but he had managed to ruin that for her too.

She gaped at him with giant eyes.

He nodded. "Her name is Mariana, and I went out with her three times after you broke up with me. The second time I had sex with her."

Lena winced.

"I am a stupid bastard."

She had never heard him sound bitter like this before. She stared at him quietly. She didn't have very much to add to that.

"She is pregnant and I am at fault. So I am taking responsibility."

"Do you know it is . . ." She had trouble finishing the sentence. " . . . yours?"

He looked at her levelly. "This is not America. This is an old-fashioned place. This is what a gentleman does."

She remembered when he'd used that word with her. She couldn't help feeling, somewhat discordantly, that his efforts at being a gentleman were not adding to the overall happiness in his life.

Slowly, looking at the water, Lena tried to reassemble the last few weeks, knowing all this.

"Will you go back to London with her?"

He shook his head. "Not for now. We'll stay here."

Lena knew what a blow that was to him. He wanted to get off the island and make a life for himself in a bigger place connected to the bigger world. She knew he had always dreamed of that.

"Do you live together?" she asked.

"Not yet. She is looking for a place in Fira."

"Do you love her?" Lena asked.

Kostos looked at her. He closed his eyes for a minute or two. "I could never imagine feeling about anyone the way I feel about you." He opened his eyes to see her. "But I'll do what I can."

Lena was going to cry soon. She knew she couldn't keep this up for long. The reality was catching up fast, hard on her heels, gripping her wrists. She wanted to get away from him before it happened.

She got up to leave, but he took hold of her hands and pulled her to him. With a stifled cry he crowded her to his chest with both arms around her, his mouth on her hair, his breathing rough.

"Lena, if I've broken your heart, I've broken my own a thousand times worse." She could hear that he was crying, but she didn't want to look. "I would do anything I could to change this, but I can't see a way out."

She let out an orphan sob, a small release as she struggled to hold the rest of it back.

"I'll let myself say this now, and not again. It goes against the commitment I made, but Lena, I have to tell you this. Everything I ever said to you was true and is true. I didn't lie. It's truer and bigger and more powerful than you'll ever know. Remember what I said."

His voice was desperate. He clutched her, almost too roughly. "You will go along, I know you will. And I will spend my whole life not having you."

She needed to get away. She pulled herself away from him and hid her face.

"I love you. I'll never stop," he promised, just as he had done a few weeks before on the sidewalk outside her house.

That time it had been a treasure. This time it was a curse.

She turned and she ran.

Tibby agreed to get a pedicure. She had never pegged herself as a pedicure kind of girl, but her mother had wanted her to come, and it was hard to hate a free foot massage. Plus, as they sat side by side with their feet swirling in miniature Jacuzzis, Tibby realized this was the longest time she'd spent with her mom all summer long. Maybe that was the idea here. Maybe you had to tag along sometimes to get what you needed.

Her mother chose dark red for her toenails. Tibby

chose clear. But then she changed her mind and chose dark red too.

"Sweetie, I wanted to show you something," her mom said, pulling an envelope out of her purse.

She unfolded the letter, handwritten on thick, fancy paper. "It's from Ari."

Tibby winced. She thought of Lena, of course, and she also thought of the whole stupid blowup.

"It made me cry," Alice said, seeming to summon up a bit of wetness in the eyes to demonstrate. Tibby could tell it wasn't a sad kind of crying.

"Before they left for Greece, she wrote the dearest apology for the whole mess. She's a sweet person. She always has been." Alice's face seemed to grow sentimental, and Tibby suddenly felt sentimental too.

"I remember when you and Ari used to play tennis on Wednesdays against Marly and Christina, and you always took turns winning."

Alice laughed. "We did not take turns," she said.

"Maybe it was just a coincidence," Tibby said, knowing it wasn't.

She remembered the four Septembers as little girls, playing for hours every Wednesday afternoon at the crummy playground on Broadbranch Road next to the public court while their mothers whacked the ball around. It had about two pieces of climbing equipment, as Tibby recalled. The Good Humor man had always stopped his truck there, and their mothers had almost always let them get ice cream bars.

"I wonder if she still plays?" Alice said more to the air than to Tibby. "Anyway." She took the envelope out of her purse. "Here's what I wanted to show you." She passed Tibby a three-by-five color photograph.

"*Ohhhh.*" Tibby held it and studied it, letting the pleasure warm her all the way down to her dark red toenails. "I love this," she said. "Can I please, please have it?"

There was a serious, actually fatal, infection called endocarditis, which was an inflammation of the heart. Lena's great-grandmother had died of it as a young woman, and Lena was pretty sure she had it.

Lena lay in bed deep into the morning, monitoring the ache and the swell.

Sometime around lunch, her mother tiptoed into the room, took off her heels, and crawled into bed with Lena. She was still wearing her navy silk suit. Lena's resistance evaporated. She felt herself slip back to being a three-year-old as her mother put her arms around her and pulled her protectively to her chest. Lena smelled her unique, powerful, mother smell, and she melted away. She cried and she shook and her nose ran disgustingly as her mother stroked her hair and wiped her face. Lena might have even fallen asleep for a while, strangely enough. She left off being a conscious creature altogether.

Her mother was as patient as the earth. She didn't say one thing until the light had changed in the room and the pink of late day crept in the window. When her mother sat up a little more in the bed, Lena noticed she'd gotten snot on her mother's best outfit.

"Would it be okay with you if I told you a little bit about Eugene?" her mother asked very softly.

Lena sat up a little too, and nodded. She'd cared so much about Eugene early in the summer, and now she could hardly remember why.

Ari fiddled with her rings for a while before she started talking—her wedding ring, her diamond engagement ring, her fifteen-year-anniversary emerald. "I met him in church in Athens when I was seventeen, and I fell madly in love."

Lena nodded again.

"He went to America to go to college—to American University. Right near home."

Lena nodded.

"I stayed in Athens. For four years I ached every day and every night we were apart. I felt like I only lived those few weeks of the year when we were together."

Lena nodded again. She understood this.

"When I was twenty-one, after university in Athens, I moved to America to be with him. My mother forbade me, and she was furious when I went. I waited tables and I waited for Eugene. He was busy with his life and finishing up school. I was willing to take any part of him that he would give me."

Her mother looked upward and thought about that for a while.

"He asked me to marry him, and of course I said yes.

He gave me a ring with a tiny pearl, and I cherished it like it was a religious icon. We lived together like we were already married. If my mother had known that, she would have died. Three months later, Eugene left suddenly and went back to Greece."

"Mmmm," Lena hummed in sympathy.

"His father had cut off the money and told Eugene he'd better come home and put his expensive education to some kind of use. I didn't actually know that at the time."

Lena nodded.

"For a year I longed for him miserably. He kept saying he would come back next month and next month and next. I lived in an ugly one-room apartment over a pet store on Wisconsin Avenue. I was as poor and lonely as could be. And, God, the place really stank. So many times I wanted to go home. But I thought Eugene would come back to me, that we would be married like he'd promised. And of course I didn't want to prove my mother right."

Lena nodded yet again. She could understand how that might be.

"I enrolled in graduate school at Catholic University that autumn. The first day of classes, I got a call from my sister. She told me the thing that everybody else knew and had known for weeks. Eugene had met another girl. He had no plans to come back to me."

Lena's chin quivered in overwhelming empathy. "Poor you," she murmured.

"I dropped out of school the very first day. I took to my bed."

Lena nodded solemnly. That sounded very practical to her. "Then what?"

"I had a truly good-hearted advisor at graduate school. She called me at home. She made me come back."

"And then?" Lena had a feeling they were about to get to the part of the story she knew.

"On Thanksgiving I met your father. We were the two confused, countryless Greeks eating alone at Howard Johnson's."

Lena smiled. She knew this part. The often-told story of her parents' first meeting, as it arose in this context, felt as dear to her as an old sweater. "And you got married four months later."

"We did."

And yet, Lena's parents' famous whirlwind meeting and marriage had a different, darker shading now that Lena knew all the facts.

"But unfortunately it wasn't the end of Eugene."

"Oh." Lena sensed that this was where it got tricky.

Her mother seemed to consider her strategy for a minute or two. Finally she said, "Lena, I will explain this to you as a nearly seventeen-year-old young woman and not as a daughter. That is, if you want me to."

Lena wanted that infinitely, but she also didn't. The wanting prevailed. She nodded.

Ari let out a breath. "I thought about Eugene often in the early years of my marriage. I loved your father, but I distrusted that love." She rubbed her finger over the top of her lip, gazing into hazy middle distance. "I felt ashamed of the hasty rebound, I guess. I believed our union was connected to Eugene and tainted by him. I was afraid I had transferred my feelings from Eugene to your father out of emotional necessity."

Lena's head felt heavy as she nodded. Her mother was trained in psychology, and sometimes it showed.

"When you were almost one, Eugene called me from New York. It was the first time I had heard his voice in four years. It sent me into a tailspin."

Lena was starting to get nervous about where this was going.

"He wanted me to go up and see him."

Lena ground her back teeth. She felt sorry for her one-year-old self.

"I agonized for three days. And then I went. I made an excuse to your father, left you with Tina and Carmen, and got on the train."

"Oh, no," Lena muttered.

"Your father still doesn't know about it, and I'd strongly prefer that you not tell him."

Lena nodded, feeling both the intoxication of knowing something about your mother that your father didn't even know and also the deep revulsion of it.

"I remember walking toward him in Central Park, touching that awful pearl ring I'd brought in my coat pocket. Honestly, in that moment, I did not know how the rest of my life was going to go."

Lena closed her eyes.

"The three hours we spent walking in the park were

possibly the most valuable three hours I have ever spent."

Lena didn't want to hear this.

"Because I left there and I came home to you and Daddy, and I knew from then on that I loved your father for being your father and I no longer loved Eugene."

Lena felt her heart begin to lift. "So nothing . . . happened."

"I did kiss him. That was it."

"Oh," said Lena, almost disbelieving she was having this conversation with her mother.

"I was so happy to be home that evening. I'll never forget the feeling." Her mother's voice took on an amused and almost conspiratorial tone. "I believe Daddy and I made Effie that very night."

Lena was starting to need to go back to being the daughter again.

"And you more or less know the rest."

This struck Lena all of a sudden. It made a kind of cosmic sense that her conception and babyhood had been spent in an atmosphere of worry and distrust, and Effie had cruised in on a wave of perfect happiness. It made a sick kind of sense.

"So that was the end of Eugene," Lena said.

"It wasn't quite as easy as that. He called me a half-dozen times over the next few years. He was usually drunk. Your father really loathes that man." Ari rolled her eyes at the memory. "That's why Tina and Alice and—" Lena knew her mother had been about to say *Marly*, but she'd stopped herself. "That's why my close friends knew about Eugene. I would dread those calls and the fights they provoked with your father. I still don't mention his name around Daddy. That's partly why I reacted the way I did when you brought him up."

Lena nodded. "But Daddy shouldn't worry, should he?"

"Oh, no." Ari shook her head emphatically. "Your father is a magnificent man and a fine father. Eugene is a fool. I look back at that heartbreak, and I feel like it was the best thing that could have happened."

Ari looked significantly at her daughter. "And that, my love, is what I want you to remember."

Tibberon: Talked to Lenny late. Awful, unbelievable shit. Have you talked to her yet?

Carmabelle: Just talked to her. Cannot even think. Poor, poor Lenny. What can we do? Stay there. I'm coming over.

Bridget knew it was time to get home. Now that she knew what was going on with Lena, she needed to be with her. On her last day in Burgess she lay with Greta on the back porch. They munched on ice cubes and talked about future home-improvement projects instead of saying good-bye.

And yet three o'clock still rolled around, and it was still time for Bridget to go.

Greta was being careful. She didn't want to start the crying.

Bridget was never careful, so she said what she was thinking. "You know what, Grandma, if I didn't have three friends I loved, I would stay here with you. This feels like home now."

Greta started tearing up right on schedule. Bridget did too.

"I'll miss you, honey. I really will."

Bridget nodded. She hugged Greta maybe too hard.

"And you'll bring your brother when you come at Christmas, you promise me?"

"I promise you," Bridget said faithfully.

"Remember," Grandma said in her ear when at last she let her go, "I'll always be here loving you."

After she gathered her things, Bridget turned around on the sidewalk to look at the house one last time. It had seemed so plain when she'd arrived, but it looked beautiful to her now. She could make out the shape of Greta standing inside the darkened front window. Her grandmother was crying hard, and she didn't want Bridget to see.

She loved this house. She loved Greta. She loved Greta for her bingo on Monday and her TV on Friday and her lunch at twelve o'clock every single day.

Maybe Bridget didn't have much of a home with her dad and Perry. But she had made herself a home here.

Lenny,

You're still in Greece, so I know you won't get this letter for a while, but I need to do something. I need to feel like I'm with you in some way.

I'm so sorry about Bapi. I cried for you this morning when I heard. You've always been steady, Len, and so good to messed-up me. I wish I could take care of you, for once.

All my love,
Bee

Two important things happened on Lena's fourth and last day in Greece. The first thing was that Grandma gave Lena Bapi's hideous white tasseled shoes, and amazingly, they fit Lena's giant feet. Grandma looked aghast, like she hadn't actually meant for Lena to put them on, but Lena was very pleased.

"I vas going to put them in the casket, but I thought you might like them, lamb."

"I do, Grandma. Thank you. I love them."

The second thing was that as night fell, Lena sat on the little wall outside her grandma's house and made a painting for Bapi. She had the idea she would bury it with him.

It was the full moon hanging over the smooth Caldera that inspired her. She set out her paints and her panel and started uniting various blobs of paint into swirly night colors. She'd never made a painting in the dark before, and she probably never would again, because it was basically impossible.

But she managed to capture two glowing moons, the

one in the sky and its twin in the water. They looked the same, and in her painting, they were the same.

As she was shoving around the mess of oils on her palette, she saw that Kostos had come to stand behind her and watch her work.

He watched very patiently for a man who had just ruined both their lives.

"Moony night," he said to no one in particular, after he'd studied it for a long time.

It was funny, because that was just what she'd thought to call it, but fear of hubris had made her back down. She couldn't connect anything of hers to Van Gogh, especially not to the painting of his she loved best of all. She thought about her mother and Eugene and wondered whether she would ever be able to think Kostos was a fool. She kind of doubted it.

"Bapi will love it," he said.

Okay, she doubted it even more.

She willed herself not to cry again, and even more, willed her nose not to start flowing. She knew this was the last time she would see him maybe ever. She turned around and stood up to get a long, thirsty look at his face, to soak it in.

The night before, she had felt stifled and hostile and numb, but now, for whatever reason, she didn't.

"Good-bye," she said.

She realized he was drinking in the look of her just as thirstily. Her eyes, her hair, her mouth, her neck, her breasts, her paint-spattered pants, Bapi's white shoes. It would have been entirely inappropriate if this had been hello and not good-bye. Maybe it was inappropriate even so.

"The things you said to me last night," she began.

He nodded.

She cleared her throat. "Same here."

She had to hand it to herself. She couldn't have found a less poetic way of putting it.

He nodded again.

"I'll never forget you." She thought about that. "Well, hopefully, I'll forget you a little." She scuffed the toe of Bapi's shoe. "Otherwise it will be awfully hard going."

His eyes were full now. The corners of his mouth quivered downward.

She put her palette and her brush down on the wall. She rose up onto her very tiptoes, put her hands on his shoulders for balance, and kissed him on the cheek. No matter the placement, she kissed him like a lover and not like a friend. But maybe it could pass. He held her in his arms, harder and closer than he should have. He didn't want to let her go.

A while after Kostos left, Effie appeared. She had her Walkman on, and she looked suspiciously disheveled.

"You sure cry a lot more than you used to," Effie pointed out.

Lena could almost have laughed. "And you found the waiter, didn't you?"

Effie shrugged coyly. Of course Effie could take up last summer's love interest as though no time had passed. Effie could revel in a robust make-out session and when it was time to leave, she could bid her crush good-bye, no worse for wear.

Lena studied her sister in amazement. Effie was bobbing her head around to some dumb song coming through her earphones.

Different people were good at different things, Lena mused. Lena was good at writing thank-you notes, for instance, and Effie was good at being happy.

We are born not once, but

again and again.

—William Charles

B ridget had wanted to carry her bags the quarter mile to the bus station, but when Billy suddenly appeared next to her on the sidewalk and took the two heavy ones, she wasn't mad.

"I wish you weren't going," he said.

"They need me at home," she said. "We'll see each other around, though."

She looked at Billy standing there in the bus station, holding her bags, wishing she weren't going. He liked her, she felt sure. She watched him for signs of physical yearning. She wanted that, didn't she? She liked herself enough again to feel like she deserved it.

But she wondered. Did she really want that? Hadn't she had enough boys look at her that way? Would she partly hate him if he changed the way he liked her because she was pretty and blond?

Anyway, he wasn't looking at her like that. He was looking at her like she was Bee, who he'd known since he was six. He was looking at her the way he looked at her when she screamed at him on the soccer field. Wasn't he?

He touched the soft underpart of her wrist.

Or was he?

She'd thought the Bee she'd been when she was six and the Bee she was now were a world apart, separated by her tragedies. She'd thought the Bee who was his friend and the Bee who was his potential crush were different and opposite girls. Now she wasn't sure what she thought.

But when he kissed her full on her lips, he sent a tingle from her hair to her toenails, and she knew she liked it.

In a flash of wonderment she saw firm, continuous ground under her feet, stretching from back then to right now and on and on as far as her eyes could take her.

It was a pretty weird idea, actually. But Carmen had always liked things that went around and came around. Her mother was out with David being happily ever after. Carmen had done her penance, spending her days worrying about Lena and watching her mother be joyful. She'd had a lot of time to devote to it too, since the Morgans were spending these last two weeks of the summer at the beach.

Porter had left a couple of messages the week before inviting her to some jock party in Chevy Chase. So Carmen figured maybe now that she'd gotten herself straightened out about her mom, she could start to like him for real.

He sounded surprised when she called him and asked him out on such late notice. But he did say yes and offer to take her to Dizzy's Grill, so that meant he didn't completely hate her. Or maybe he did hate her and was sneakily planning to present her with the bill at the end of the night. Carmen made a mental note to stick an extra twenty in her wallet.

She put on the Traveling Pants for the first time since the fateful night when Christina had fallen in love with David and Carmen had not fallen in love with Porter. Tonight, who knew? With the Pants, this night might very well be fateful too.

She was just plucking a stray eyebrow hair when the phone rang.

According to caller ID, she was being called by a pay phone at Union Station.

"Hello?"

"Hi. It's Paul."

She was pretty sure Paul was supposed to be on his way from Charleston, where he'd been hanging out at home for two weeks, back to school in Philadelphia.

"Hi. What are you doing?"

"Missing my train."

"Oh, no. What happened?"

"I got lost on the subway."

Carmen let out a hooting laugh. "You didn't!"

"I didn't."

"Oh."

"I got a ride with a friend as far as D.C., and then I did miss my train."

"Oh."

Carmen considered what this meant. This meant Paul had nowhere to stay tonight and she would need to look after him.

"Uhhh." She tapped the phone, thinking. "Meet me at Dizzy's Grill on Wisconsin and Woodley. Just whenever you get there. Have you eaten?"

"No."

"Good. See you there." Poor Porter. This was going to be a strange date, what with the extra guy and all.

Carmen had finally gotten her tweezers around the offending hair for the second time when the phone rang again.

"Jeez!" she shouted, throwing the tweezers at the wall.

This call came from Lena's house. Was Lena home? Carmen snatched the phone from its holder.

"Lena!"

"No, it's Effie." Effie was whispering.

"You're home?"

"Yeah, like an hour ago."

"How's Lena?"

Carmen could feel her heart beating in her temples. Lena was home. Lena would need her. Well, that was that. She hoped Paul and Porter would enjoy each other's company.

Effie paused. "Mmmmm. Can't tell."

"Is she walking? Is she talking?"

"Yes and no."

"What do you mean?"

"Yes walking, no talking."

"Oh. I'll come right over."

"No, you need to take her out."

"I do?"

"Yeah," Effie said. "That's what she needs."

"Ooookay. You sure about that?" Effie was a boss and Carmen was a boss. They didn't always mix.

"Yes. Half her room is covered with letters. The other half with pictures. That's how it is. We left in a hurry. You need to take her out and distract her, and I need to put all that stuff away. Like down the garbage disposal. Ha ha."

Carmen was silent. Effie never cared if nobody else laughed at her jokes.

"Did you talk to Tibby?" Carmen asked.

"Not home."

"Okay, Ef. I'll be over to pick her up in fifteen minutes." Carmen smacked the phone down.

She shook her head as she raced around her room, stuffing her things into her purse. She would just have to bring Lena to Dizzy's Grill also. That was the only thing to do.

And anyway, crazy Carmen's date with two guys at the same time would be nothing if not distracting.

A long time afterward, Carmen tried to replay every nuance of that strange meeting. She wanted to pinpoint exactly when it happened. How it happened. Why it happened. Whether it happened.

Carmen was wearing the Pants. She was holding hands with Lena. Lena was wearing soft flannel drawstring pants and a shirt. From three feet away it looked like a regular white T-shirt, straight and simple. But if you got closer, it had this very small ruffle running along the neckline. It had struck Carmen right away. The T-shirt was classic Lena, but the ruffle was not.

Lena looked particularly thin. She was thin from torment, but Carmen couldn't help envy it anyway. Lena's eyes were large and light-filled and seemed to be focused on some vague middle distance, not here, not there. She blinked and looked around the restaurant like a newborn. Her skin seemed tender and raw, and her eyes seemed as if they were new to seeing. And Carmen felt bad dragging her into this bustling, smoky, overstimulating scene. It was no place for a newborn.

Carmen sat Lena down at the front of the restaurant, the waiting part. She strode into the dining room, and found Porter and Paul each waiting for her at his own table. First she went to Porter. He stood up and smiled upon seeing her.

"Hi." He kissed her on the lips, but she was too distracted to analyze it.

"Hey, listen. This night has gotten sort of complicated." She grimaced apologetically. "My friend—well, my stepbrother actually—missed his train tonight and he has nowhere to go so I invited him to come along." Tentatively she touched her jaw. "Is that okay?"

He gave her a look that said, *Does it matter if it's okay?*

"And also." Carmen rushed right along. "My friend Lena? You know her. She got back from Greece tonight and she's kind of . . . well, a disaster, actually," Carmen said, lowering her voice, "and I can't leave her alone, so she's here too." Carmen raised her shoulders plaintively. "Sorry."

Porter nodded. Carmen figured there wasn't much she could do at this point to surprise or disappoint him.

By this time, Paul had spotted her. She went to him. "Hi. Come on over."

He followed.

"Porter, this is Paul. Paul, this is Porter," she said when they were within earshot.

"Hey." Porter raised one hand like an Indian chief.

She seemed to be arranging a lot of people's lives this evening. She pointed to the table where Porter had been sitting. "We can all fit here, right?"

Porter shrugged. "Sure."

"Okay. Sit. I'll go get Lena."

Paul was looking a little shell-shocked. He wasn't very social. He was probably wishing he'd stayed on a bench at Union Station.

On a chair at the front, Lena was watching her hands as the world spun around her. "Len?"

She looked up.

"Sorry to drag you around tonight, but we're having dinner with two guys you don't know." What was the use of sugar-coating it? If Lena was going to mutiny, now was the time.

Instead of crawling under a chair, as Carmen half expected, Lena got up and followed obediently. This worried Carmen more than the all-out kick-and-scream scenario.

The two of them were walking toward the table. It was around then that it happened. For some reason, Paul and Porter were sitting on the same side of the table, facing the girls as they walked over. It looked sort of comical, in a way, these two very large boys sitting side by side. She couldn't exactly say how Porter looked at the time, because she was watching Paul.

This was when the clocks stopped and the place got quiet and the colors faded into sepia. The air felt nostalgic, even though nothing had happened yet.

Paul looked at Lena. Millions of boys had looked at Lena, but no one had ever looked at her like that.

That was one of the main things Carmen wondered about later. That look of Paul's. How could a look on a face contain so many things?

Porter stood up. Paul stood up. They all sat down. Carmen said things. Porter said things. The waiter appeared and said things. It all seemed random and irrelevant, because something important was happening.

Paul and Lena, Lena and Paul. They didn't even smile at each other or say anything. Maybe they didn't even realize something was happening, but Carmen did. She just knew it.

Suddenly, in the middle of the cozy four-top, a chasm opened. On one side were the world and the restaurant and all the regular people like Porter and Carmen. On the other side were Paul and Lena. As intensely alert as she was, Carmen didn't feel like she could look at them or listen to them. She didn't belong there, on the other side.

"Do you want to share the spicy chicken wings?" Porter asked her amiably.

Carmen felt like crying.

These were the Love Pants! They were! There was pure, transforming magic around them. But it wasn't for her! It was never for her.

She was bad at love. She loved too hard.

Carmen's imagination was starting to branch out in dangerous directions. Lena would become the center of Paul's world. She could just see it. He wouldn't care about Carmen anymore. He wouldn't listen carefully to all the stupid things she said.

And what about Lena? What would that do to their friendship? To the Sisterhood? Where was this going to leave Carmen?

Anxiety was brewing somewhere down there, filling her stomach with acid, tangling up her intestines.

What was it about her and double dates? Why did Carmen have to sit on the sidelines of love when it was so close? Why did she end up losing instead of gaining?

She thought about her mother and David just then. He'd arrived at the apartment earlier that evening with bouquets of roses for both Christina and Carmen. Carmen had mostly appreciated the gesture because it had made her mom so supremely happy. David had known the word Carmen was stuck on in her crossword puzzle (Japanese dog, five letters, starting with *a*). More important, though, had been the radiance of her mother's face, even as she'd tried to appear rational. That wasn't losing. That was gaining.

Over in the world of Lena and Paul, Paul murmured something to Lena. Lena looked down at the table shyly, but when she looked up again, she had a smile as lovely as any Carmen had ever seen her wear. Some things had changed with Lena.

Carmen could ignore what she was seeing. She could feel threatened and try to stomp on it before it could dig roots.

Or maybe she could figure that Lena and Paul were two of the people she loved best on the planet, and they each deserved the love of someone as worthy as the other.

Suddenly Carmen's head snapped up. "Lena?"

Lena seemed to travel many miles to reach her.

"Yes?"

"Can you come with me for just a second?"

Both Paul and Lena seemed to look at her in wonderment at how she could be so loud and encroaching. "Just a second, I promise," Carmen added.

Once in the bathroom, Carmen unbuttoned the Pants. She shed them quickly. "Give me yours and take these, okay?"

"Why are you doing this?" Lena asked.

"Because I know it is going to be an important night for you." Carmen's heart was pounding.

"How do you know?" Lena looked almost scared.

Carmen pressed her palm to her heart. "I just do. I know it."

Lena fixed her wide eyes on Carmen's. "Important how? How do you mean?"

Carmen cocked her head. "Len. If you don't know,

you'll know soon. You've been through a lot this summer. It could take a while."

Lena looked confused. She wasn't going to argue. She pulled the Pants on. The air seemed to glimmer with them.

Thank God Lena wore drawstring pants tonight, Carmen thought, pulling them on and tying them quickly.

Lena was already floating forward, through the door and out into the restaurant. Watching Lena walk to Paul, Carmen sensed it was one of those strange points in time when the world unfolds. Maybe Carmen was the only one who could see it.

This is how it is going to be, Carmen thought. And she'd find a way to love love, however it appeared.

Lena lay in her bed at home. As usual, she was thinking restlessly about a boy. But tonight, strangely enough, the boy in question wasn't the usual one. This new one was taller and squarer and so earnest in the eyes. The way he looked at her, it felt like he could see everything, but would only take what she was ready to give. He wasn't married. He hadn't gotten anybody pregnant, so far as she knew.

Somehow or other, in the space of about ninety seconds, she'd let go of the trapeze she was flying on, hovered in heart-stopping midair, and grabbed a trapeze flying in the opposite direction.

Since when had she become a highflyer? She had to wonder. How had she gone from an emotional hermit to a trapeze artist?

She was concerned for her safety.

She called Tibby. She hadn't spoken to her since she'd gotten home, and she felt like being out loud.

"Tib, I don't know what's wrong with me," she moaned, unsure whether her moan was happy or sad. Up on the high swing, the two feelings seemed to merge, identical in their intensity.

"What is it, Len?" Tibby said as tenderly as Tibby ever said anything.

"I think I have that disease where your heart swells up."

"Well," Tibby said philosophically, "I guess I would say, Better a swollen heart than a shrunken one."

When Carmen walked in the door after dropping Lena off, she heard the phone ringing. She answered it in the kitchen.

"Hello?"

"Hey, Carmen, it's Porter."

"Hey," she said, surprised.

"Listen, I give up. I just wanted you to know that. A person can only take so much."

Carmen swallowed hard. For some reason, she felt her heart beating in all the wrong parts of her body. "Um, what do you mean?" she said timidly, dishonestly. She didn't *want* to know what he meant, but that didn't mean she didn't.

Porter let out a breath. "I'll be honest. I've had a huge crush on you for, like, two years. I was psyched to get together with you this summer. I really hoped it could work out, but Jesus, Carmen, how many times can you lead a guy on?"

Porter paused, giving her an opportunity to defend herself, but she was so stunned she couldn't activate her tongue. It just lolled there unhelpfully in her mouth.

"I was confused when you kept calling. When we went out, I could tell you weren't that into it, but then you'd call me again." He didn't sound irritable. He sounded resigned. "So anyway, I have officially given up. I can act like an idiot for only so long."

In her gaping, sputtering silence it began to dawn on Carmen that Porter was not the person she'd thought he was. Then again, had she thought at all, for even a second, about *what* kind of person he was? She had considered his objective boyfriend merit at great length, but not that he had actual feelings or that, God forbid, he would talk about them. He was a boy, a potential Boyfriend, an enviable accessory, much like a very good handbag.

Wasn't he?

"I know you were distracted by the whole thing with your mom, and I understand that. But I thought maybe after it was fixed up, we could hang out finally."

No, he wasn't.

She felt her cheeks burning. She had been so colossally off base about him she almost had to laugh.

"Porter?" she said. His name felt different to her now. She suddenly felt as if she might be talking to a friend.

"Yeah?"

"I can act like an idiot for a lot longer than you."

He laughed, albeit heavily.

They hadn't laughed together, she realized. She hadn't given him much cause to.

"I don't know what to say for myself except that I didn't realize that you are a real person," she said honestly.

"What did you think I was?"

"God . . . I don't know. A penguin?"

He laughed a little more and cleared his throat. "I'm not sure how to take that."

"I was wrong, though."

"I'm not a penguin?"

"No."

"Glad to hear it."

She took a long, sad breath.

"I'm really sorry," she said, wishing she didn't so often put herself in the position of owing people large and sincere apologies.

"Accepted," he said easily.

"Thanks," she said.

"You take care, Carmen." His voice was intimate. It was nice.

"Thanks," she said again, even more quietly, and she heard him hang up.

As she put the phone down, she knew she'd gotten what she deserved. And the sick thing was, she could imagine for the first time what it might feel like to really like him.

She smiled faintly as she pulled on her fuzzy red pajamas, the ones she wore when she was sick. She felt ashamed, but also strangely hopeful.

❖   ❖   ❖

The next morning, after having ridden through the night, Bee leaped off the bus in Bethesda, Maryland, but she didn't go home. She went straight to Lena's house. She gave Ari a wordless hug at the door and went upstairs.

Lena was lying on her bed, still in her pajamas with the green and black olives.

She sat up at the sight of Bridget. Bridget let out a small yell and almost tackled her in an embrace, then pulled away to study her more carefully.

Bridget had expected to find flat-out tragedy in her friend's face, but she didn't. She saw something more complicated than that.

"You heard about Bapi?" Lena asked.

Bee nodded solemnly.

"You heard about Kostos?"

Bee nodded again.

"I'm a mess, huh?" she said.

"Are you?" Bee asked gently, studying Lena's eyes.

Lena looked toward the ceiling. "I don't even know what I am." She flopped back onto the bed, and she smiled when Bee flopped next to her.

"I loved him so much," she said to Bee. She closed her eyes and started to cry. As she cried, she wasn't even sure which "him" she was talking about. She felt Bee's arms close around her.

"I know," Bee said soothingly. "I'm so sorry."

When Lena came up for air, Bee was looking thoughtful. "You're different, Lenny," she said.

Lena laughed a little through her tears. She touched

one of Bee's lovely yellow strands. "You're the same. I mean, you changed back into yourself."

"I'm hoping it's a harder-wearing version," Bee said.

Lena stretched her large feet out in front of her. "You know what?"

"What?"

"I asked myself, if I could erase this whole summer, would I?"

"And what did you say?" Bee asked.

"Until yesterday night, I would have said yes, please, put me back how I was."

Bridget nodded. "And now?"

"And now, I think, maybe not. Maybe I'll stay here."

Lena started crying again. She used to cry roughly three times a year. Now she seemed to cry three times before breakfast. Could that be considered progress?

She leaned into Bee, allowing Bee to support her weight. What a strange reversal it was to collapse and let Bee catch her.

But then, she hadn't just learned to love this summer — she had also learned how to need.

Let the golden age begin.

—Beck

Bee called Tibby and Carmen from Lena's, and they appeared there moments later, Carmen wearing her shirt inside out and her mother's slippers, Tibby with her feet bare. They screamed with joy when they saw each other.

Now, hours later, the sun was slanting sunset pink through the window and they still had not left the room. They had talked long and hard, all four of them lying on Lena's bed. Carmen knew that none of them wanted to break this mood, this spell. But they were also getting hungry.

Tibby and Lena finally set out on an expedition to forage in the kitchen and bring supplies back upstairs. But less than thirty seconds later the two of them burst back into the room.

"We heard people in the kitchen," Tibby explained with wide, excited eyes.

"Come down and see," Lena said. "But be quiet."

On account of their footwear, Carmen noticed, they were good at being quiet. Tibby stopped at the side of the kitchen door, and they all clustered behind her.

Carmen let out her breath when she saw the three mothers sitting at the round table. Their heads were bent, low and confidential. Christina appeared to be telling a funny story, because both Ari and Alice were laughing. Ari's hands covered her eyes in a gesture just like Lena made when the laughter was getting out of control.

Carmen also noticed the two wine bottles on the table, one empty and one half-full.

There were so many things to feel, looking at them, Carmen couldn't sort the powerfully sad from the joyful—nor did they really seem distinct. There was the comfort and familiarity of these women's poses together that brought back a rush of childhood. There was the fourth chair at the table, empty, where Marly should have been, where perhaps Greta now belonged.

Carmen looked around and saw the same rushing emotions in her friends' faces. They were each feeling the same things and probably different ones too.

Without speaking they followed Tibby out the front door to the empty lot next to the house. Carmen felt herself smiling. The sight of their mothers as friends struck her as a case of something you hoped for mightily but wouldn't allow yourself to admit you wanted.

The four of them lay on the grass until the sun finished and the stars began. Carmen wondered at the power of silence to create a stronger bond, even, than thousands and thousands of words.

❖　　❖　　❖

That night the mood at Gilda's was both sweet and dark. They held hands and improvised a séance for their dead: Marly, Bailey, Bapi. Tibby threw in Brian's dad and Lena added Kostos, too. He was somebody she needed to mourn. Bee wanted to remember her grand-father. Tibby also thought about Mimi, though she didn't say so out loud.

After the dead, they honored love. They opened a bot-tle of champagne that Tibby had stolen from her parents' basement stash. Carmen wanted to drink to romantic love, but that got tricky right away. Lena wanted to include Brian, but Tibby refused. Carmen wanted to include Paul, but Lena refused. So they widened it to general love and the number got bigger: Greta, Brian, Paul, Valia, Effie, Krista, Billy. Carmen felt virtuous adding David to the list.

Then they wanted to toast their mothers, too. Bee's eyes filled during that part. She asked if Marly could be in two categories, and they all agreed. Then she asked if Greta could be in two categories too, and they all agreed again.

For this last part, Tibby brought out a surprise. Carefully she unwrapped the photograph Ari had sent to her mother and placed it on the Traveling Pants in the middle of their circle. They all leaned and squinted to get a good look.

Four young women sat on a brick wall. They all had their arms around each other's shoulders and waists. They all overlapped their ankles, like they might burst into a cancan. They were laughing. One of them had beautiful blond hair. One had dark wavy hair and dark eyes—her smile was the widest. One had freckles and flyaway hair. The fourth had straight black hair and classic features. It was a picture of friendship, but it wasn't the Sisterhood. It was their mothers, long ago. Tibby noted with joy that all four of them were wearing jeans.